Praise for Anne Perry

and her

THOMAS AND CHARLOTTE PITT NOVELS

FARRIERS' LANE

"[A] devious affair of passion and political intrigue in Victorian London."

—*The New York Times Book Review*

BELGRAVE SQUARE

"So pulsates with the sights and sounds of Victorian London that the reader soon gets caught up in Anne Perry's picaresque story of life, love and murder that involves both the upper and lower classes of that colorful era."

—*The Pittsburgh Press*

HIGHGATE RISE

"When it comes to the Victorian mystery, Anne Perry has proved that nobody does it better. Once again, her recreation of its manners and morality, fashions and foibles is masterful."

—*The San Diego Union-Tribune*

SILENCE IN HANOVER CLOSE

"[A] complex, gripping and highly satisfying mystery . . . an adroit blend of thick London atmosphere and a convincing cast . . . a totally surprising yet wonderfully plausible finale."

—*Publishers Weekly*

PARAGON
WALK

PARAGON WALK

A CHARLOTTE AND THOMAS PITT NOVEL

ANNE PERRY

Ballantine Books　New York

2009 Ballantine Books Trade Paperback Edition

Published in the United States by Ballantine Books, an imprint of
The Random House Publishing Group, a division of
Random House, Inc., New York.

BALLANTINE and colophon are registered trademarks of Random House, Inc.
MORTALIS and colophon are trademarks of Random House, Inc.

Originally published in hardcover in the United States by St. Martin's Press in 1981.
Subsequently published by Fawcett Books,
an imprint of The Random House Publishing Group,
a division of Random House, Inc., in 1982.

ISBN 978-0-345-51397-7

Printed in the United States of America

www.mortalis-books.com

4 6 8 9 7 5

for my mother

PARAGON
WALK

One

Inspector Pitt stared down at the girl, and an overwhelming sense of loss soaked through him. He had never known her in life, but he knew and treasured all the things that now she had lost.

She was slight, with fair brown hair, a childish seventeen. Lying on the white morgue table, she looked brittle enough to have snapped if he had touched her. There were bruises on her arms where she had fought.

She was expensively dressed in lavender silk, and there was a gold and pearl chain around her throat—things he could never have afforded. They were pretty, trivial enough in the face of death, and yet he would like to have been able to give such things to Charlotte.

Thoughts of Charlotte, safe and warm at home, brought a sickness tightening in his stomach. Had some man loved this girl as he loved Charlotte? Was there someone right now for whom everything clean and bright and gentle had gone? All laughter snatched away, with the breaking of this fragile body?

He forced himself to look at her again, but his eyes avoided the wound in her chest, the stream of blood, now congealed and thick. The white face was expressionless, all surprise or horror ironed out of it. It was a little pinched.

1

She had lived in Paragon Walk, very rich and very fashionable, and no doubt also idle. He had nothing in common with her. He had worked ever since leaving the estate that had employed his father possessing nothing but a cardboard box with a comb and a change of shirt and an education shared with the son of the great house. He had seen the poverty and the despair that teemed just behind the elegant streets and squares of London, things this girl had never dreamed of.

He pulled a face as he remembered with a twist of humor how horrified Charlotte had been when he had first described them to her, when he was merely the policeman investigating the Cater Street murders, and she a daughter of the Ellison house. Her parents had been appalled even to have him in the establishment, let alone to address him socially. It had taken courage for Charlotte to marry him, and at the thought of it the warmth burst up inside him again, and his fingers clenched on the edge of the table.

He looked down at the girl's face again, furious at the waste, the wealth of experience she would never know, the chances gone.

He turned away.

"Last night after dark," the constable beside him said glumly. "Ugly business. Do you know Paragon Walk, sir? Very 'igh class neighborhood, that. Most of it is, around there."

"Yes," Pitt said absently. Of course, he knew it; it was part of his district. He did not add that he knew Paragon Walk especially, because Charlotte's sister had her town house there and so it had remained in his mind. As Charlotte had married socially beneath her, so Emily had married above and was now Lady Ashworth.

"Not the sort of thing you'd expect," the constable went on, "not in a place like that." He made a slight click of disapproval with his tongue. "I don't know what things is coming to, what with General Gordon killed by that there dervish, or whatever, in January, and now we got rapists loose in a place like Paragon Walk. Shockin', I call it, poor young girl like that. Looks as innocent as a lamb, don't she?" He stared down at her mournfully.

Pitt turned round. "Did you say raped?"

"Yes, sir. Didn't they tell you that at the station?"

"No, Forbes, they did not," Pitt was sharper than he meant to be, to cover the new misery. "They just said murder."

"Oh, well, she's been murdered, too," Forbes added reasonably. "Poor creature." He sniffed. "I suppose you'll be wanting to go to Paragon Walk now it's morning, like, and talk to all them people?"

"Yes," Pitt agreed, turning to leave. There was nothing more he could do here. The means of death was obvious, a long, sharp-bladed knife at least an inch broad. There was only one wound, which had to have been fatal.

"Right," Forbes followed him up the steps, his heavy feet loud on the stone.

Outside Pitt gulped at the summer air. The trees were in full leaf and already at eight o'clock it was warm. A hansom cab clopped by at the end of the road, and an errand boy whistled about his business.

"We'll walk," Pitt said, striding out, coat flapping, hat jammed on the top of his head. Forbes was obliged to trot to keep up with him, and long before they were at Paragon Walk the constable was distressingly out of breath and wishing fervently his duty had landed him with anybody but Pitt.

Paragon Walk was a Regency road of great elegance, facing an open park with flowerbeds and ornamental trees. It curved gently for about a thousand yards. This morning it looked white and silent in the sunlight, and there was not even a footman or a gardener's boy to be seen. Word of the

3

tragedy would have spread, of course; there would be huddles in kitchens and pantries and embarrassed platitudes over the breakfast tables upstairs.

"Fanny Nash," Forbes said, catching his breath for the first time as Pitt stopped.

"Pardon?"

"Fanny Nash, sir," Forbes repeated. "That was 'er name."

"Oh, yes." The sense of loss returned for a moment. This time yesterday she would have been alive, behind one of those classic windows, probably deciding what to wear, telling her maid what to lay out for her, planning her day, whom to call on, what gossip to tell, what secrets to keep. It was the beginning of the London Season. What dreams had crowded through her mind such a little while ago?

"Number Four," Forbes prompted at his elbow.

Inwardly Pitt cursed Forbes for his practicality, though he knew that was unfair. This was a foreign world to Forbes, stranger than the back streets of Paris or Bordeaux would have been. He was used to women in plain, stuff dresses who worked from waking to sleeping, large families living in a few, overfurnished rooms with the smell of cooking everywhere and the intimate usage of faults and pleasures. He could not think of these people as the same, under their silks, and their rigid, stylized manners. Without the discipline of work, they had invented the discipline of etiquette, and it had become just as ruthless a master. But Forbes could not be expected to understand that.

As a policeman, Pitt knew it was customary for him to present himself at the tradesman's entrance, but he would not now begin something he had refused all his life.

The footman who came to the front door was grim and stiff-faced. He stared at Pitt with unaffected dislike, although the superciliousness of the look was somewhat spoiled by the fact that Pitt was several inches taller.

4

"Inspector Pitt, of the police," Pitt said soberly. "May I speak with Mr. and Mrs. Nash?" He assumed assent and was about to go in, but the footman stood his ground.

"Mr. Nash is not at home. I will see if Mrs. Nash will receive you," he said with distaste, then backed half a step. "You may wait in the hall."

Pitt looked around him. The house was larger than it had appeared from outside. He could see a wide stairway with landings leading from it on either side, and there were half a dozen doors in the hall. He had learned something of art from working on the recovery of stolen goods, and he judged the pictures on the walls to be of considerable value, if too stylized for his own taste. He preferred the modern, more impressionistic school, with blurred lines, sky and water merging in a haze of light. But there was one portrait, after the manner of Burne-Jones, that caught his attention, not for its artist, but for its subject, a woman of exceptional beauty—proud, sensuous and dazzling.

"Cor!" Forbes let out his breath in amazement, and Pitt realized he had not been inside a house such as this before, except perhaps in the servants' hall. He was afraid Forbes's gaucheness would embarrass them both, and perhaps even handicap his questioning.

"Forbes, why don't you go and see what you can learn from the servants?" he suggested. "Perhaps a footman or a maid was out? People don't realize how much they notice."

Forbes was torn. Part of him wanted to stay and examine this new world, not to be shut out of anything, but a larger part wanted to escape to the more familiar and do something he was confident in. His hesitation was brief and came to a natural end.

"Right, sir! Yes, I'll do that. Might try some of the other houses, too. Like you say, never know what they've seen, till you try, like?"

When the footman returned, he conducted Pitt into the

morning room and left him. It was five minutes before Jessamyn Nash appeared. Pitt knew her immediately; she was the woman from the portrait in the hall, with those wide, direct eyes, that mouth, that radiant hair, thick and soft as summer fields. She was dressed in black now, but it did nothing to dim her brilliance. She stood very straight, her chin high.

"Good morning, Mr. Pitt. What is it you wish to ask me?"

"Good morning, ma'am. I'm sorry to have to disturb you in such tragic circumstances—"

"I appreciate the necessity. You do not need to explain." She walked across the room with exquisite grace. She did not sit, nor did she invite him to do so. "Naturally you must discover what happened to Fanny, poor child." Her face froze for just an instant, stiff. "She was only a child, you know, very innocent, very—young."

It was the same impression he had had, extreme youth.

"I'm sorry," he said quietly.

"Thank you." He had no idea from her voice whether she knew he meant it, or if she took it as a simple courtesy, the automatic thing to say. He would like to have assured her, but then she would not care about the feelings of a policeman.

"Tell me what happened." He looked at her back as she stood at the window. She was slender, shoulders delicately soft under the silk. Her voice, when it came, was expressionless, as though she were repeating something rehearsed.

"I was at home yesterday evening. Fanny lived here with my husband and myself. She was my husband's half sister, but I presume you know that. She was only seventeen. She was engaged to marry Algernon Burnon, but that was not to be for three years at least, when she became twenty."

Pitt did not interrupt. He seldom interrupted; the slightest remarks that seemed irrelevant at the time could turn out to

6

mean something, betraying a feeling if nothing else. And he wanted to know all he could about Fanny Nash. He wanted to know how other people had seen her, what she had meant to them.

"—that may seem a long engagement," Jessamyn was saying, "but Fanny was very young. She grew up alone, you see. My father-in-law married a second time. Fanny is—was—twenty years younger than my husband. She seemed forever a child. Not that she was simple." She hesitated, and he noticed that her long fingers were fiddling with a china figurine from the table, twisting it around and around. "Just—" She fumbled for the word. "—ingenuous—innocent."

"And she was living here with you and your husband, until her marriage?"

"Yes."

"Why was that?"

She looked round at him in surprize. Her blue eyes were very cool, and there were no tears in them.

"Her mother is dead. Naturally we offered her a home." She gave a tiny, icy smile. "Young girls of good family do not live alone, Mr.—I'm sorry—I forget your name."

"Pitt, ma'am," he said with equal chill. He was ruffled, surprised that he was still capable of feeling slighted after all these years. He refused to show it. He smiled within himself. Charlotte would have been furious; her tongue would have spoken as quickly as the words came to her mind. "I thought she might have remained with her father."

Something of his humor must have softened his face. She mistook it for a smirk. The color rose in her exquisite cheeks.

"She preferred to live with us," she said tartly. "Naturally. A girl does not wish to enter the Season without a suitable lady, preferably of her own family, to advise and accompany her. I was happy to do so. Are you sure this is

7

relevant, Mr.—Pitt? Are you not merely indulging your curiosity? I appreciate our way of life is probably quite unknown to you."

An acid reply came to his mind, but anger was irrevocable, and he could not yet afford to commit himself to her enmity.

He pulled a face. "Perhaps it has nothing to do with it. Please continue with your account of yesterday evening."

She took a breath to speak, then apparently changed her mind. She crossed over to the mantel shelf, piled with photographs, and began again in the same flat voice.

"She had spent a perfectly usual day. She had no household affairs to attend to, of course—I do all that. She wrote letters in the morning, consulted her diary, and kept an appointment with her dressmaker. She lunched here at home, and then in the afternoon she took the carriage and went calling. She did tell me upon whom, but I forget. It is always the same sort of people, and as long as one remembers oneself, it really hardly matters. I dare say you can find out from the coachman, if you wish. We dined at home. Lady Pomeroy called, a most tiresome person, but a family obligation—you wouldn't understand."

Pitt controlled his face and regarded her with continued polite interest.

"Fanny left early," she went on. "She has very little social ability, as yet. Sometimes I think she is too young for a Season! I have tried to teach her, but she is very artless. She seems to lack any natural ability to invent. Even the simplest prevarication is a trial to her. She went on some small errand, a book for Lady Cumming-Gould. At least, that is what she said."

"And you do not think it was so?" he inquired.

A slight flicker crossed her face, but Pitt did not understand it. Charlotte might have interpreted it for him, but she was not here to ask.

"I should think it was precisely so," Jessamyn replied. "As I have tried to explain to you, Mr.—er—" She waved her hand irritably. "Poor Fanny had no art to deceive. She was a guileless as a child."

Pitt had seldom found children guileless; tactless perhaps—but most he could remember were possessed of the natural cunning of a stoat and the toughness in a bargain of a moneylender, although certainly some were blessed with the blandest of countenances. It was the third time Jessamyn had referred to Fanny's immaturity.

"Well, I can ask Lady Cumming-Gould," he replied with what he hoped was a smile as guileless as Fanny's.

She turned away from him sharply, lifting one slender shoulder, as if his face had somehow reminded her who he was and that he must be recalled to his proper position.

"Lady Pomeroy had gone and I was alone when—" her voice wavered, and for the first time she seemed to lose her composure. "—when Fanny came back." She made an effort not to gulp, and failed. She was obliged to fumble for a handkerchief, and the clumsiness of it brought her back. "Fanny came in and collapsed in my arms. I don't know how the poor child had had the strength to come so far. It was amazing. She died but a moment afterward."

"I am sorry."

She looked at him, her face devoid of expression, almost as if she were asleep. Then she moved one hand to brush at her heavy taffeta skirt, perhaps in memory of the blood on her the night before.

"Did she speak at all?" he asked quietly. "Anything?"

"No, Mr. Pitt. She was nearly dead by the time she got so far."

He turned slightly to look at the French doors. "She came in through there?" It was the only possible way without having passed the footman, and yet it seemed natural to ask.

She shivered minutely.

9

"Yes."

He walked over toward them and looked out. The lawn was small, a mere patch, surrounded by laurel bushes and a herbaceous walk beyond. There was a wall between this garden and the next. No doubt, by the time he had closed this case, he would know every view and corner of all these houses—unless there was some pathetic, easy answer, but none presented itself yet. He turned back to her.

"Is there any way your garden connects with the others along the Walk, a gate or door in that wall?"

Her face looked blank. "Yes, but it is hardly the way she would choose to come. She was at Lady Cumming-Gould's."

He must send Forbes to all the gardens to see if there was any sign of blood. A wound such as that must have left some stain. And there might even be broken plants or footprints in gravel or grass.

"Where does Lady Cumming-Gould live?" he asked.

"With Lord and Lady Ashworth," she replied. "She is an aunt, I believe, and is visiting for the Season."

With Lord and Lady Ashworth—so Fanny Nash had been to Emily's house the night she was murdered. Memories came rushing back of Charlotte and Emily as he had first known them in Cater Street when he was investigating the hangman murders. Everyone had been afraid, looking with new eyes at friends, even at family; suspicions had been born that could otherwise have lain silent all life long. Old relationships had faltered and broken under the weight. Now violence and obscene and ugly secrets were close again, perhaps inside the very house. All the nightmares would return, the cold questions one was afraid even to think, and yet could not shut out.

"Is there access between all the gardens?" he asked carefully, forcing the fog and terror of Cater Street from his

10

mind. "Might she have returned that way? It was a pleasant summer evening."

She looked at him with light surprize.

"I hardly think it likely, Mr. Pitt. She was wearing a dinner dress, not pantaloons! She went and returned by the road. She must have been accosted by some lunatic there."

A ridiculous thought flashed through his mind to ask her how many lunatics lived in Paragon Walk, but perhaps she would not know there had been coachmen lounging around at one end waiting for their masters and mistresses to leave a party, and a constable on the beat at the other.

He eased his weight from one foot to the other and stood a little straighter.

"Then I had best go and see Lady Cumming-Gould. Thank you, Mrs. Nash. I hope we will be able to clear up the matter quickly and not need to distress you for long."

"I hope so," she agreed with formal coolness. "Good day."

At the Ashworth house he was shown into the with-drawing room by a butler whose face mirrored his social dilemma. Here was a person who admitted to being of the police, and therefore undesirable, and should not be allowed to forget he was here on sufferance only, a most unpleasant necessity due to the recent tragedy. Yet, on the other hand, he was quite extraordinarily also Lady Ashworth's brother-in-law! Which is what comes of marrying beneath one! In the end the butler settled for a pained civility and withdrew to fetch Lord Ashworth. Pitt was too entertained by the man's predicament to be annoyed.

But when the door opened, it was not George but Emily herself who came in. He had forgotten how charming she could be, and at the same time how utterly different from Charlotte. She was fair and slight, dressed at the height of fashion and expense. Where Charlotte was disastrously forthright, Emily was far too practical to speak without thinking, and could be exquisitely devious when she chose, in a good cause, of course. And she usually considered Society to be an excellent cause. She could lie without a tremor.

She came in now and closed the door behind her, looking straight at him.

"Hello, Thomas," she said wanly. "You must be here about poor Fanny. I didn't dream we should have the good fortune that it should be you to investigate it. I've been trying to think if I knew anything that would be of help, as we did in Callander Square." Her voice lifted for a moment, "Charlotte and I were rather clever there." Then her tone dropped again, and her face took on a pinched, unhappy look. "But that was different. We didn't know the people to start with. And the ones who were dead were dead before we ever knew of them. When you didn't know people alive, it doesn't hurt the same way." She sighed. "Please sit down, Thomas. You tower there, sort of flapping. Can't you do up your coat, or something? I must speak to Charlotte. She lets you come out without—" She looked him up and down and gave up the whole idea.

Pitt ran his hands through his hair and made it worse.

"Did you know Fanny Nash well?" he asked, sitting on the sofa and seeming to spread over it, all coattails and arms.

"No. And I'm ashamed to say it now, but I didn't especially like her either." She made an apologetic little face. "She was rather—dull. Jessamyn's enormous fun. At least half of me can't bear her, and I'm constantly diverted by thinking what I might do next to annoy her."

He smiled. There were so many echoes of Charlotte in her that he could not help warming to her.

"But Fanny was too young," he finished the sentence for her. "Too naive."

"Quite. She was almost insipid." Then her face changed, filling with pity and embarrassment, because she had momentarily forgotten death, and the manner of it. "Thomas, she was the last kind of creature in the world to invite such an abominable thing! Whoever did it must be quite insane. You must catch him, for Fanny's sake—and for everyone else's!"

All sorts of answers ran through his mind, reassurance about strangers and vagrants, long gone now, and they all died on his tongue. It was quite possible that the murderer was someone who lived or worked here in Paragon Walk. Neither the constable on duty at one end nor the servants waiting at the other had seen anyone pass. It was not the sort of area where people wandered unremarked. The probability was that it had been some coachman or footman from the party, inflamed with drink and with time on his hands, allowing a foolish impulse, perhaps when she threatened to cry out, to become suddenly an ugly and appalling crime.

But it was not the crime itself; it was the attendant investigation that frightened, and the haunting fear that it might not be a footman but some man on the Walk, one of themselves with a violent and obscene nature lying under the mannered surface they knew. And police investigations uncovered not only the major crimes, but so often the smaller sins, the meannesses and deceits that hurt so much.

But there was no need to tell her that. For all her title and her assurance, she was still the same girl who had been so vulnerable in Cater Street, when she had seen her father frightened and stripped of his pretenses.

"You will, won't you?" Her voice cut across his silence, demanding an answer. She was standing in the middle of the floor, staring at him.

"We usually do." It was the best thing he could say and be honest. And even if he had wished to, it was not much use lying to Emily. Like many practical and ambitious

13

people, she was disastrously perceptive. She was well accomplished in the art of polite lies, and she read them like a book in others.

He recalled himself to the purpose of his visit.

"She came to see you that evening, didn't she?"

"Fanny?" Her eyes widened a little. "Yes. She returned a book, or something, to Aunt Vespasia. Do you want to speak to her?"

He took the chance immediately.

"Yes, please. Perhaps you had better stay. In case she is distressed, you would be of comfort to her." He imagined an elderly female relative of excessively gentle birth with a correspondingly tender susceptibility to the vapors.

For the first time Emily laughed.

"Oh, my dear," she put her hand over her mouth. "You can't imagine Aunt Vespasia!" She picked up her skirts and swept to the door. "But I shall most certainly stay. It is precisely what I need!"

George Ashworth was handsome enough, with bold dark eyes and a fine head of hair, but he could never have been an equal for his aunt. She was over seventy now, but there were still the remnants of a startling beauty in her face—the strength of the bones, the high cheeks and long, straight nose. Blue-white hair was piled on her head, and she wore a dress of deep lilac silk. She stood in the doorway and looked at Pitt for several minutes, then moved into the room, picking up her lorgnette, and studied him more closely.

"Can't really see without the damn thing," she said irritably. She snorted very gently, like an extremely well-bred horse. "Extraordinary," she breathed out. "So you are a policeman?"

"Yes, ma'am." For an instant even Pitt was at a loss for words. Over his shoulder he saw Emily's face alight with amusement.

14

"What are you looking at?" Vespasia said sharply. "I never wear black. It doesn't suit me. Always wear what suits you, regardless. Tried to tell Emily that, but she doesn't listen. The Walk expects her to wear black, so she does. Very silly. Don't let other people expect you into doing something you don't wish to." She sat down on the sofa opposite and stared at him, her fine, gray eyebrows arched a little. "Fanny came to see me the night she was killed. I assume you knew that, and that is why you have come."

Pitt swallowed and tried to compose his face.

"Yes, ma'am. At what time, please?"

"I've no idea."

"You must have some idea, Aunt Vespasia," Emily interrupted. "It was after dinner."

"If I say I have no idea, Emily, then I have no idea. I don't watch clocks. I don't care for them. When one gets to my age, one doesn't. It was dark, if that is of any help."

"A great help, thank you." Pitt calculated quickly. It must have been after ten, at this time of the year. And Jessamyn Nash had sent the footman for the police at a little before quarter to eleven. "What did she come for, ma'am?" he asked.

"To get away from an excessively boring dinner guest," Vespasia replied immediately. "Eliza Pomeroy. Knew her as a child, and she was a bore even then. Talks about other people's ailments. Who cares? One's own are tedious enough!"

Pitt hid a smile with difficulty. He dared not look at Emily.

"She told you that?" he inquired.

Vespasia considered whether to be patient with him—because he was foolish—and decided against it. The thought was plain in her face.

"Don't be ridiculous!" she said smartly. "She was a

child of quite moderate breeding, neither good enough nor bad enough to be frank. She said she was returning some book or other.''

"You have the book?" He did not know what made him ask, except habit to check every detail. It was almost certainly immaterial.

"I should imagine so," she replied with slight surprise. "But I never lend books I expect to require again, so I couldn't say. She was an honest child. She hadn't the imagination to lie successfully, and she was one of those comfortable people who know their own limitations. She would have done quite nicely, had she lived. No pretensions and no spite, poor little creature."

The humor and the pleasantness vanished as suddenly as winter sun, leaving a chill in the room behind it.

Pitt felt obliged to speak, but his voice was remote, and it sounded trivial, meaningless.

"Did she make any remark about calling upon anyone else?"

Vespasia seemed to have been touched by the same coldness.

"No," she said solemnly. "She had stayed here long enough to serve her purpose. If Eliza Pomeroy had chanced still to be at the Nashes, she could quite easily have excused herself and gone straight up to bed without discourtesy. From her conversation before leaving here, I gathered she intended to go straight home."

"She took her leave of you some time after ten?" Pitt confirmed. "How long do you judge she was here?"

"A little above a half an hour. She came in the early dusk and left when it was fully dark."

That would be roughly quarter to ten until about quarter past, he thought. She must have been attacked somewhere in the short journey down Paragon Walk. They were large houses with broad frontages, carriageways, and shrubbery deep enough to hide a figure, but even so there were only three between Emily's and the Nashes'. She could not have been on the street for more than minutes—unless she had called somewhere else after all?

"She was engaged to marry Algermon Burnon?" His mind searched for possibilities.

"Very suitable," Vespasia agreed. "A pleasant enough young man of quite adequate means. His habits are sober and his manners good, if a trifle boring, so far as I know. Altogether a suitable choice."

Pitt wondered inwardly how much good sense appealed to seventeen-year-old Fanny.

"Do you know, ma'am," he said aloud, "if there was anyone else who especially admired her?" He hoped his meaning was plain under such genteel disguise.

She looked at him with a slight puckering of her eyebrows, and over her shoulder he could see Emily wince.

"I can imagine no one, Mr. Pitt, who held such feelings for her as to precipitate last night's tragedy, which I presume is what you are trying to say?"

Emily shut her eyes and bit her lip to stop herself from laughing.

Pitt was aware he had fallen into precisely the strain of language he despised, and both women knew it. Now he must avoid overcompensating.

"Thank you, Lady Cumming-Gould." He stood up, "I'm sure if anything comes to your mind that you believe could help us, you will let us know. Thank you, Lady Ashworth."

Vespasia nodded slightly and permitted herself a faint smile, but Emily came around the table from the back of the sofa and held out both her hands.

"Please give my love to Charlotte. I shall be calling upon her directly, but not until the worst of this is over. But perhaps that won't be long?"

"I hope not." He touched her hand gently, but he had no belief that it would be so brief, or so easy. Investigations were not pleasant, and things were seldom the same afterwards. There was always hurt.

He visited several of the other houses along the Walk and found at home Algernon Burnon, Lord and Lady Dilbridge, who had held the party, Mrs. Selena Montague, a very handsome widow, and the Misses Horbury. By half past five he left its quiet dignity and made his way back to the scruffy, heelworn utility of the police station. By seven he was at his own front door. The facade of the house was narrow, tidy, but there was no carriageway, no trees, only a scrubbed and whitened step and the wooden gateway through to the back yard.

He opened the door with his key, and at once the same little bubble of pleasure that rose inside him every time burst in warmth, and he found himself smiling. Violence and ugliness slipped away.

"Charlotte?"

There was a clatter in the kitchen, and his smile broadened. He went down the passage and stopped in the doorway. She was on her knees on the scrubbed floor, and two saucepan lids were still rolling just out of her reach under the table. She was in a plain dress with a white apron over it, and her shining, mahogany hair was coming out of its knot in long, trailing strands. She looked up and pulled a face, grabbing at the lids and missing. He bent and picked them up for her, holding out his other hand. She took it, and he pulled her up and toward him. As she relaxed in his arms, he dropped the lids on the table. It was good to feel her, the warmth of her body, of her answering mouth on his.

"Who have you been chasing today?" she asked after a moment.

He pushed the hair off her face.

"Murder," he said quietly. "And rape."

"Oh," her face stiffened a little, perhaps memory. "I'm sorry."

It would have been easy to have left it at that, not to have told her that it was someone Emily knew, living in Emily's street, but she would have to know sometime. Emily would be bound to tell her. Perhaps they would solve it quickly after all—a drunken footman.

But she had already noticed his hesitation.

"Who was it?" she asked. Her first guess for his concern was wrong. "Was she someone with children?"

He thought of little Jemima, asleep upstairs now.

She saw the easing of his face, the shadow of relief.

"Who, Thomas?" she repeated.

"A young woman, a girl—"

She knew that was not all. "You mean a child?"

"No—no, she was seventeen. I'm sorry, love, she lived in Paragon Walk, just a few doors from Emily. I saw Emily this afternoon. She sent her love."

Memories of Cater Street came back, of the fear that had ultimately reached into everything, touching and tainting everyone. She spoke the first fear that came to her mind.

"You don't think George was—had anything to do with it?"

His face fell.

"Good heavens no! Of course not!"

She went back to the stove. She skewered the potatoes savagely to see if they were cooked, and two of them fell apart. She would like to have sworn at them, but she would not in front of him. If he still cherished her as a lady, let him keep his illusions. Her cooking was enough of a hurdle to overcome at one time. She was still enough in love with him to hunger for his admiration. Her mother had taught her how to govern a house most excellently and see that all the tasks were properly performed, but she had never foreseen that Charlotte would marry so far beneath her as to require that she actually do the cooking herself. It had been an experience not without its difficulties. It was to Pitt's credit that he had laughed at her so little and only once lost his temper.

"Your dinner is nearly ready," she said, carrying the pan to the sink. "Was Emily all right?"

"She seemed to be." He sat on the edge of the table. "I met her Aunt Vespasia. Do you know her?"

"No. We don't have an Aunt Vespasia. She must be George's."

"She ought to be yours," he said with a sudden grin. "She is exactly as you might be when you get to be seventy or eighty."

She let the pan go in her surprize and turned to stare at him, his body like some enormous flightless bird, coattails trailing.

"And the thought didn't appall you?" she asked. "I'm surprized you still came home!"

"She was marvelous," he laughed. "Made me feel a complete fool. She said precisely what she thought without a qualm."

"I don't do it without a qualm!" she defended herself. "I can't help it, but I feel awful afterward."

"You won't by the time you're seventy."

"Get off the table. I'm going to put the vegetables on it."

He moved obediently.

"Who else did you see?" she continued when they were in the dining room and the meal was begun. "Emily has told me something of the people in the Walk, although I've never been there."

"Do you really want to know?"

"Of course, I do!" Why on earth did he need to ask? "If someone has been raped and murdered next door to Emily, I have to know about it. It wasn't Jessamyn something-or-other, was it?"

"No. Why?"

"Emily can't abide her, but she would miss her if she were not there. I think disliking her is one of her main entertainments. Although I shouldn't speak like that of someone who might have been killed."

He was laughing at her inside himself, and she knew it, "Why not?" he asked.

She did not know why not, except she was quite sure her mother would have said so. She decided not to answer. Attack was the best form of defense.

"Then who was it? Why are you avoiding telling me?"

"It was Jessamyn Nash's sister-in-law, a girl called Fanny."

Suddenly gentility seemed irrelevant.

"Poor little child," she said quietly. "I hope it was quick, and she knew little of it."

"Not very. I'm afraid she was raped and then stabbed. She managed to make her way to the house and died in Jessamyn's arms."

She stopped with a forkful of meat halfway to her mouth, suddenly sick.

He saw it.

"Why the hell did you ask me in the middle of dinner?" he said angrily. "People die every day. You can't do anything about it. Eat your food."

It was on the tip of her tongue to point out that that did not make it any better. Then she realized that he had been hurt by it himself. He must have seen the body—it was part of his duty—and talked with those who had loved her. To Charlotte she was only imaginary, and imagination could be denied, while memory could not.

Obediently she put the food in her mouth, watching him. His face was calm, the anger entirely gone, but his shoulders were tense and he had forgotten to take any of the gravy she had so carefully made. Was he so moved by the death of the girl—or was it something far worse, fear that the investigations would uncover things uglier, close to him, something about George?

Two

The following morning Pitt went first to the police station, where Forbes was waiting with a lugubrious face.

"Morning, Forbes," Pitt said cheerfully. "What's the matter?"

"Police surgeon's been looking for you," Forbes replied with a sniff. "Got a message about that corpse from yesterday."

Pitt stopped.

"Fanny Nash? What message?"

"I don't know. 'E wouldn't say."

"Well, where is he?" Pitt demanded. What on earth could the man have to say beyond the obvious? Was she with child? It was the only thing he could think of.

"Gone to 'ave a cup of tea," Forbes shook his head. "I suppose we're going back to Paragon Walk?"

"Of course, we are!" Pitt smiled at him and Forbes looked glumly back. "You can see a little more of how the gentry live. Try all the staff at that party."

"Lord and Lady Dilbridge?"

"Precisely. Now I'm going to find that surgeon." He swung out of the office and went to the little eating house on the corner where the police surgeon in a dapper suit was sitting over a pot of tea. He looked up as Pitt came in.

"Tea?" he inquired.

Pitt sat down.

"Never mind the breakfast. What about Fanny Nash?"

"Ah." The surgeon took a long gulp from his cup. "Funny thing, that. May mean nothing at all, but thought I should mention it. She has a scar on her buttock, left buttock, low down. Looks pretty recent."

Pitt frowned.

"A scar? Healed. So what does that matter?"

"Probably not at all," the surgeon shrugged. "But it's sort of cross-shaped, long bar with shorter cross bar toward the lower end. Very regular, but the funny thing about it is that it's not a cut." He looked up, his eyes very brilliant. "It's a burn."

Pitt sat perfectly still.

"A burn?" he said incredulously. "What on earth could burn her like that?"

"I don't know," the surgeon replied. 'So help me, I don't even care to think."

Pitt left the tea house puzzled, unsure if it meant anything at all. Perhaps it was no more than a perverse and rather ridiculous accident. Meanwhile he must continue the dreary task of establishing where everyone had been at the time the murder was committed. He had already seen Algernon Burnon, the young man engaged to marry Fanny, and found him pale but as composed as was proper in the circumstances. He claimed to have been in the company of someone else all that evening, but refused to say whom. He implied it was a matter of honor that Pitt would not understand, but was too delicate to phrase it quite so plainly. Pitt could get no more from him and for the present was content to leave it so. If the wretched man had been indulging in some other affair at the very time his fiancée was being ravished, he would hardly care to admit it now.

Lord and Lady Dilbridge had been with company since

seven o'clock, and could be written off. The household of the Misses Horbury contained no men at all. Selena Montague's only manservant had been either in the servants' hall or in his own pantry in view of the kitchen all the relevant time. That left Pitt with three more houses to call on and then the distressing duty of going back to the Nashes' to see Jessamyn's husband, the half brother of the dead girl. Lastly there was the personally awkward necessity of asking George Ashworth to account for his time. Pitt hoped, above anything else in the case, that George could do so.

He wished he could have got that interview over with first, but he knew that George would not be available so early in the morning. More than that, there was a foolishness in him that hoped he might discover some strong clue before he came to the necessity, something so urgent and pointed he could avoid asking George at all.

He began at the second house in the Walk, immediately after the Dilbridges'. At least this unpleasant task could be put behind him. There were three Nash brothers, and this was the house of the eldest, Mr. Afton Nash and his wife, and the youngest, Mr. Fulbert Nash, as yet single.

The butler let him in with weary resignation, warning him that the family was still at breakfast, and he must oblige him to wait. Pitt thanked him and, when the door was closed, began slowly to walk around the room. It was traditional, expensive, and yet made him feel uncomfortable. There were numerous leather-bound volumes in the bookcase in such neat order as to look unused. He ran his finger along them to see if there was dust on them, but they were immaculate, more to the credit of the housekeeper, he guessed, than of any reader. The bureau held the usual clutter of family photographs. None of them smiled, but that was usual; one had to hold a pose for so long that smiling was impossible. A sweetness of expression was the best that could be hoped for, and it had not been achieved here.

An embroidered sampler hung above the mantel, a single, baleful unblinking eye, and underneath it in cross stitch, "God sees all."

He shivered and sat down with his back to it.

Afton Nash came in and closed the door behind him. He was a tall man, becoming portly, with strong, straight features. But for a certain heaviness and a tightening in the mouth, it should have been a handsome face. Curiously, it was not even pleasing.

"I don't know what we can do for you, Mr. Pitt," he said coldly. "The poor child lived with my brother Diggory and his wife. Her moral welfare was their concern. Perhaps on hindsight it would have been better if we had taken her, but it appeared a perfectly adequate arrangement at the time. Jessamyn cares for Society more than we do, and therefore was more suitable to introduce Fanny."

Pitt should have been used to it, the defensive drawing together, the protestations of innocence, even of noninvolvement. They came in some form or other every time. And yet this was peculiarly repellent to him. He remembered the girl's face, so unmarked by life; she had hardly begun, and she was destroyed so quickly. Here in the comfortless room her brother was talking about "moral welfare" and looking to exonerate himself from whatever blame there turned out to be.

"One cannot 'make arrangements' against murder," Pitt could hear the edge in his own voice.

"One can surely make arrangements against rape," Afton answered tartly. "Young women of virtuous habits do not court such an end."

"Have you some reason to suppose your sister was not of virtuous habits?" Pitt had to ask, although everything in him already knew the answer.

26

Afton turned round and regarded him with a curl of distaste.

"She was raped before she was murdered, Inspector. You must know that as well as I. Please do not be coy. It is disgusting. You would be better employed speaking to my brother Diggory. He has some curious tastes. Though I would have expected even he would not infect his sister with them, but I could be mistaken. Perhaps one of his less salubrious friends was in the Walk that night? I assume you will do your best to ascertain precisely who was here?"

"Of course," Pitt agreed with equal coolness. "We shall be determining the whereabouts of everyone we can."

Afton's eyebrows rose a little.

"The residents of the Walk can hardly interest you—the servants perhaps, although I doubt it. I, for one, am most particular about the type of manservant I employ, and I do not allow my women servants to have followers."

Pitt felt a twinge of pity for the servants, and the bleak, joyless lives they must lead.

"A person might be in no way involved," he pointed out, "and yet possibly have seen something of significance. The smallest observation may help."

Afton grunted in irritation that he had not seen the point for himself. He flicked a nonexistent crumb from his sleeve.

"Well, I was at home that night. I remained in the billiard room most of the evening, with my brother Fulbert. I neither saw nor heard anything."

Pitt could not afford to give up so easily. He must not let his dislike of the man show. He had to struggle.

"Perhaps you noticed something earlier, in the last few weeks—" he began again.

"If I had noticed such a thing, Inspector, do you not imagine I should have done something about it?" Afton's heavy nose twitched minutely. "Apart from the unpleasant-

27

ness for all of us of such a thing happening here, Fanny was my sister!"

"Of course, sir—but with the perception of hindsight?" Pitt finished the question.

Afton considered again.

"Not that I can recollect," he said carefully. "But if something does occur, I shall inform you. Was there anything else?"

"Yes, please I would like to speak to the rest of your family."

"I think if they had observed anything they would have spoken to me of it," Afton said with impatience.

"Nevertheless, I would like to see them," Pitt persisted.

Afton stared at him. He was a tall man, and they looked eye to eye. Pitt refused to waver.

"I suppose it is necessary," Afton conceded at last, his face sour. "I do not wish to set a bad example. One must consider one's duty. I would ask you to be as delicate as you are capable with my wife."

"Thank you, sir. I shall do my best not to distress her."

Phoebe Nash was as different from Jessamyn as possible. If there had ever been fire in her, it long since had been damped. She was dressed in tired black, and there was no artificial color in her pale face. At another time she might have been pleasing enough, but now she looked very much the recently bereaved, eyes a little pink, nose puffed, her hair orderly but far less than elegant.

She refused to sit, and stood staring at him, holding her hands tightly together.

"I doubt I can help you, Inspector. I was not even at home that evening. I was visiting an elderly relative who had been unwell. I can give you her name if you wish?"

"I do not doubt you for a moment, ma'am," he said, smiling as much as he dared without appearing to show undue levity in the face of death. He felt a nameless, sad pity for her. He wanted to put her at ease and did not know how. She was a sort of woman he did not understand. All her feelings were inward, tightly governed; gentility was everything.

"I wondered if perhaps Miss Nash might have confided in you," he began, "being her sister-in-law, if perhaps someone had paid her unwelcome attention, or passed an offensive remark? Even if she had seen a stranger in the neighborhood?" He kept on trying, "Or if you have yourself?"

Her hands jerked into a knot, and she stared at him, appalled.

"Oh dear heaven! You don't imagine he's still here, do you?"

He hesitated, wanting to take away her fear, which at least was a familiar emotion, and yet he knew it was foolish to lie.

"If he's a vagrant, I don't doubt he'll have moved on by now," he settled for a truth that was without meaning. "Only a fool would stay, when the police are here and looking for him."

She relaxed visibly, even permitting herself to sit down on the edge of one of the bulging chairs.

"Thank goodness. You've made me feel so much better. Of course I should have thought of that for myself." Then she frowned, drawing her light brows together. "But I don't recall seeing any strangers in the Walk, at least not of that type. Had I done so, I should have sent the footman to get rid of them."

He would only terrify and confuse her if he tried to explain that rapists did not necessarily appear different from anyone else. Crime so often surprised people, as if it were not merely an outward act born from the inward selfishness, greed, or hate that had grown too big inside, the dishonesties suddenly without restraint. She expected it to be

29

recognizable, different, nothing to do with the people she knew.

It would be pointless and hurtful to try to change her. He wondered why after so many years he even noticed it, still less allowed it to disturb him.

"Perhaps Miss Nash confided in you?" he suggested. "If anyone had distressed her, or made improper remarks?"

She did not even bother to consider it.

"Certainly not! If such a thing had happened, I should have spoken to my husband, and he would have taken steps!" Her fingers were winding round a handkerchief in her lap, and she had already torn the lace.

Pitt could imagine what Afton Nash's "steps" might have been. Still he could not quite give up.

"She expressed no anxieties at all, mentioned no new acquaintance?"

"No." She shook her head vehemently.

He sighed and stood up. There was nothing more to be gained from her. He had a feeling that, if he frightened her with the truth, she would simply banish it from her mind and dissolve all reason and memory in blind fear.

"Thank you, ma'am, I'm sorry to have had to distress you with the matter."

She smile with something of an effort.

"I'm sure it is perfectly necessary, or you would not have done so, Inspector. I suppose you wish to see my brother-in-law, Mr. Fulbert Nash? But I'm afraid he was not at home last night. I dare say, if you call this afternoon, he may have returned."

"Thank you, I shall do that. Oh," he remembered the peculiar burn the surgeon had remarked, "do you happen to know if Miss Nash had had an accident recently, a burn?" He did not wish to describe the place of the injury if it was avoidable. He knew it would embarrass her exquisitely.

"Burn?" she said with a frown.

"Quite a small burn," he described its shape as the police surgeon had described it to him. "But fairly deep, and recent."

To his amazement, every vestige of color fled from her face.

"Burn?" her voice was faint. "No, I cannot imagine. I'm sure I know nothing of it. Perhaps—perhaps she had—" she coughed "—had taken some interest in the kitchen? You must ask my sister-in-law. I—I really have no idea."

He was puzzled. She was plainly horrified. Was it simply that she knew the site of the injury and was agonized with embarrassment by it because he was a man, and an infinitely inferior person in her social hierarchy? He did not understand her well enough to know.

"Thank you, ma'am," he said quietly. "Perhaps it is of no importance." And with further polite murmurings he was shown out by the footman into the light and sun again.

He stood for several minutes before deciding whom to call upon next. Forbes was somewhere in the Walk, talking to the servants, relishing his new importance in investigating a murder, and indulging a long cherished curiosity about the precise workings of the households of a social order beyond all his previous experience. He would be a mine of information tonight, most of it useless, but in all the welter of trivial habit, there might be some observation that led to another—and another. He smiled broadly as he thought of it, and a passing gardener's boy stared at him with amazement, and a little awe for one who was obviously not a gentleman and yet could stand idle in the street and grin at himself.

In the end he tried the central house, belonging to one Paul Alaric, and was told very civilly that Monsieur Alaric was not expected home until dark, but if the Inspector would care to call then, no doubt Monsieur would receive him.

He had not yet composed in his mind what he meant to say to George, so he shelved it and tried the house further on, belonging to a Mr. Hallam Cayley.

Cayley was still at a very late breakfast but invited him in, offering him a cup of strong coffee, which Pitt declined. He preferred tea anyway, and this looked as thick as the oiled water in the London docks.

Cayley smiled sourly and poured himself another cupful. He was a good-looking man in his early thirties, although excellent, somewhat aquiline features were spoiled by a deeply pocked skin, and already there was a shade of temper, a slackness, marking itself around his mouth. This morning his eyes were puffed and a little bloodshot. Pitt guessed at a heavy engagement with the bottle the evening before, perhaps several bottles.

"What can I do for you, Inspector?" Cayley began before Pitt asked. "I don't know anything. I was at the Dilbridges' party most of the night. Anyone'll tell you that."

Pitt's heart sank. Was everyone going to be able to account for themselves? No, that was foolish. It did not matter, it was almost certainly some servant who had had too much to drink, got above himself, and then when the girl had screamed, he had knifed her in fear, to keep her quiet, perhaps not even meaning to kill. Forbes would probably find the answers. He himself was merely asking the masters because someone had to, as a matter of form, so they would know the police were doing their jobs—and better he than Forbes, with his awkward tongue and his glaring curiosity.

"Do you happen to recall who you were with about ten o'clock, sir?" he recalled himself to his questions.

"Actually, I had a row with Barham Stephens," Cayley helped himself to yet more coffee and shook the pot irritably when it did no more than half-fill his cup. He slammed it down, rattling the lid. "Fool said he didn't lose at cards. Can't stomach a bad loser. No one can." He glared at his crumb strewn plate.

"You had this disagreement at ten o'clock?" Pitt asked.

Cayley remained staring at the plate.

"No, bit before, and it was more than a disagreement. It was a bloody row." He looked up sharply. "No, not what you would call a row, I suppose. No shouting. He may not behave like a gentleman, but we're both sufficiently wellbred not to brawl in front of women. I went outside for a walk to cool off."

"Into the garden?"

Cayley looked down at the plate again.

"Yes. If you want to know if I saw anything—I didn't. There were loads of people milling around. Dilbridges have some peculiar social tastes. But I suppose you've got a guest list? You'll probably find it was some footman hired for the evening. Some people do hire carriages, you know, especially if they're only up for the Season." His face was suddenly very grave, and he looked at Pitt unblinkingly. "I honestly haven't an idea who could have murdered poor Fanny." His face crumpled a little with a strange pain, subtler than simple pity. "I know most of the men on the Walk. I can't say I care for all of them, but neither can I honestly believe any of them capable of sticking a knife into a woman, a child like Fanny." He pushed his plate away with repugnance. "I suppose it could be the Frenchman, odd sort of fellow, and a knife sounds a French kind of thing. But it doesn't really seem likely."

"Murder often isn't," Pitt said softly. Then he thought of the filthy, teeming rookeries squatting just behind stately streets, where crime was the road to survival, infants learned to steal as soon as they could walk, and only the cunning or the strong made it to adulthood. But all that was

33

irrelevant in Paragon Walk. Here it was shocking, alien, and naturally they sought to disown it.

Cayley was sitting quite still, eaten up with some inner moil of emotions.

Pitt waited. Outside, carriage wheels crunched on the gravel and passed.

At last Cayley looked up.

"Who on earth would want to do that to a harmless little creature like Fanny?" he said quietly. "It's so bloody pointless!"

Pitt had no answer for him. He stood up.

"I don't know, Mr. Cayley. Presumably she recognized the rapist, and he knew it. But why he assaulted her in the first place, only God knows."

Cayley banged a hard, tight fist on the table, not loudly, but with tremendous power.

"Or the devil!" He put his head down and did not look up again, even when Pitt went out of the door and closed it behind him.

Outside the sun was warm and clear, birds chattered in the gardens across the Walk, and somewhere out of sight beyond the curve a horse's hooves clattered past.

He had seen the first open grief for Fanny, and although it was painful, a reminder that the mystery was trivial, the tragedy real—that long after everyone knew who had killed her, and how, and why, she would still be dead—yet he felt cleaner for it.

He went to see Diggory Nash. It was the middle of the afternoon when he could no longer put off going back to Emily and George. He had learned nothing that would allow him to avoid asking the question. Diggory Nash had offered nothing positive either. He had been away from home, gambling, so he said, at a private party, and was reluctant to name the other players. Pitt was not prepared at this stage to insist.

Now he must see George. Not to do so would be as obvious and thereby as offensive as any questions he could ask.

Vespasia Cumming-Gould was taking tea with Emily and George when Pitt was announced. Emily took a deep breath and asked the parlormaid to have him shown in. Vespasia looked at her critically. Really, the girl was wearing her corset far too tightly for one in her stage of pregnancy. Vanity was all very well in its place, but child-bearing was not its place, as every woman should know! When the opportunity arose, she must tell her what apparently her own mother had neglected to. Or was the poor girl so fond of George, and so unsure of his affection, as to be trying still to capture his interest? If she had been a little better bred she would have been brought up to expect the weaknesses of men and take them in her stride. Then she could have treated the whole thing with indifference, which would have been far more satisfactory.

And now this extraordinary creature, the police inspector, was coming into the withdrawing room, all arms and legs and coattails, with hair like the scullery maid's mop, falling in every direction.

"Good afternoon, ma'am," Pitt said courteously.

"Good afternoon, Inspector," she replied, extending him her hand without rising. He bent over and brushed it with his lips. It was a ridiculous gesture from a policeman, who after all was more or less a tradesman, but he did it without an iota of self-consciousness, even a kind of odd grace. He was not as uncoordinated as he appeared. Really, he was the oddest creature!

"Please sit down, Thomas," Emily offered. "I shall send for more tea." She rang the bell as she spoke.

"What is it you wish to know this time?" Vespasia enquired. Surely the fellow could not be paying a social call?

35

He turned a little to face her. He was uncommonly plain, and yet she found him not displeasing. There was great intelligence in his face and a better humor than she had observed in anyone else in Paragon Walk, except perhaps that marvelously elegant Frenchman all the women were making such fools of themselves about. Surely that could not be why Emily was tying herself in? Could it?

Pitt's reply cut across her thoughts.

"I was not able to see Lord Ashworth when I called before, ma'am," he answered.

Of course. Suppose the wretched man had to see George. It would appear odd if he did not.

"Quite," she agreed. "I suppose you want to know where he was?"

"Yes, please?"

She turned to George, sitting a little sideways on the arm of one of the easy chairs. Wish he would sit properly, but he never had since he was a child. Always fidgeted, even on a horse; only saving grace was that he had good hands, didn't haul an animal about. Got it from his mother. His father was a fool.

"Well!" she said sharply, turning to him. "Where were you, George? You weren't here!"

"I was out, Aunt Vespasia."

"Obviously!" she snapped. "Where?"

"At my club."

There was something in the way he was sitting that made her feel uncomfortable and distrust his answer. It was not a lie, and yet it was somehow incomplete. She knew it from the way he shifted his bottom a little. His father had done exactly the same as a child when he had been in the butler's pantry trying the port. The fact that the butler had imbibed the majority of it himself was immaterial.

"You have several clubs," she pointed out tartly. "Which were you at on that occasion? Do you wish to send Mr. Pitt

36

scouring all the gentlemen's clubs in London asking after you?"

George colored.

"No, of course not," he said with irritation. "I was at Whyte's, I think, most of the evening. Anyway, Teddy Aspinall was with me. Although I don't suppose he kept time, any more than I did. But I suppose you could ask him, if you have to?" He twisted to look at Pitt. "Although I'd rather you didn't press him. He was pretty well soaked, and I don't suppose he can remember much. Rather embarrassing for him. His wife is a daughter of the Duke of Carlisle, and a bit straitlaced. Make things rather unpleasant."

The old Duke of Carlisle was dead, and anyway Daisy Aspinall was as used to her husband's drinking as she had been to her father's. However, Vespasia forbore from saying so. But why did George not want Pitt to ask? Was he nervous that Pitt would let fall that he was George's brother-in-law? No doubt George would get ragged about it, but one was not accountable for the peculiar tastes of one's relatives, as long as they were discreet about it. And so far Emily had been excellently discreet, as much as loyalty to her sister would allow. Vespasia admitted to a rapidly mounting curiosity about this sister she had never seen. Why had Emily not invited her? Since they were sisters, surely the girl had been tolerably well brought up? Emily certainly knew how to behave like a lady. Only someone of Vespasia's immense and subtle experience would have known she was not—not quite.

She had missed some of the conversation. Hope to heavens she was not becoming deaf! She could not bear to be deaf. Not to hear what people were saying would be worse than being buried alive!

"—time you came home?" Pitt finished.

George scowled. She could remember the same expression on his face when doing sums as a child. He always chewed the ends of his pencils. Disgusting habit. She had told his mother to soak them in aloes, but the softhearted woman had refused.

"I'm afraid I didn't look," George answered after a few moments. "I think it was pretty late. I didn't disturb Emily."

"What about your valet?" Pitt enquired.

"Oh—yes," George seemed uncertain. "I doubt he'll remember. He'd fallen asleep in my dressing room. Had to waken him up." His face brightened. "So it must have been pretty late. Sorry, I can't help you. Looks as if I was miles away at the time that matters. Didn't see a thing."

"Were you not invited to the Dilbridges' party?" Pitt asked with surprise. "Or did you prefer not to go?"

Vespasia stared at him. Really, he was a most unexpected person. He was sitting now on the couch, taking up more than half of it in pure untidiness. None of his clothes seemed to fit him properly, poverty, no doubt. In the hands of a good tailor and barber he might even have looked quite well. But there was a suppressed energy about him that was hardly decent. He looked as if he might laugh at any time, any inappropriate time. Actually, when she thought about it, he was quite entertaining. Pity it had taken a murder to bring him here. On any other occasion he would have been a distinct relief from the boredom of Eliza Pomeroy's ailments, Lord Dilbridge's excesses, as recited by Grace Dilbridge, Jessamyn Nash's latest gown, Selena Montague's current involvement, or the general decay of civilization as monitored by the Misses Horbury and Lady Tamworth. The only other diversion was the rivalry between Jessamyn and Selena as to who should attract the beautiful Frenchman, and so far neither of them had made any progress that she had heard about. And she would have heard. What was the point in making a conquest if one could not tell everybody about it, preferably one by one and in the strictest

38

confidence? Success without envy was like snails without sauce—and, as any cultivated woman knew, the sauce is everything!

"I preferred not to go," George said, his brow wrinkled. He also failed to see the relevance of the question. "It was not the sort of occasion to which I would wish to take Emily. The Dilbridges have some—some friends of decidedly vulgar tastes."

"Oh, do they?" Emily looked surprized. "Grace Dilbridge always looks so tame."

"She is," Vespasia said impatiently. "She does not write the guest list. Not that I think she would object to it. She is one of those women who like to suffer; she has made a career of it. If Frederick were to behave properly, she would have nothing to talk about. It is the sole source of her importance—she is put upon."

"That's terrible!" Emily protested.

"It's not terrible," Vespasia contradicted. "She is perfectly happy with it, but it is extremely tedious." She turned to Pitt. "No doubt that is where you will find your murderer, either among Frederick Dilbridge's guests, or among their servants. Some of the most reprehensible persons can drive a carriage-and-pair extraordinarily well." She sighed. "I can remember my father had a coachman who drank like a sot and bedded every girl in the village, but he could drive better than Jehu—best hands in the south of England. Gamekeeper shot him in the end. Never knew whether it was an accident or not."

Emily looked helplessly at Pitt, anxiety driving the laughter out of her eyes.

"That's where you'll find him, Thomas," she said urgently. "No one in Paragon Walk would have done it!"

There was still time for Pitt to see Fulbert Nash, the last brother, and he was fortunate to find him at home a little

39

before five. Apparently, to judge from Fulbert's face, he had been expected.

"So you are the police," Fulbert looked him up and down with undisguised curiosity, as one might regard some new invention, but without the desire to purchase it.

"Good afternoon, sir," Pitt said a little more stiffly than he had intended.

"Oh, good afternoon, Inspector." Fulbert mimicked the tone very slightly. 'Obviously you are here about Fanny, poor little creature. Do you want her life history? It's pathetically short. She never did anything of note, and I don't suppose she ever would have. Nothing in her life was as remarkable as her death.''

Pitt was angered by his flippancy, although he knew how often people covered grief they could not bear with apparent indifference, or even laughter.

"I have no reason yet, sir, to suppose she was anything but a chance victim, and therefore her life story need not be inquired into so far. Perhaps if you would tell me where you were on that evening, and if you saw or heard anything that might help us?''

"I was here," Fulbert replied with slightly raised eyebrows. He was more reminiscent of Afton than of Diggory, having something of Afton's faintly supercilious expression, features that should have been handsome, but were not. Diggory, on the other hand, was less well constructed, but there was a pleasingness in the irregularity, character in the stronger, darker brows, something altogether warmer.

"All evening," Fulbert added.

"In company, or alone?" Pitt asked.

Fulbert smiled.

"Didn't Afton say I was with him, playing billiards?"

"Were you, sir?"

"No, as a matter of fact, I wasn't. Afton's several inches

40

taller than I am, as I dare say you've noticed. It irritates the hell out of him that he can't beat me, and Afton in a bad temper is more than I care to put up with.''

"Why don't you let him beat you?" The answer seemed obvious.

Fulbert's light-blue eyes opened wide, and he smiled. His teeth were small and even, too small for a man's mouth.

"Because I cheat, and he's never been able to work out how. It's one of the few things I do better than he does,'' he answered.

Pitt was a little lost. He could not imagine any pleasure in a competition to see who could cheat the best. But then he did not enjoy games himself. He had never had time in his youth, when he might have learned the skills. Now it was too late.

"Were you in the billiard room all evening, sir?''

"No, I thought I just told you that! I wandered round the house a bit, library, upstairs, into the butler's pantry and had a glass of port, or two." He smiled again. "Long enough for Afton to have nipped out and raped poor Fanny. And since she was his sister, you'll be able to add incest to the charge—'' He saw Pitt's face. "Oh, I've offended your sensibilities. I forgot how puritanical the lower classes are. It's only the aristocracy and the guttersnipes who are frank about everything. And on reflection, perhaps we are the only ones who can afford to be. We are so arrogant we think no one can shift us, and the guttersnipes have nothing to lose. Do you really imagine my painfully self-righteous brother crept out between billiard balls and raped his sister in the garden? She wasn't stabbed with a billiard cue, was she?''

"No, Mr. Nash," Pitt said coldly and clearly. "She was stabbed with a long knife, sharp point and probably single-edged.''

Fulbert shut his eyes, and Pitt was glad he had hurt him at last.

"How revolting," he said quietly. "I didn't go out of the house, which is what you want to know, nor did I see or hear anything odd. But you can be damned sure that if I do, I'll look a good deal harder! I suppose you're working on the hypothesis it is some lunatic? Do you know what a hypothesis is?"

"Yes, sir, and so far I am merely collecting evidence. It is too early for hypotheses." He deliberately used the plural to show Fulbert that he knew it.

Fulbert observed and smiled.

"I'll lay you odds two to one it is not! I'll lay you it's one of us, some nasty, grubby little secret that snapped through the civilized veneer—and rape! She saw him, and he had to kill her. Look into the Walk, Inspector, look at us all very, very carefully. Sift us through a small sieve, and comb us with a fine-tooth comb—and see what parasites and what lice you turn up!" He giggled very lightly with amusement and met Pitt's angry eyes squarely, brilliantly. "Believe me, you'll be amazed what there is!"

Charlotte was waiting anxiously for Pitt all afternoon. From the time she had put Jemima upstairs for her afternoon sleep, she found herself repeatedly glancing at the old brown clock on the dining room shelf, going up to it to listen for the faint tick to make sure it was still going. She knew perfectly well it was foolish, because he could not return before five at the very earliest, and more likely six.

The reason for her concern was Emily, of course. Emily was newly with child, her first, and, as Charlotte could remember only too well, those first months could be very trying. Not only did one feel a natural unsureness at one's new condition, but there were nausea and the most unreasonable depressions to overcome.

She had never been to Paragon Walk. Emily had invited her, naturally, but Charlotte was not sure if she had really wished her to go. Ever since they were girls, when Sarah had been alive, and they had lived in Cater Street with Mama and Papa, Charlotte's lack of tact had been a social liability. Mama had found umpteen suitable young men for her, but Charlotte had had no ambitions, like the others, to make her curb her tongue and seek to impress. Of course, Emily loved her, but she was also aware that Charlotte would not be comfortable in the Walk. She could not afford the clothes, nor the time from her household tasks. She knew none of the gossip, and her life would soon be seen to be utterly different.

Now she wished she could go, to see for herself that Emily was quite well and not afraid because of the appalling crime. Of course her sister could always remain at home, go out only with a servant, and in daylight, but that was not the real terror. Charlotte refused to remember or think of that.

It was after six when she finally heard Pitt at the door. She dropped the potatoes she was straining in the sink and knocked over the salt and pepper on the edge of the table running out to meet him.

"How's Emily?" she demanded. "Have you seen her? Have you discovered who killed that girl?"

He closed her in a hard hug. "No, of course I haven't. I've barely begun. And yes, I saw Emily, and she seemed quite well."

"Oh." She pulled away. "You haven't discovered any-thing! But you know at least that George had nothing to do with it, don't you?"

He opened his mouth to answer, but she saw the indecision in his eyes before he found the words.

"You don't!" It came out as an accusation. She was aware even as she said it, and she was sorry, but there was

43

no time to apologize now. "You don't know! Why haven't you found out where he was?"

He moved her aside gently and sat down at the table.

"I asked him," he said. "I haven't had time to check yet."

"Check?" she was at his elbow. "Why? Don't you believe him?" Then she knew that was unfair. He did not have the choice of belief, and anyway belief was not what she needed, not what Emily needed. "I'm sorry." She touched his shoulder with her hand, feeling the hardness of it under his coat. Then she moved away back to the sink and picked up the potatoes again. She tried to keep her voice casual, but it came out ridiculously high. "Where did he say he was?"

"At his club," he replied. "Most of the time. He can't remember how long he was there, or precisely which other clubs he went to."

She went on mechanically dishing the potatoes, the fine-chopped cabbage and the fish she had been so careful to bake in cheese sauce. It was something she had only just learned how to make successfully. Now she surveyed its perfection without interest. Perhaps it was foolish to be afraid. George might be able to prove exactly where he had been all the time, but she had heard about men's clubs, the games, the conversations, people sitting around drinking, or even asleep. How could anyone remember who had been there at a particular time, or even a particular evening? How was one evening different from another to recall it with surety?

It was not that she thought George might have killed the girl, nothing so appalling as that, but she knew from the past what damage even suspicion can do. If George was telling the truth, he would resent it if Emily did not utterly and immediately believe him. And if he had evaded the truth, left out something, like a flirtation, a foolish party,

44

some excess in drink, then he would feel guilty. One lie would lead to another, and Emily would become confused and in the end perhaps suspect him even of the crime itself. The truth could be full of so many uglinesses. It was unforeseeably painful to strip away the small deceits that made life comfortable and allowed you not to see what you preferred to pretend you did not know.

"Charlotte," Pitt's voice came from behind her. She forced the fear out of her mind and served the food. She set it on the table in front of him.

"Yes?" she said innocently.

"Stop it!"

It was no use trying to deceive him, even with a thought. He read her too easily. She sat down with her own plate.

"You will prove it wasn't George as soon as you can, won't you?" she asked.

He stretched out his hand across the table to touch hers.

"Of course, I will. As soon as I can, without making it look as if I suspect him."

She had not even thought of that! Of course—if he pursued George first of all, it would make it even worse. Emily would think—oh goodness only knew what Emily would think.

"I shall go and call on Emily." She speared a potato with her fork and sliced it hard, unconsciously making the pieces smaller than usual, as if she were already dining in Paragon Walk. "She is often inviting me." She started to think which of her dresses she could possibly make suitable for the occasion. If she called in the morning, her dark gray would be well enough. It was a good muslin and not too obviously last year's cut. "After all, one of us should go, and Mama is busy with Grandmama's illness. I think it is an excellent idea."

Pitt did not answer her. He knew that she was talking to herself.

Three

Charlotte had already worked out in her mind exactly what she meant to do, and, as soon as Pitt had gone, she tidied the kitchen and then dressed Jemima in her second-best clothes, cotton, trimmed with lace Charlotte had carefully salvaged from one of her own old petticoats. When she was all ready, Charlotte picked her up and took her out into the warm, dusty street and over to the house opposite. The net curtains were twitching behind a dozen windows, but she refused to turn her head and betray that she knew it. Balancing Jemima on one arm, she knocked on the door.

It opened almost immediately, and a gaunt little woman in a plain, stuff pinafore stood on the mat just inside.

"Good morning, Mrs. Smith," Charlotte said with a smile. "I just heard yesterday evening that my sister is unwell, and I feel I should go and see her. Perhaps I can help." She did not want to lie so directly as to imply that Emily had no one else to care for her, as might have been her own situation, but she did want to suggest a certain urgency. Her feelings conflicted; she was faintly ashamed on this woman's doorstep, looking at the shabby hall and knowing that Emily could ring a bell and have a maid come if she were ill, or send a footman for a doctor. Yet she needed to make the summons seem important.

"Would you be good enough to look after Jemima for me today?"

The woman's face lit in an answering smile, and she held out her arms. Jemima hesitated for a moment, drawing back a little, but Charlotte had no time for tears or cajolings today. She gave her a quick kiss and passed her over.

"Thank you very much. I expect I shall not be long, but, if things are worse than I fear, I may not be home until the afternoon.

"Don't you worry, love." The woman cuddled Jemima easily, setting her weight on her bony hip, as she had done with countless bundles of laundry and with all eight of her own children, except the two who had died before they were old enough to sit at all. "I'll take care of 'er, give 'er 'er dinner. You just go and see to your sister, poor soul. I 'ope as it isn't anything bad. I always reckons this 'ot weather's to blame for a lot. Ain't natural."

"No," Charlotte agreed hastily. "I like the autumn best myself."

"More like furrin' weather, I should think," Mrs. Smith went on. "Leastways from what one 'ears. I 'ad a brother what was a sailor. Terrible places 'e's bin to. Well, you go and see to yours sister, dear. I'll take care o' Jemima till you comes back."

Charlotte gave her a dazzling smile. It had taken her a long time to learn any sort of ease with these people, who were so different from those she had known before her marriage. Of course, there had been working people before, but the only ones she had known personally had been servants, as familiar in the house as the furniture or the pictures, as much accommodated to the family's ways, and as easy to regard or ignore. They had brought nothing of their own lives into the drawing room or upstairs. Their

47

families were known of, naturally, as part of their references, but they were no more than names and reputations; there were no faces, and still less any ambitions or tragedies, and feelings.

Now she had to accommodate herself to them, learn to cook, to clean, to shop wisely—above all to need and be needed. Neighbors were everything through the long days while Pitt was away; they were laughter, the sound of voices, help when she did not know how to manage things, when Jemima was cutting teeth and she had no idea what to do. There were no nursery maids to call, no nanny, only Mrs. Smith with her old woman's remedies and years of practice. Her ordinariness, her passive resignation to hardship and obedience infuriated Charlotte, and yet her patience soothed her, that and her sureness of what to do in the daily small crises that Charlotte had never been taught to handle.

To begin with, the whole street had thought Charlotte arrogant, aloof to the point of coldness, not realizing she was as shy of them as they of her. It had taken nearly two years for them to accept her. The annoying thing was that in their own way they were just as prim as Mama and her friends, just as full of genteel expressions to avoid a truth that offended and every whit as conscious of social differences in all the subtlest of shades. Charlotte had quite unintentionally outraged them with her opinions, spoken in total innocence.

Mama's withdrawing room seemed a long time ago: the afternoon teas, the polite visits, exchanging gossip, trying to learn something about eligible young men, other people's social and financial affairs, always in the most circumlocutory manner, of course.

Now she must try to recapture at least the semblance of grace again, sufficient not to embarrass Emily.

She hurried home and changed into the gray muslin with

white spots. Last year she had saved from the housekeeping for it, and the style was so plain as to have dated little. Of course that was why she had chosen it, that, and so as not to seem above herself to the rest of the street.

The day was already hot by ten o'clock when she dismounted from the cab in Paragon Walk, thanked the cabbie and paid him, then crunched her way slowly up the gravel to Emily's door. She was determined not to stare; someone would see her. There was always someone about, a housemaid bored with dusting, daydreaming out of a window, a footman or coachman on an errand, a gardener's boy.

The house was large, and after her own street it seemed positively palatial. Of course, it was built for a full staff of servants as well as the master and mistress, their children and whatever relatives might care to come up for the Season.

She knocked on the door, and then sudddenly felt terribly afraid that she would let Emily down, that their lives had become so separate since Cater Street that they would be strangers. Even that business at Callander Square was more than a year ago now. They had been close then, sharing danger, horror, even a sort of excitement. But that had not been in Emily's home, among her friends.

She was wrong to have thought the gray muslin was all right; it was dull, and there was a tear near the hem that showed where she had mended it. She did not think her hands were red, but she had better keep her gloves on just in case. Emily would be bound to notice; Charlotte's hands had always been beautiful, one of the things she had been proud of.

The maid opened the door, surprize in her face at seeing a stranger.

"Good morning, ma'am?"

"Good morning," Charlotte stood very straight and

49

forced herself to smile. She must speak slowly; it was idiotic to be nervous calling upon one's own sister, and one's younger sister at that. "Good morning," she repeated. "Will you be good enough to inform Lady Ashworth that her sister, Mrs. Pitt, has called?"

"Oh." The girl's eyes widened. "Oh, yes, ma'am. If you'd like to come in, ma'am, I'm sure as her ladyship'll be pleased to see you."

Charlotte followed her in and waited in the morning room for only a few minutes before Emily came bursting in.

"Oh, Charlotte! How marvelous to see you!" She threw her arms around Charlotte's neck and hugged her, then stood back. Her eyes glanced over the gray muslin, then at Charlotte's face. "You look well. I have been meaning to come and see you, but you must know what an awful thing has happened here. Thomas will have told you all about it. Thank heaven it is nothing to do with us this time." She shuddered and shook her head in a little gesture of denial. "Does that sound terribly callous?" She turned back to Charlotte again with a wide, slightly guilty look.

Charlotte was honest as always.

"I suppose it does, but it is the truth, if we would all but admit it. There is a sort of thrill in horror, as long as it is not too close. People will talk about how dreadful it is and how the mere mention of it distresses them beyond conceivable opportunity."

Emily's face relaxed in a smile.

"I'm so glad you're here. I dare say it is quite irresponsible of me, but I shall love to hear your opinions of the Walk, although I shall never be able to view them in the same way afterwards. They are all so very careful, they bore me terribly at times. I've an awful feeling I have forgotten how to think frankly myself!"

Charlotte linked her arm in Emily's, and they walked

through the French doors and onto the lawn at the back. The sun was hot on their faces and dazzled from a peerless sky.

"I doubt it," Charlotte answered. "You were always able to think one thing and say another. I am a social catastrophe because I can't."

Emily giggled as memories came back to her, and for a few moments they talked together over disasters of the past that had made them blush at the time but were only bonds of laughter and shared affection now.

Charlotte had even forgotten her real reason for coming when sudden mention of Sarah, their older sister who had been a victim of the Cater Street hangman, made her remember murder, its close, suffocating terror, and the corroding acid of suspicion it brought in its wake. She had never been able to be subtle, least of all with Emily who knew her so well.

"What was Fanny Nash like?" She wanted a woman's opinion. Thomas was clever, but so often men missed the real things in a woman, things that were perfectly obvious to another woman. The number of times she had seen men taken in by a pretty girl who chose to seem vulnerable, when Charlotte knew really she was as strong and as hard as a kitchen pot!

The laughter died out of Emily's face.

"Are you going to play detective again?" she said warily.

Charlotte thought of Callander Square. Emily had wanted to detect then. She had even insisted on it, and there had been times when it was a kind of adventure—before the frightening, horrifying end.

"No!" she said immediately. Then, "Well, yes. I can't help caring, can I? But I'm not going to go around asking questions, of course not! Don't be foolish. I mean, that would be most unseemly. You should know I wouldn't do that to you. I can be tactless, I admit, but I am not quite stupid!"

Emily relented, probably because she also was curious and the whole thing was not close enough to be ugly yet.

"Of course, I know that. I'm sorry. I am a little highly strung at the moment," she colored very faintly at her reference to her condition; she had not yet be come accustomed to it, and it was not a subject one discussed. "Fanny was rather ordinary, really. I suppose you do want the truth? She was the last person in the world I would have thought to provoke such a passion in anyone. I can only presume he was quite mad, poor creature. Oh." She tightened her lip, caught in a social gaffe herself. She took pride that since her marriage she had made herself immune to such things. Charlotte's influence must be contagious. "I suppose one shouldn't sympathize with him," she corrected. "That is quite wrong. Except that, if he is mad, of course, he cannot help it. Will Thomas catch him?"

Charlotte did not know how to reply. She could say simply that she did not know, but that was no answer at all. What Emily was really asking was: did Thomas have any knowledge; was it inside or outside the Walk; could they all dismiss it as a tragedy, but something beyond their own affairs, a brief intrusion, now entirely of the past, something that had happened in the Walk, but could as easily have occurred anywhere else in the mad creature's path?

"It's too early to say," she temporized. "If he is quite mad, he could be anywhere by now, and since there was no reason for selecting Fanny, except that she was there, he will be very hard to recognize—even when we find him."

Emily looked directly at her.

"Are you saying it is possible it was not someone mad?"

Charlotte avoided her eyes.

"Emily, how can I know? You say Fanny was very— ordinary, not in the least a flirt—"

"No, no one less so. She was not plain, exactly. But you know, Charlotte, the older I get, the more I believe beauty is

52

not so much a matter of what your features or your coloring may be, but the way you behave and what you believe of yourself. Fanny behaved as though she were plain. Whereas Jessamyn, if you look at her dispassionately, is not really so very beautiful, and yet she behaves as if she were quite marvelous. Therefore everyone sees her so! She believes it—and so we do too."

It was very perceptive of Emily to know that. Charlotte wished she could have known it herself when she was younger and cared desperately. She could recall with painful clarity how wretched she had felt at fifteen when Sarah and Emily seemed so pretty and she felt plain, all elbows and feet. She was already the tallest, and still growing. She might become perfectly gigantic, and no man would ever care for her. She would look over the tops of their heads! She thought young James Fortescue so attractive, but she knew she was at least two inches taller than he was and found herself unable to say anything at all in his presence. He had ended up by admiring Sarah instead.

"You are not listening!" Emily accused.

"I'm sorry, what did you say?"

"That Thomas has been up and down the Walk asking questions of all the men. He even asked George where he was."

"Of course," Charlotte said reasonably. This was the part she had been fearing since the beginning. "He has to. After all, George may have seen something that appeared quite usual at the time, but now that we know what happened, he would recognize it as important." She was pleased with the way she had phrased that. It was immediate and yet completely rational. It did not sound contrived to make Emily comfortable.

"I suppose so," Emily conceded. "Actually George wasn't even here that evening. He was in town at his club, so he couldn't be any help."

Charlotte was saved the necessity of answering by the arrival of the most magnificent old lady she had ever seen, with hair piled immaculately and back as straight as a ramrod. Her nose was a shade too long, and her eyes a little hooded, and yet the remnant of beauty was unmistakable, and her intimate knowledge of it and its power even more so.

Emily got to her feet with a trifle more haste than dignity. It was a long time since Charlotte had seen her the least out of composure, and it was telling. She hoped it was not anxiety that she would not know how to behave, and thus let her down.

"Aunt Vespasia," Emily said quickly. "May I present my sister, Charlotte Pitt?" She looked at Charlotte penetratingly. "My great aunt-in-law, Lady Cumming-Gould."

Charlotte had no need of warning.

"How do you do, ma'am," she inclined her head very slightly, enough for courtesy and too little for obsequiousness.

Vespasia extended her hand, and her eyes regarded Charlotte frankly from toe to top, ending with a direct stare from her flittering old eyes.

"How do you do, Mrs. Pitt," she answered levelly. "Emily has often spoken of you. I am pleased that you have been able to call." She did not add "at last," but it was in her voice.

Charlotte doubted that Emily had spoken of her at all, still less that it had been often. It would have been most injudicious—and Emily had never been injudicious in her life—but she could hardly argue. Neither could she think of a suitable answer. "Thank you" seemed so foolish.

"It is kind of you to make me welcome," she heard herself saying.

"I hope you are staying to luncheon?" It was a question.

"Oh yes," Emily rushed in quickly before Charlotte had

54

time to flounder. "Of course, she will stay. And this afternoon we shall go calling."

Charlotte drew breath to make some excuse. She could not possibly go around Paragon Walk with Emily, dressed in gray muslin. Momentarily she was angry with Emily for putting her in such a position. She turned to glare at her.

Aunt Vespasia cleared her throat sharply.

"And who, precisely, did you have it in mind to call upon?"

Emily looked at Charlotte, realized her mistake, and fished herself out of it with aplomb.

"I thought Selena Montague. She admires herself in plum pink, and Charlotte will look so much better in it I should enjoy putting her in my new silk, and obliging Selena to look at her. I do not care for Selena," she added as an aside to Charlotte, quite unnecessarily. "And the dress will fit you excellently. The foolish dressmaker got her fingers muddled and made it much too long for me."

Aunt Vespasia allowed her a small smile of admiration.

"I thought it was Jessamyn Nash you disliked," she remarked casually.

"I like irritating Jessamyn," Emily waved a hand. "That is not really the same thing. I have never thought whether I like her or not."

"Whom do you like?" Charlotte inquired, wanting to know more about the Walk. Now that she was freed from the immediate problem of dress, her mind went back to Fanny Nash and the fear that the others seemed to have forgotten.

"Oh," Emily considered for a moment. "I quite like Phoebe Nash, Jessamyn's sister-in-law, if she would be a little more definite. And I like Albertine Dilbridge, although I have no patience with her mother. And I like Diggory Nash, but I do not know why. I can think of nothing in particular to say about him that is good."

Luncheon was announced, and the three of them departed for the dining room. Charlotte had not seen a meal of such simple grace for a long time, perhaps not ever. It was all cold, and yet of such delicacy that it must have taken hours to prepare. In the still heat it was delicious just to contemplate the cold soups, fresh salmon with minute cold vegetables, ices, sherbets and fruit. She was halfway through eating it, elegantly, as if she ate such things every day, when she remembered Pitt would probably be chewing through heavy bread sandwiches with a little cold meat in them, if he was fortunate, if not, then cheese, dry and clogging in the mouth. She put her fork down, the peas rolling away. Neither Emily nor Vespasia noticed.

It took half an hour, much critical surveying by Emily, and a least a dozen pins, before Charlotte was satisfied that she looked acceptable in the plum silk and could go calling to the Walk. Actually she was rather more than satisfied. It was a very good quality silk indeed, and the color was remarkably flattering to her. The warmth of it against the honey of her skin and the richness of her hair was enough to carry her away in a flight of vanity. It was going to hurt to take it off and give it back to Emily at the end of the afternoon. The gray muslin had lost all its appeal. It no longer looked smart, merely drab and very much last year's.

Aunt Vespasia complimented her with dry humor as she came down the stairs, but she met the old lady's eyes without a flicker and hoped she had no idea how many pins there were in it, or how hard she had relaced her stays to get into Emily's old waist.

She thanked Vespasia and walked with Emily out into the sunlight on the carriageway, head high and back very straight. Actually it was more than a little uncomfortable to hold herself in any other way, and she would have to sit with care.

It was only a hundred yards or so to Selena Montague's

house, and Emily said very little on the way. They knocked at the door and were let in immediately by a smart maid in black and lace, obviously poised to expect callers. Apparently Mrs. Montague was in the garden at the back, and they were invited to join her. The house was elegant and expensive, although Charlotte's practiced eye could see tiny economies, a mend in the fringe of a lampshade, a cushion whose upholstery had obviously been turned, the new piece from the underside darker against the faded wings. She had done the same herself and knew the signs.

Selena was sitting in a wicker chaise lounge, her arms dangling over the sides, her face lifted upward, but protected from the harsh sun by a floppy, flower-decked hat. She had excellent features, although her nose was perhaps a trifle sharp. Her eyes were wide and brown, long lashed, and she opened them with intense interest when she saw Charlotte.

"My dear Selena," Emily began in her best voice. "How charming you look, and so cool! May I present my sister, Charlotte Pitt, who has called upon me?"

Selena did not move, but surveyed Charlotte with barely disguised curiosity. Charlotte had an unpleasant feeling that nothing had been missed, from her rather worn best boots to every pin in her dress.

"How delightful," Selena said at last. "So," she glanced down at Charlotte's boots again "—considerate—of you to have come. I am sure we shall all enjoy your company."

Charlotte felt her temper rise instantly. Above all things she hated to be patronized.

"I hope I shall also enjoy yours," she said with a cool smile.

The implication was not missed by Selena, and from the pressure of Emily's fingers on her arm Charlotte knew that she too had taken the point.

"You must come and dine with us sometime," Selena

57

went on. "These summer evenings are so warm we frequently eat out here. The strawberries are quite delicious this year, don't you think so?"

Strawberries were utterly beyond Charlotte's budgeting.

"Very sweet," she agreed. "Perhaps it is the sun."

"No doubt," Selena was not interested in where they came from. She looked up at Emily. "Please sit down. I'm sure you would like some refreshment, you must be dreadfully hot—" Charlotte saw Emily's face tighten at the implication, and her cheeks did look flushed. "Perhaps a sherbet?" Selena smiled. "And you, Mrs. Pitt? Something cooling?"

"Whatever you care for yourself, Mrs. Montague," Charlotte put in before Emily could speak. "I would not wish to put you to inconvenience."

"I assure you it is no inconvenience!" Selena said with a touch of tartness. She reached out and rang a small bell on the table, and its sharp sound was answered by a maid in starched white. Selena gave elaborate orders. Then she turned to Emily again. "Have you seen poor Jessamyn?"

Emily sat in a white wrought-iron chair, and Charlotte perched on another beside her, carefully, so as not to burst a pin.

"No," Emily replied. "I did leave my card, of course, and a small letter to express my condolences."

Selena struggled to hide her disappointment and failed.

"Pour soul," she murmured. "She must be feeling quite dreadful. One simply cannot imagine it! I hoped perhaps you had seen her and could tell me something."

Emily knew immediately that Selena had not seen her either and was consumed with curiosity.

"One doesn't even wish to try," She shivered. "I'm sure she has the sympathy of absolutely everyone. I have no doubt each of us will call upon her in the next weeks, it would be inhuman not to. Even gentlemen will call, I'm sure. It would be the least they could do to comfort her."

The nostrils flared on Selena's sharp little nose.

"I would not have thought any comfort possible after one's sister-in-law has been violated practically on one's doorstep and has staggered in to die literally in one's arms." There was an unspecified criticism of Emily in her tone. "I think I should retire altogether if such a thing happened to me. I might even become quite deranged." She said it very certainly, as if she were in no doubt that such a thing had already happened to Jessamyn.

"Good gracious!" Emily affected horror. "Surely you don't imagine it will happen again, do you? I didn't even know you had a sister-in-law."

"I don't!" Selena snapped. "I was merely saying how I sympathize with poor Jessamyn, and that we must not expect too much of her. We must be understanding if she seems a little odd—at least I am sure I shall be."

"I'm sure you will, my dear." Emily leaned forward, her voice cooing. "I'm sure you would never intentionally be unkind to anyone."

Charlotte wondered if Emily were not giving her credit for rather many "accidents."

"It must be very difficult to know what to say," Charlotte suggested. "I should not know whether avoiding the subject might seem as if I were indifferent to her loss, or then on the other hand discussing it might appear like curiosity, which would be so vulgar."

Selena's face hardened, taking the inference perfectly.

"How very frank of you," she said with wide-eyed surprize, as if she had discovered something alive in the salad. "Are you always so—candid—about your thoughts, Mrs. Pitt?"

"I'm afraid so. It is my greatest social disadvantage." Now let her find a civil answer to that!

"Oh! Well, I dare say it cannot be too serious," Selena replied cooly. "Your sister does not appear even to be aware of it."

"I am inured to it." Emily smiled dazzlingly at her. "I have suffered disaster upon disaster. Now I only bring her to call upon friends I know I can trust." She met Selena's brown eyes squarely.

Charlotte nearly choked, trying to maintain a sober face. Selena was outmaneuvered, and she knew it.

"How kind," she murmured pointlessly. She took the tray from the maid. "Do have some sherbet."

There was a natural silence after this for a little while, as they dipped their spoons into the cool delicacy. Charlotte wanted to use the opportunity to learn something more about the people, perhaps something that Pitt, as an obvious policeman, could not observe, but all the questions in her head were too clumsy. And she had not decided precisely what she needed to know. She sat with the sherbet dish in her hand and stared at the roses on the far wall. It reminded her a little of Cater Street and her parents' home, only this was grander, lusher. It seemed such an unlikely place for a sordid crime like rape. Embezzlement or fraud she could have understood, or of course burglary. But did men who lived in houses like these ever rape anyone? Surely no matter how eccentric their tastes, or even perverted—she had heard that there were such things—men from Paragon Walk could afford to pay to indulge them. And there were always people who catered, everywhere, from the teeming rookeries to the expensive brothels, even boys and children.

Unless, of course, some particular woman was tormenting them, teasing, and flaunting herself. But from everyone's descriptions, Fanny Nash had been anything but a flirt—in fact, decidedly gauche. Thomas had said Jessamyn made as much a point of it as was only just short of unkindness, and Emily had borne her out.

She was still thinking about it, convincing herself it had been some drunken coachman from the Dilbridges' party and nothing to touch Emily, when she was distracted by voices across the lawn. She turned to see two elderly ladies, dressed in identical turquoise muslin and lace, although the styles were different, as suited their vastly different figures. One was tall and gaunt, flat-chested, the other small and rotund with a high, overstuffed bosom and plump little hands and feet.

"Miss Lucinda Horbury," Selena introduced the small one, "and Miss Laetitia Horbury." She turned to the taller. "I am sure you have not met Lady Ashworth's sister, Mrs. Pitt."

Greetings were exchanged with elaborately concealed curiosity, and more sherbet was brought. When the maid had left, Miss Lucinda turned to Charlotte.

"My dear Mrs. Pitt, how good of you to call. Of course you have come to comfort poor Emily after the dreadful happening! Isn't it too appalling?"

Charlotte made polite noises, scrambling to think of something useful to ask, but Miss Lucinda did not really require a reply.

"I really don't know what things are coming to!" she went on, warming to the subject. "I'm sure when I was young such things never occurred in decent society. Although, of course—" she glanced at her sister "—we did have those among us whose morals were not without fault!"

"Indeed?" Miss Laetitia's faint eyebrows rose. "I don't recall that I knew any, but perhaps you had a wider circle than I?"

Miss Lucinda's plump face tightened, but she ignored the remark, lifting her shoulder slightly and looking toward Charlotte.

"I expect you have heard all about it, Mrs. Pitt? Poor dear Fanny Nash was vilely assaulted and then stabbed to death. We are all quite shattered! The Nashes have lived in the Walk for years, I dare say for generations, a very good family, indeed. I was talking to Mr. Afton, that's the eldest

61

of the brothers, you know, only yesterday. He has such dignity, don't you think?" She flushed and looked at Selena, then Emily, and returned to Charlotte. "He is such a sober man," she continued. "One can hardly imagine his having a sister who would meet with such an end. Of course, Mr. Diggory is a good deal more—more liberal—" she pronounced the word carefully "—in his tastes. But I always say, there are things a man may acceptably do, even if they are not very pleasant, which would be quite unthinkable in a woman—even of the loosest order." Again she lifted her shoulder a little and glanced momentarily at her sister.

"Are you saying that Fanny somehow invited her attack?" Charlotte asked frankly. She felt the ripple of amazement in the others and ignored it, keeping her eyes on Miss Lucinda's pink face.

Miss Lucinda sniffed.

"Well, really, Mrs. Pitt, one would hardly expect such a nature of thing to happen to a woman who was—chaste! She would not allow herself to be put in such a circumstance. I am sure that you have never been molested! And neither have any of us!"

"Perhaps that is no more than our good fortune?" Charlotte suggested, then added, lest she embarrass Emily too much, "If he were a madman, he might imagine all sorts of things that were entirely false, might he not, utterly without reason?"

"I have no acquaintance with madmen," Miss Lucinda said fiercely.

Charlotte smiled. "Nor I with rapists, Miss Horbury. Everything I say is only a surmise."

Miss Laetitia flashed her a smile so quick it was gone almost as soon as it had appeared.

Miss Lucinda sniffed harder. "Naturally, Mrs. Pitt. I hope you did not imagine for a moment that anything I said was from any kind of personal knowledge! I assure you, I was no more than sympathizing with poor Mr. Nash—to have such a disgrace within his family."

"Disgrace!" Charlotte was too angry even to try to control her tongue. "I see it as a tragedy, Miss Horbury, a terror, if you like, but hardly a disgrace."

"Well!" Miss Lucinda bridled. "Well, really—"

"Is that what Mr. Nash said?" Charlotte pressed, ignoring a sharp nudge from Emily's boot. "Did he say it was a disgrace?"

"Really, I do not recall his words, but he was most certainly aware of the—the obscenity of it!" She shuddered and snorted down her nose. "I am quite terrified at the mere thought myself. I believe, Mrs. Pitt, if you lived in the Walk, you would feel as we do. Why, our maid, poor child, fainted clean away this morning, when the next door bootboy spoke to her. That's another three of our best cups gone!"

"Perhaps you could reassure her that the man is probably miles away from her now?" Charlotte suggested. "After all, with the police investigating and everyone looking for him, this is the last place he would be likely to remain."

"Oh, one must not lie, Mrs. Pitt, even to servants," Miss Lucinda said sharply.

"I don't see why not?" Miss Laetitia put in with mildness. "If it is for their good."

"I always said you had no sense of morals!" Miss Lucinda glared at her sister. "Who can say where the creature is now? I am sure Mrs. Pitt cannot! He is obviously possessed by uncontrollable passions, abnormal hungers too dreadful for a decent woman to contemplate."

Charlotte was tempted to point out that Miss Lucinda had done little else but contemplate them since she had arrived, and it was only sensibility for Emily that prevented her.

Selena shivered.

"Perhaps he is some depraved creature from the underworld, excited by women of quality, satins and laces, cleanliness?'' she said to no one in particular.

"Or perhaps he lives here in the Walk, and naturally chooses his own to prey upon—who else?'' It was a gentle, light voice, but distinctly masculine.

They all whirled round as one, to see Fulbert Nash only two yards from them on the grass, a dish of sherbet in his hand.

"Good afternoon, Selena, Lady Ashworth, Miss Lucinda, Miss Laetitia.'' He looked at Charlotte with raised eyebrows.

"My sister, Mrs. Pitt,'' Emily said tightly. "And that is an appalling thing to say, Mr. Nash!''

"It is an appalling crime, ma'am. And life can be appalling, have you not observed?''

"Not, mine, Mr. Nash!''

"How charming of you,'' he sat down opposite them.

Emily blinked. "Charming?''

"That is one of the most restful qualities of women,'' he replied. "The ability to see only what is pleasant. It makes them so comfortable to be with. Don't you think so, Mrs. Pitt?''

"I should think it would make for extreme insecurity,'' Charlotte replied with candor. "One would never know whether one was dealing with the truth or not. Personally I should be forever wondering what it was I did not know.''

"And so, like Pandora, you would open the box and let disaster loose upon the world.'' He looked over the sherbet at her. He had very fine hands. "How unwise of you. There are so many things it is safer not to know. We all have our secrets.'' His eyes flickered round the small group. "Even in Paragon Walk. 'If any man says he is without sin, he deceives himself.' You didn't expect to hear me quote from the Good Book, did you, Lady Ashworth? If you stroll along the Walk, Mrs. Pitt, your naked eye will see perfect houses, stone upon stone, but your spiritual eye, if you have one, will see a row of whited sepulchers. Is that not so, Selena?"

Before Selena could reply, there was a slight clatter as a maid jiggled yet more sherbet on her tray, and they turned to see a most beautiful woman coming across the grass, seeming almost to gloat as the faint, warm air moved the white and water-green silk of her dress. Selena's face hardened.

"Jessamyn, how charming to see you. I had not expected you to have such fortitude to be about. How I admire you, my dear. Do join us and meet Mrs. Pitt, Emily's sister from—?" She lifted her eyebrows, but no one answered her. There were brief acknowledgements. "What an attractive gown," Selena went on, looking at Jessamyn again. "Only you could get away with wearing such a—an anaemic color. On me I swear it would look quite disastrous, so, so washed out!"

Charlotte turned to Jessamyn and observed from her expression that she understood Selena's meaning perfectly. Her composure was exquisite.

"Don't be depressed, my dear Selena. We cannot all wear the same things, but I'm sure there must be some colors which will suit you excellently." She looked at the gorgeous gown Selena was wearing, lavender appliqued with plum-pink lace. "Not that, maybe," she said slowly. "Had you thought of something a little cooler, perhaps blue? So flattering to the higher complexion in this trying weather."

Selena was furious. Her eyes spat something that looked as deep as hatred. Charlotte was surprised and a little taken aback to see it.

"We go to too many of the same places," Selena said between her teeth. "And I should dislike above all things to be thought to ape your tastes—in anything. One should at all costs be original, do you not agree, Mrs. Pitt?" She turned to Charlotte.

Charlotte, acutely conscious of Emily's made-over dress, full of pins, could not summon a reply. She was still shaken by the hatred she had seen, and Fulbert Nash's ugly remark about whited sepulchers.

Oddly, it was Fulbert who rescued her.

"Up to a point," he said casually. "Originality can so easily become outlandish, and one can end up a positive eccentric. Don't you think so, Miss Lucinda?"

Miss Lucinda snorted and declined to reply.

Emily and Charlotte excused themselves shortly afterwards, and, as Emily obviously did not feel like making any further calls, they went home.

"What an extraordinary man Fulbert Nash is," Charlotte commented as they climbed the stairs. "Whatever did he mean about 'whited sepulchers'?"

"How should I know?" Emily snapped. "Perhaps he has a guilty conscience."

"Over what? Fanny?"

"I've no idea. He is a thoroughly horrible person. All the Nashes are, except Diggory. Afton is perfectly beastly. And whenever people are horrible themselves, they tend to think everyone else is too."

Charlotte could not leave well enough alone.

"Do you think he really does know something about all the people in the Walk? Didn't Miss Lucinda say the Nashes had lived here for generations?"

"She's a silly old gossip!" Emily crossed the landing and went into her dressing room. She took Charlotte's old muslin dress off its hanger. "You should have more sense than to listen to her."

Charlotte began searching for the pins in the plum silk, taking them out slowly.

"But if the Nashes have lived here for years, then maybe Mr. Nash does know a lot about everyone. People do, when they live close to each other, and they remember."

"Well, he doesn't know anything about me! Because there isn't anything to know!"

At last Charlotte was silent. The real fear was out. Of course Mr. Nash did not know anything about Emily, but then no one would suspect Emily of rape and murder. But what did he know about George? George had lived here every summer of his life.

"I wasn't thinking of you." She slipped the plum dress to the floor.

"Of course not," Emily picked it up and passed her the gray muslin. "You were thinking of George! Just because I'm with child, and George is a gentleman and doesn't have to work like Thomas, you think he's out gambling and drinking at his club and having affairs, and that he could have taken a fancy to Fanny Nash and refused to be put off!"

"I don't think anything of the kind!" Charlotte took the muslin and put it on slowly. It was more comfortable than the plum, and she had let her stays out an inch, but it looked inexpressibly drab. "But it seems that you are afraid of it."

Emily whirled around, her face red.

"Rubbish! I know George, and I believe in him!"

Charlotte did not argue; the fear was too high in Emily's voice, the sharp corrosive poison of anxiety eating away. In weeks, perhaps days, it would turn to question, doubt, or even actual suspicion. And George was bound to have made some mistakes somewhere, said or done something foolish, something better forgotten.

"Of course," she said softly. "And hopefully Thomas will soon find whoever did it, and we can begin to forget the whole thing. Thank you for lending me your dress."

Four

Emily spent a miserable evening. George was at home, but she could think of nothing to say to him. She wanted to ask him all sorts of questions, but they would have betrayed her doubts so openly that she dared not. And she was afraid of his answers, even if he kept his patience with her and was neither hurt nor angry. If he told her the truth, would there be something she would wish with all her heart she had never known?

She had no illusions that George was perfect. She had accepted when she had first determined to marry him that he gambled and occasionally drank more than was good for him. She even accepted that from time to time he would flirt with other women, and normally she regarded it as harmless enough, the same sort of game she indulged in herself, just a sort of practice, a refining of one's skills, so as not to become too domestic and taken for granted. It had been hard at times, even confusing, but she had accommodated to his manner of life with great skill.

It was only that lately she had been most unlike herself, upset over trivialities and even inclined to weep, which was appalling. She had never had patience with weepy women, or those given to fainting, for that matter—and this last month she had done both.

She excused herself and went to bed early, but although she fell asleep straight away, she awoke several times through the night, and in the morning felt miserably sick for over an hour.

She had been most unfair to Charlotte, and she knew it. Charlotte wanted to learn all she could about the Walk because she wished to protect Emily from the very things that gnawed at the back of her mind now. Part of her loved Charlotte for it, and for a hundred other reasons, but there was a loud, strident voice in her just now that hated her, because even in her old-fashioned, dull gray muslin she was secure and comfortable, with no ugly fears at the back of her mind. She knew perfectly well that Thomas was not out flirting with anyone else. No social behavior of Charlotte's would ever make him wonder if he had been wise to marry beneath him, or if Charlotte could maintain his social position and be a credit to him. There was no pressure to produce a son to carry on the title.

Admittedly Thomas was a policeman, of all things, and quite the oddest creature, as homely as a kitchen pot and wildly untidy. But he knew how to laugh, and Emily had a knowledge inside her she kept unspoken that he was cleverer than George. Perhaps he was clever enough to find out who murdered Fanny Nash before suspicions uncovered all kinds of old guilts and wounds in the Walk, and they could keep up the small, chosen masks no one really wanted to see behind.

She could not stomach any breakfast, and it was luncheon before she saw Aunt Vespasia.

"You look very peaked, Emily," Vespasia said with a frown. "I hope you are eating sufficiently. In your condition, it is most important."

"Yes, thank you, Aunt Vespasia." Indeed she was hungry now and took herself a very liberal portion.

"Hmph!" Vespasia picked up the tongs and helped

herself to half the amount. "Then you are worrying. You must not mind Selena Montague."

Emily looked up at her sharply.

"Selena? Why should you think I am worrying about Selena?"

"Because she is an idle woman who has neither husband nor child to concern herself with," Vespasia said tartly. "She has set her cap, unsuccessfully so far, at the Frenchman. Selena does not care for failure. She was her father's favorite child, you know, and she has never got over it."

"She is perfectly welcome to Monsieur Alaric, as far as I am concerned," Emily replied. "I have no interest in him."

Vespasia gave her a sharp look.

"Nonsense, child, every healthy woman has an interest in a man like that. When I look at him, even I can remember what it was like to be young. And believe me, when I was young, I was beautiful. I would have made him look at me."

Emily felt the laughter inside her.

"I'm sure you would, Aunt Vespasia. I wouldn't be surprized if he preferred your company even now!"

"Don't flatter me, child. I'm an old woman, but I haven't lost my wits."

Emily remained smiling.

"Why didn't you tell me about your sister before?" Vespasia demanded.

"I did. I told you about her the day after you came, and later I told you she had married a policeman."

"You said she was not conventional, I grant you. Her tongue is a disaster, and she walks as though she thought herself a duchess. But you did not say that she was so handsome."

Emily suppressed a desire to giggle. It would be most unfair to mention the pins or the stays.

"Oh yes," she agreed. "Charlotte was always striking, for better or worse. But many people find her too striking to be comfortable. Only traditional beauty is admired by most people, you know. and she does not know how to flirt."

"Unfortunate," Vespasia agreed. "It is one of the arts that cannot possibly be taught. Either you have it, or you have not."

"Charlotte hasn't."

"I hope she calls again. It should prove most entertaining. I am bored with everyone here. Unless Jessamyn and Selena improve their battle over the Frenchman, we shall have to create some diversion of our own, or the summer will become intolerable. Are you well enough to go to the funeral of that poor child? Have you remembered it is the day after tomorrow?"

Emily had not remembered.

"I expect I shall be fine, but I think I shall ask Charlotte if she will accompany me. It is bound to be trying, and I should like to have her there." Also it would be an opportunity to apologize to her for yesterday's unfairness. "I shall write straightaway and ask her."

"You will have to lend her something black," Vespasia warned. "Or perhaps you had better find something of mine, I believe we are more of a height. Get Agnes to alter that lavender for her. If she starts now she should have it quite acceptable by then."

"Thank you, that is very kind of you."

"Nonsense. I can always have another one made if I wish. You had better find her a black hat and shawl as well. I haven't got any, can't bear black."

"Won't you wear black to the funeral yourself?"

"Haven't got any. I shall wear lavender. Then your sister will not be the only one. No one will dare criticize her if I wear lavender also."

* * *

71

Charlotte received the letter from Emily with surprize, and then when she opened it a wave of relief spread through her. The apology was simple, not a matter of good manners but a genuine expression of regret. She was so happy she nearly missed the part about the funeral, and not to worry about a dress, but would she please come because Emily would greatly value her presence at such a time. A carriage would be sent in the morning to collect her, if she would prepare herself by having someone take care of Jemima.

Of course she would go, not only because Emily wanted her to but also because all the Walk surely would be there, and she could not resist the opportunity of seeing them. She told Pitt about it that evening, as soon as he was through the door.

"Emily asked me to go to the funeral with her," she said, her arms still round him in welcome. "It's the day after tomorrow, and I shall leave Jemima with Mrs. Smith—she won't mind—and Emily will send a carriage, and she has a dress organized for me!"

Pitt did not question how one "organized" a dress, and, as she was wriggling to free herself in order the better to explain, he let her go with a wry smile.

"Are you sure you want to?" he asked. "It will be a grim affair."

"Emily wants me to be there," she said it as if it were a complete answer.

He knew immediately from the luminous rationality in her eyes that she was evading the issue. She wanted to go, out of curiosity.

She saw his wide smile and knew she had not fooled him in the least. She shrugged and relaxed into a smile herself.

"All right, I want to see them. But I promise I shall do no more than look. I shan't interfere. What have you discovered? I have a right to ask, because it involves Emily."

His face closed over, and he sat down at the table, leaning

his elbows on it. He looked tired and rumpled. Suddenly she realized her selfishness in ignoring his feelings and thinking only of Emily. She had just learned how to make good lemonade without all the quantity of expensive fresh fruit that she would have used before her marriage. She kept it in a bucket of cold water on the stones near the back door. Quickly she poured him some and put the glass in front of him. She did not ask the question again.

He drank the whole glassful and then answered her.

"I've been trying to check where everyone was. I'm afraid no one remembers whether George was at his club on that evening or not. I pressed as hard as I dared, but they don't recall one evening from another. In fact, I'm not honestly sure how much they recall one person from another. A lot of them look and sound much the same to me." He smiled slowly. "Silly, isn't it—I suppose most of us look the same to them?"

She sat silent. It was the one thing she had been praying for, that George would be cleared beyond question, quickly, completely.

"I'm sorry," he reached out and touched her hand. She closed her fingers over his hand.

"I'm sure you tried. Did you clear anyone else?"

"Not really. Everyone can account for themselves, but it can't be proved."

"Surely some can!"

"Not proved," he looked up, his eyes clouded. "Afton and Fulbert Nash were at home and together most of the time, but not all—"

"But they were her brothers," she said with a shudder. "Surely you don't think they could possibly be so depraved, do you?"

"No, but I suppose it isn't impossible. Diggory Nash was gambling, but his friends are peculiarly reticent about exactly who was where, and when. Algernon Burnon implies he was on a matter of honor, which he won't divulge. I imagine that means he was having an affair, and in the circumstances he dares not say so. Hallam Cayley was at the Dilbridges' party and had a row. He went for a walk to cool off. Again, it's not likely he left the garden and somehow found Fanny, but it is possible. The Frenchman, Paul Alaric, says he was at home alone, and that's probably true, but again we can't prove it."

"How about the servants? After all, they are far more likely." She must keep it in proportion, not let Fulbert's words warp her thinking. "Or the footmen and coachmen from the party?" she added.

He smiled slightly, understanding her thoughts.

"We're working on them. But nearly all of them stayed together in groups, swapping gossip and bragging, or else were inside, getting something to eat. And servants are too busy to have much time unaccounted for."

She knew that was true. She could remember from the days when she had lived in Cater Street that footmen and butlers did not have spare time in the evenings to go wandering outside. A bell might summon them at any moment to open the door or bring a tray of port or perform any other of a dozen tasks.

"But there must be something!" she protested aloud. "It's all so—nebulous. Nobody's guilty, and nobody's really innocent. Something must be provable!"

"Not yet, except for most of the servants. They can account."

She did not argue anymore. She stood up and began to serve his meal, placing it carefully, trying to make it look delicate and cool. It was nothing like Emily's, but then she had made it for a twentieth of the price, all except for the fruit—she had been a little extravagant to buy that.

* * *

74

The funeral was the most magnificently somber affair Charlotte had ever been to. The day was overcast and sultry hot. She was collected by Emily's carriage before nine in the morning and taken straight to Paragon Walk. She was welcomed quickly, Emily's eyes warm with relief to see her and to know that the outburst of the other day was forgotten.

There was no time for refreshments or gossip. Emily rushed her upstairs and presented her with an exquisite deep-lavender dress, far more elaborate and formal than anything she had seen Emily wear. There was a sort of grand dame effect to it she could not reconcile with Emily as she knew her. She held it up and stared over its regal neckline.

"Oh," Emily sighed with a faint smile. "It's Aunt Vespasia's. But I think you will look wonderful in it, very stately." Her smile widened, then she flushed with guilt, remembering the occasion. "I think you are very like Aunt Vespasia, in some ways—or you might be, in fifty years."

Charlotte remembered that Pitt had said much the same thing and found herself rather flattered.

"Thank you." She put the dress down and turned for Emily to unbutton her own dress so that she might change. She was all prepared to reach for pins again, but was amazed to find that none were necessary. It fitted her almost as well as any of her own; it could have done with an inch more across the shoulder, but other than that it was perfect. She surveyed herself in the cheval glass. The effect was quite startling, and really very handsome.

"Come on!" Emily said sharply. "There isn't time to stand there admiring yourself. You must put black over it, or it will hardly be decent. I know lavender is mourning as well, but you look like a duchess about to receive. There's this black shawl. Don't fidget! It's not in the least hot, and it darkens the whole thing. And black gloves, of course. And I've found a black hat for you."

Charlotte did not dare ask where she had "found" it. Perhaps she would be happier not to know. Still, it was church, so it was necessary to wear a hat, apart from the obligations of fashion.

When the hat came it was extravagant, broad brimmed, feathered and veiled. She set it on her head at rather a rakish angle and started Emily giggling.

"Oh, this is awful! Please, Charlotte, do watch what you say. I'm so nervous about it you make me laugh when I don't mean it at all. Inside I am doing everything I can not to think of that poor girl. I'm occupying my mind with all sorts of other things, even silly things, just to keep the thought of her away."

Charlotte put her arm around her.

"I know. I know you're not heartless. We all laugh sometimes when we really want to cry. Tell me, do I look ridiculous in this hat?"

Emily put out both her hands and altered the angle a little. She was already in the soberest black herself.

"No, no, it looks very well. Jessamyn will be furious, because afterward everyone will look at you and wonder who you are. Bring the veil down a little, and then they will have to come closer to see. There, that's perfect! Don't fiddle with it!"

The cortege was awe-inspiring in the deadest black: black horses pulling a black hearse, black-crepe-ribboned coachmen and black-plumed harness. The chief mourners followed immediately behind in another black, fluttering carriage, and then the rest of the attendants. Everything moved at the most august walk.

Charlotte sat with Emily, George, and Aunt Vespasia in their carriage and wondered why a people who profess a total belief in resurrection should make a melodrama out of death. It was rather like bad theater. It was a question she frequently had considered, but had never found anyone appropriate to ask. She had hoped one day to meet a bishop, although there seemed little chance of it now. She had mentioned it to Papa once and received a very stiff reply, which silenced her completely but in no way provided an answer—except that Papa obviously did not know either and found the whole matter grossly distasteful.

Now she climbed out of the carriage, taking George's hand to alight gracefully, without tipping the black hat to an even more rakish angle, then, side by side with Aunt Vespasia, followed Emily and George through the gate of the churchyard and up the path to the door. Inside, the organ was playing the death march, with rather more exuberance than was entirely fitting and with several notes so wrong that even Charlotte winced to hear them. She wondered if the organist were the regular one, or an enthusiastic amateur drafted in ignorance for the occasion.

The service itself was very dull, but mercifully short. Possibly the vicar did not wish to mention the manner of death, in all its worldly reality, in such an unworldly place. It did not belong with stained-glass windows, organ music, and little sniffles into lace handkerchiefs. Death was pain and sickness, and terror of the long, blind, last step. And there had been nothing resigned or dignified in it for Fanny. It was not that Charlotte did not believe in God, or the resurrection; it was the attempt to soothe away the ugly truths with ritual that she hated. All this elaborate, expensive mourning was for the conscience of the living, so that they might feel they had paid due tribute and now could decently forget Fanny and continue with the Season. It had little to do with the girl and whether they had cared for her or not.

Afterward they all went out to the graveyard for the interment. The air was hot and heavy, as if it had already been breathed, and tasted faintly stale. The soil was dry from long weeks without rain, and the gravediggers had had to hack at it to break it. The only damp spot anywhere was under the yew trees, settling lower and lower to the earth, and it smelled old and sour, as if the roots had fed on too many bodies.

"Ridiculous things, funerals," Aunt Vespasia whispered sharply from beside her. "Greatest fit of self-indulgence in society; it's worse than Ascot. Everyone seeing who can mourn the most conspicuously. Some women look very well in black and know it, and you'll see them at all the fashionable funerals, whether they were acquainted with the deceased or not. Maria Clerkenwell was always doing that. Met her first husband at the funeral of his cousin. He was the chief mourner because he inherited the title. Maria had never heard of the dead man before she read it in the society pages and decided to go."

Secretly Charlotte admired her enterprise; it was something Emily might have done. She stared across the open grave past the pallbearers, red-faced and glistening with sweat, to Jessamyn Nash standing erect and pale at the far side. The man closest to her was less then handsome, but there was something pleasing in his face, a readiness to smile.

"Is that her husband?" Charlotte asked softly.

Vespasia followed her eye.

"Diggory," she agreed. "Bit of a rake, but always was the best of the Nashes. Not that that is granting him much."

From what Charlotte had heard of Afton and seen of Fulbert, she could not disagree. She continued to stare, trusting to her veil to disguise the fact. Really, veils were of very practical convenience. She had never tried one before, but she must remember it for the future. Diggory and Jessamyn were standing a little apart; he made no effort to touch her or support her. In fact his attention seemed to be turned rather toward Afton's wife Phoebe, who looked perfectly awful. Her hair seemed to have slipped to one side and her hat to the other, and although she made one or two feeble gestures to readjust it, each time she made it worse.

Like everyone else, she was in black, but on her it seemed dusty, the black of the sweep, rather than the glossy, raven's-wing black of Jessamyn's gown. Afton stood to attention by her side, his face expressionless. Whatever he felt, it was beneath his dignity to display it here.

The vicar held up his hand for attention. The faint whisperings stopped. He intoned the familiar words. Charlotte wondered why they intoned. It always sounded so much less sincere than to speak in a normal voice. She had never heard people who were really emotionally moved speak in such a fashion. They were too much consumed in the content to take such pains with the manner. Surely God was the last person to be swayed by dressing up and affecting airs.

She looked up through her veil and wondered if anyone else was thinking the same things, or were they all properly impressed? Jessamyn had her head down; she was stiff, pale and beautiful as a lily, a little rigid, but very appropriate. Phoebe was weeping. Selena Montague was becomingly pale, although to judge from her lips she had not altogether left nature unaided, and her eyes were as bright as fever. She was standing beside the most singularly elegant man Charlotte had ever seen. He was tall and slender, but there was a litheness to him as if his body were hard, far from the foppish, rather feminine grace of so many fashionable people. He was bareheaded, as were all the other men, and his black hair was thick and smooth. She could see when he turned how perfectly it grew in the nape of his neck. She did not need to ask Vespasia who he was. With a little tingle of excitement she knew—that was the beautiful Frenchman— the one Selena and Jessamyn were fighting over!

She could not tell who was winning at the moment, but he was standing next to Selena. Or perhaps she was standing next to him? But it was Jessamyn who was the center of attention. At least half the heads in the congregation were turned toward her. The Frenchman was one of the few who was looking at the coffin as it was lowered clumsily into the open grave. Two men with shovels stood respectfully back, accustomed enough to such rituals to fall into the right attitude without conscious thought.

One of the few others who seemed to be genuinely caught in the turmoil of some emotion was a man on the same side of the grave as Charlotte and Vespasia. She only noticed him at first because of the angle of his shoulders, which had a tightness to them, as if all his muscles were clenched inside. Without thinking, she moved a little forward to catch sight of his face, should he turn when the earth was thrown in.

The vicar's sing-song voice went through the old words about earth to earth and dust to dust. The man swiveled to watch the hard clay rattle on the lid, and Charlotte saw his profile, and then his full features. It was a strong face with skin marred by smallpox and at the moment was in the grip of some deep and twisting pain. Was it for Fanny? Or for death in general? Or was it even grief for the living, because he knew or guessed something of the "whited sepulchers" Fulbert had spoken of? Or was it fear?

Charlotte stepped back and touched Vespasia's arm.

"Who is he?"

"Hallam Cayley," Vespasia replied. "Widower. His wife was one of the Cardews. She died about two years ago. Pretty woman, lot of money, but not much sense."

"Oh." So that explained his tight body and the confusion of pain in his face. Perhaps she herself was staring around at all these people, occupying her mind with questions to keep it from the memory of other funerals, personal ones that hurt too much to bear recalling?

The ceremony was over. Slowly, with extreme decorum, they all turned as if on a single pivot and began the walk back to the road and the carriages. They would meet at

Paragon Walk again at Afton Nash's for the obligatory baked meats. Then the ritual could be considered accomplished.

"I see you remarked the Frenchman," Vespasia observed under her breath.

Charlotte considered feigning innocence, and decided it would not work.

"Next to Selena?"

"Naturally."

They walked, or rather processed, down the narrow path, through the gateway, and out onto the footpath. Afton, as the eldest brother, embarked into his carriage first, then Jessamyn, with Diggory a few moments behind her. He had been talking to George, and Jessamyn was obliged to wait for him. Charlotte saw the flicker of irritation pass across her face. Fulbert had come in a separate carriage for the occasion and had offered a ride to the Misses Horbury, dressed in ornate and antique black. It took them several moments to seat themselves satisfactorily.

George and Emily were next, and Charlotte found herself moving before she was really ready to leave. She looked across at Emily. Emily caught her eye and smiled wearily in return. Charlotte was happy to see that she had slipped her hand into George's and he was holding it protectively.

The funeral breakfast was very splendid, as she had expected it to be. There was nothing ostentatious—one did not draw attention to a death that had come about in such an appalling manner—but there was enough to feed half of Society on the great table, and Charlotte thought at a quick estimation that every man, woman, and child on her own street could have lived on it for a month, with care.

People split into little groups, whispering together, no one wishing to be the first to begin.

"Why do we always eat after funerals?" Charlotte asked, unconsciously frowning. "I've never felt less like it."

"Convention," George replied, looking at her. He had the finest eyes she had ever seen. "It's the only sort of hospitality everyone understands. Anyway, what else could one do? We can't simply stand here, and we can hardly dance!"

Charlotte suppressed a desire to giggle. It was as formal and ridiculous as an old-fashioned dance.

She glanced around the room. He was right; everyone was a little awkward, and eating eased the tension. It would be vulgar to show emotion, at least for men. Women were expected to be frail, though weeping was frowned upon, because it was embarrassing and no one knew what to do about it. But one could always faint; that was quite acceptable and gave one the perfect excuse to retire. Eating was an occupation that covered the hiatus between obvious mourning and the time when one could decently go and leave the whole matter of death behind.

Emily put out her hand to claim Charlotte's attention. She turned, to find herself facing a woman in extremely expensive black with a rather heavyset man beside her. "May I present my sister, Mrs. Pitt? Lord and Lady Dilbridge."

Charlotte responded with the usual courtesies.

"Such a dreadful affair," Grace Dilbridge said with a sigh. "And such a shock! One would never have expected it of the Nashes."

"Surely one cannot expect such a thing of anyone," Charlotte rejoined, "except the most wretched and desperate of people." She was thinking of the slums and rookeries Pitt had spoken of, but even he had told her little of the real horror. She had only guessed, as much from the hollow look of his face and his long silences as from anything he had said.

"I always thought poor Fanny such an innocent child,"

Frederick Dilbridge went on, as if in answer to her. "Poor Jessamyn. All this is going to be very hard for her."

"And for Algernon," Grace added, looking out of the corner of her eye to where Algernon Burnon was turning away a baked pie and helping himself to another glass of port from the footman. "Poor boy. Thank God he was not yet married to her."

Charlotte could not entirely see the relevance.

"He must be very grieved," she said slowly. "I cannot imagine a worse way to lose one's fiancée."

"Better than a wife," Grace insisted. "At least he is now free—after a decent interval, of course—to find himself someone more suitable."

"And the Nashes had no other daughter," Frederick also took a glass as the footman hovered. "That's something to be thankful for."

"Thankful?" Charlotte could hardly believe it.

"Of course," Grace looked at her with raised eyebrows. "You must be aware, Mrs. Pitt, how hard it is to get one's daughters married well as it is. To have a scandal such as this in the family would make it well nigh impossible! I should not wish any son of mine to marry a girl whose sister was—well—" She coughed delicately and glared at Charlotte for obliging her to put into words something so crass. "All I can say is, I am vastly relieved my son is already married. A daughter of the Marchioness of Weybridge, a delightful girl. Do you know the Weybridges?"

"No," Charlotte shook her head, and, mistaking her meaning, the footman whisked the tray away and she was left with an empty hand outstretched. No one took any notice, and she withdrew it. "No, I don't."

There was no polite reply to this, so Grace returned to the original subject.

"Daughters are such an anxiety, until one has them married. My dear," she turned to Emily, reaching out her hand, "I do so hope that you have only sons—so much less vulnerable. The world accepts the weaknesses of men, and we have learned to put up with them. But when a woman is weak, all Society completely abhors her. Poor Fanny, may she rest in peace. Now, my dear, I must go and see Phoebe. She looks quite ill! I must see what I can do to comfort her."

"That's monstrous!" Charlotte said as soon as they were gone. "Anyone would think from the way she speaks that Fanny went out whoring!"

"Charlotte!" Emily said sharply. "For goodness' sake don't use words like that here! Anyway, only men go out whoring."

"You know what I mean! It's unforgivable. That girl is dead, abused and murdered here in her own street, and they are all talking about marriage opportunities and what Society will think. It's disgusting!"

"Sh!" Emily's hand gripped her hand, her fingers digging in painfully. "People will hear you, and they wouldn't understand." She smiled with rather more force than charm, as Selena approached them. By her side George breathed in deeply and let it out in a sigh.

"Hello, Emily," Selena said brightly. "I must compliment you. It must be a most trying experience, and looking at you one could hardly tell. I do admire your fortitude." She was a smaller woman than Charlotte had realized, fully eight or ten inches shorter than George. She looked up at him through her eyelashes.

George passed some trivial remark. There was a faint flush on the bones of his cheeks.

Charlotte glanced at Emily and saw her face tighten. For once Emily seemed to think of nothing to say.

"We must also admire you," Charlotte stared at Selena pointedly. "You carry it so well. Indeed, if I did not know

84

you must naturally be distressed, I would swear you were positively gay!"

There was a sharp intake of breath from Emily, but Charlotte ignored her. George shifted from one foot to the other.

Color rushed up Selena's face, but she chose her words carefully.

"Oh, Mrs. Pitt, if you knew me better, you could not imagine me callous. I am a most warmhearted person! Am I not, George?" again she looked at him with her enormous eyes. "Please do not let Mrs. Pitt think I am cold. You know it is not so!"

"I—I am sure she does not believe it," George was palpably uncomfortable. "She only meant that—er—that you comport yourself admirably."

Selena smiled at Emily, who stood frozen.

"I should not care for anyone to think I was unfeeling," she added the last little touch.

Charlotte moved closer to Emily, wanting to protect her, guessing vividly what the threat was, feeling it in Selena's dazzling eyes.

"I am flattered you care so much what I should think of you," Charlotte said coolly. She would like to have forced a smile, but she had never been good at acting. "I promise you I shall not make any hasty judgements. I am sure you are capable of great—" She looked directly at Selena, allowing her to see she picked the word intentionally with all its shades of meaning. "—generosity!"

"I see your husband is not with you!" Selena's reply was vicious and unhesitating.

Charlotte was able to smile this time. She was proud of what Thomas was doing, even though she knew they would have held it in contempt.

"No, he is otherwise engaged. He has a great deal to do."

"How unfortunate," Selena murmured, but without conviction. The satisfaction was gone out of her.

It was not long after that that Charlotte got her opportunity to meet Algernon Burnon. She was introduced by Phoebe Nash, whose hat was now straight, though her hair still looked uncomfortable. Charlotte knew the sensation all too well: a pin or two in the wrong place, and it could feel as if all the weight of one's hair were attached to one's head with nails.

Algernon bowed very slightly, a courteous gesture Charlotte found a little discomposing. He seemed more concerned for her comfort than his own. She had prepared herself for grief, and he was asking her about her health, and if she found the heat trying.

She swallowed the sympathy she had had on the edge of her tongue and made as sensible a reply as she could. Perhaps he found it all too painful to dwell on and was glad of the chance to speak to someone who had not known Fanny. How little one could really tell from faces.

She was floundering, too conscious that he had been close to Fanny and too busy with her own confusion, wondering whether he had loved her, or if it had been a very much arranged affair, or if perhaps he even was relieved to be free of it. She hardly noticed his conversation, though part of her brain was telling her it was both literate and easy.

"I'm sorry," she apologized. She had no idea what he had just said.

"Perhaps Mrs. Pitt finds our baked meats a little diverse—as I do?"

Charlotte turned sharply to find the Frenchman only a few feet away from her, his fine, intelligent eyes carefully hiding a smile.

She was not quite sure what he meant. He could not possibly have known the wanderings of her mind—or was he thinking the same things, perhaps even knowing them? Honesty was the only safe retreat.

"I am not experienced in them," she replied. "I have no idea what they usually are."

If Algernon had any understanding of the ambiguity in her words, he did not betray it.

"Mrs. Pitt, may I present Monsieur Paul Alaric," he said easily. "I don't believe you have met? Mrs. Pitt is Lady Ashworth's sister," he added by way of explanation.

Alaric bowed very slightly.

"I am well aware who Mrs. Pitt is." His smile removed any discourtesy from his words. "Did you imagine such a person could visit the Walk and not be talked of? I'm sorry it is a tragic occasion that has afforded us the opportunity to meet you."

It was ridiculous, but she found herself coloring under his calm gaze. For all his grace, he was unusually direct, as if his intelligence could penetrate the polite, rather empty mask of her face and see all the confused feelings behind. There was nothing unkind in his stare, only curiosity and faint amusement.

She pulled herself together sharply. She must be very tired from the heat and all this mourning to be so stupid.

"How do you do, Monsieur Alaric," she said stiffly. Then, because that did not seem enough. "Yes, it is unfortunate that it frequently takes tragedy to rearrange our lives."

His mouth curled in the slightest, most delicate smile.

"Are you going to rearrange my life, Mrs. Pitt?"

The heat scorched up her face. Please heaven, the veil would hide it.

"You—you misunderstand me, monsieur, I meant the tragedy. Our meeting can hardly be of importance."

"How modest of you, Mrs. Pitt," Selena drifted up, wafting black chiffon behind her, her face bright. "I judged from your marvelous gown that you had imagined otherwise. Do they always wear lavender for mourning where you come from? Of course, it is easier to wear than black!"

"Why, thank you," Charlotte forced a smile and feared it might be more like bared teeth. She looked Selena up and down. "Yes, I imagine it is. I'm sure you would find it flattering, too."

"I do not go around from funeral to funeral, Mrs. Pitt, only to those of people I know," Selena snapped back with tart meaning. "I don't imagine I shall be requiring it again before this style has gone quite out of fashion."

"Sort of 'one funeral per Season,'" Charlotte murmured. Why did she dislike this woman so much? Was it only an identification with Emily's fears, or some instinct of her own?

Jessamyn moved towards them, pale but entirely composed. Alaric turned toward her, and a look of venom momentarily hardened Selena's face before she mastered it and ironed it out. She spoke quickly, preempting Alaric.

"Dear Jessamyn, what a terrible ordeal for you. You must be devastated, and you have comported yourself so well. The whole affair has been so dignified."

"Thank you," Jessamyn took the glass Alaric handed her from a waiting footman's tray and sipped at it delicately. "Poor Fanny is at rest. But I find it hard to accept it as I suppose one should. It seems so monstrously unjust. She was such a child, so innocent. She did not even know how to flirt! Why her, of all people?" Her eyelids lowered slightly over her wide, cool eyes, and she did not quite look at Selena, but some minute gesture of her shoulder, an arch in her body, seemed addressed to her. "There are other people so—so much more—likely!"

Charlotte stared at her. The hatred between the two women was so tangible she could not believe Paul Alaric was unaware of it. He stood elegantly, with a slight smile, and made some innocuous answer, but surely he must feel as uncomfortable as she did? Or did he enjoy it? Was he flattered, excited to be fought over? The thought hurt her; she wanted him to be above such a demeaning vanity, to be embarrassed by it, as she was.

Then another thought occurred to her as Jessamyn's words sank in, ". . . other people so much more likely." That was a dig at Selena, of course, but could it have been precisely Fanny's innocence that had attracted the rapist? Perhaps he was tired and bored with sophisticated women who were only too available. He wanted a virgin, frightened and unwilling, so he could dominate her. Maybe that was what excited, sent his blood racing, the touch and the smell of terror!

It was an ugly thought, but then the intimate violence in the dark, the humiliation, the symbolic, stabbing knife, the blood, the pain, life gushing away—they were all ugly. She shut her eyes. Please, dear God, it had nothing to do with Emily! Don't let George be anything worse than easygoing, a little foolish, a little vain!

They were talking across her, and she had not heard them. She was conscious only of the prickling hostility and of Alaric's elegant black head as he half listened to one, then the other. Somehow it seemed to Charlotte as if his eyes were on her, and there was an understanding in them which was uncomfortable and at the same time stirring.

Emily found her again. She was looking very tired, and Charlotte thought she had already been standing too long. She was about to make some suggestion of returning home when she saw, behind Emily, Hallam Cayley, the only man she had observed to be moved by Fanny's death beyond the usual trappings of observance. He was facing toward Jessamyn, but his expression was vacant, as if he were unaware of her. Indeed, the whole room, with its shafts of sunlight under the half drawn blinds, its glittering table spread with the debris of food, its clusters of murmuring figures in black, seemed to make no impression on his senses at all.

Jessamyn caught sight of him. Her face changed, the full lower lip came forward and the skin tightened fractionally across her cheeks. For a moment it was frozen. Then Selena spoke to Alaric, smiling, and Jessamyn turned back.

Charlotte looked at Emily.

"Haven't we paid all respects necessary now? I mean, surely we could decently go home? The heat in here is oppressive, and you must be tired."

"Do I look it?" Emily asked.

Charlotte lied immediately and without thought.

"Not at all, but surely better to leave before we do. I know I feel it!"

"I expected you would be enjoying yourself, trying to solve the mystery." There was a faint cutting edge in Emily's voice. Indeed, she was tired. The skin under her eyes looked papery.

Charlotte pretended not to notice.

"I don't think I have learned a thing, except what you had already told me—that Jessamyn and Selena hate each other over Monsieur Alaric, that Lord Dilbridge has very liberal tastes, and Lady Dilbridge enjoys being put upon because of them. And that none of the Nashes are very pleasant. Oh, and that Algernon is behaving himself with great dignity."

"Did I tell you all that?" Emily smiled faintly. "I thought it was Aunt Vespasia. But I suppose we may as well go home. I admit, I have had enough. I find myself much more affected by it than I had thought to be. I didn't care much for Fanny when she was alive, but now I can't help thinking of her. This is her funeral, and do you know, hardly anybody has really spoken of her!"

It was a sad and pathetic observation; yet it was true.

They had spoken of the effect of her death, its manner and their own feelings, but no one had spoken of Fanny herself. Lost, and a little sick, Charlotte followed Emily to where George was half waiting for them. He, too, seemed eager to leave. Aunt Vespasia was deep in conversation with a man about her own age, and since it was only a few hundred yards, they left her to come when she chose.

They found Afton and Phoebe in desultory expression of mutual sympathies with Algernon. They all three stopped as George approached.

"Leaving?" Afton enquired. His eyes flickered over Emily and then Charlotte.

Charlotte felt her stomach curl up and instantly longed to be outside. She must control herself and leave with courtesy. After all, the man must be under great strain.

George was muttering something to Phoebe, a ritual politeness about the hospitality.

"How kind of you," she replied automatically, her voice high and tight. Charlotte saw that her hands were clenched across the billows of her skirt.

"Don't be ridiculous," Afton snapped. "A few are here out of courtesy, but most are no more than inquisitive. Rape is a better scandal than mere adultery any day. Besides, adultery has become so common that, unless there is something ludicrous attached to it, it is hardly worth recounting anymore."

Phoebe colored uncomfortably, but she seemed incapable of finding an answer.

"I came out of affection for Fanny." Emily looked up at him coldly. "And for Phoebe!"

Afton inclined his head a little.

"I'm sure she'll appreciate it. If you are able to call upon her some afternoon, she will no doubt regale you with her feelings in the matter. She is quite convinced there is some madman lurking around, just waiting for the chance to leap upon her and ravish her next."

"Please!" Phoebe tugged at his sleeve, her face painfully red. "I do not think so at all."

"Did I misunderstand you?" he inquired, not lowering his voice, but staring at George. "I thought from the way you disported yourself that you suspected his presence on the upstairs landing last night. You had your gown so wrapped around you I feared you might strangle yourself if you were to turn carelessly. What on earth did you call the footman for, my dear? Or should I not ask you such a thing in front of others?"

"I didn't call the footman. I—I merely—well, the curtain blew in the wind. I was startled, and I suppose—," her face was scarlet now, and Charlotte could imagine the foolishness she was feeling, almost as if the whole company could see her frightened and disheveled in her nightclothes. She burned to think of something crushing to say for her, to cut at Afton with equally lacerating words, but nothing came.

It was Fulbert who spoke, lazily, a slow smile on his face. He put his arm around Phoebe, but his eyes were on Afton.

"There's no need for you to be afraid, my dear. What you were doing is quite your own affair." His face softened into amusement, some secret laughter inside him. "I really doubt it is one of your footmen, but, if it were, he would hardly be reckless enough to attack you in your own house. And you are more fortunate than any other woman in the Walk—at least you know perfectly well it wasn't Afton. We all do!" He smiled across at George. "Would God the rest of us could be as far beyond suspicion?"

George blinked, unsure of his meaning, but knowing it held cruelty somewhere.

Charlotte instinctively turned to Afton. She had no idea what occasioned it, but cold, irrevocable hatred flared up in his eyes, and the shock of it rippled through her, leaving her feeling sick. She wanted to grip hold of Emily's arm, touch something warm, human, and then run out of the glittering black-crepe room into the air, into the green summer, and keep on running until she was home in her own narrow, dusty little street with its whited steps, shoulder-to-shoulder houses, and women who worked all day.

Five

Charlotte could hardly wait until Pitt came home. She rehearsed a dozen times in her mind what she meant to tell him, and each time it came out differently. She completely missed the bookshelves in her dusting and forgot to salt the vegetables. She gave Jemima two lots of pudding, much to the child's delight, but at least she did have her changed and sound asleep when Pitt finally came.

He looked tired, and the first thing he did was to take his boots off and empty his pockets of the enormous number of things he had shoved into them throughout the day. She brought him a cold drink, determined not to make the same mistake as last time.

"How was Emily?" he asked after a few minutes.

"Well enough," she answered, almost holding her breath to avoid plunging into the story. "The whole affair was rather horrible. I suppose they felt the same as we would underneath, but nothing showed. It was all—empty."

"Did they talk about her—Fanny?"

"No!" She shook her head. "No, they didn't. You'd hardly have known whose funeral it was. I hope when I die whoever's there talks about me all the time!"

He smiled suddenly, a broad grin like a child.

"Even if they do absolutely all the time, my darling," he replied, "it will still seem quiet without you!"

She looked around for something harmless to throw at him, but the only thing to hand was the lemonade jug, which would hurt, not to mention break the jug, which they could ill afford. She had to settle for making a face.

"Didn't you learn anything?" he pressed.

"I don't think so. Only what Emily had already told me. I got lots of odd impressions, but I don't know what they mean, or even if they mean anything at all. I had umpteen things to tell you before you came, but now they seem to have frittered away. All the Nashes are unpleasant, except perhaps Diggory. I didn't really get to meet him, but he has a bad reputation. Selena and Jessamyn loathe each other, but that can't be relevant; it's all to do with the most gorgeous Frenchman. The only people who seemed to be really upset were Phoebe—she really was terribly white and shaky—and a man called Hallam Cayley. And I don't know whether he was upset for Fanny, or because his own wife died only a little while ago." It had seemed so much when it was all a tumult of feelings in her mind, but now that she wanted to put words to it, there was nothing. It sounded so silly, so ephemeral that she was a little ashamed. She was a policeman's wife, she should have had something concrete to tell him. How did he ever solve a case if all witnesses were as woolly as she was?

He sighed and stood up, walking in his socks over to the kitchen sink. He ran the cold water and put his hands under it, then splashed it up over his face. He held out his hands for the towel, and she brought it.

"Don't worry." He took it from her. "I didn't expect to learn anything there."

"You didn't expect to?" She was confused. "You mean you were there?"

He dried his face and looked up at her over the towel.

"Not to learn anything—just—because I wanted to."

She felt the tears prickle hot behind her eyes and her throat ache. She had not even seen him. She had been busy watching everyone else, and thinking how she looked in Aunt Vespasia's dress.

At least Fanny had had one real mourner, someone who was simply sorry she was dead.

Emily had no one with whom she could discuss her feelings. Aunt Vespasia did not consider it good for her to dwell on such things. It would produce a melancholic baby, she said. And George was unwilling to speak of it at all. In fact, he went noticeably out of his way to avoid it.

Everyone else in the Walk seemed determined to forget the entire subject, as if Fanny had merely gone away for a holiday and might be expected to return at any time. They resumed their lives, as much as propriety would permit, still wearing sober dress, of course, as to do anything else would be tasteless. But there appeared to be an unspoken consensus that the very indecency of the manner of death made the usual observances of mourning a reminder of it, and therefore a little vulgar, possibly even offensive to others.

The only exception was Fulbert Nash, who had never minded giving offense. In fact, he appeared at times positively to relish it. He made sly, delicate suggestions about almost everyone. There was nothing decisive, nothing that one could question him with, but the swift color in people's faces betrayed when he had hit a mark. Perhaps they were old secrets he was referring to; everyone had something of which they were ashamed, or at least would very much perfer to keep from their neighbors. Perhaps the secrets were not witty so much as merely foolish? But then no one wished to be laughed at either, and some would go to great lengths to prevent it. Ridicule could be as deadly to one's social aspirations as a report of any of the ordinary sins.

It was a week after the funeral, and still hot, when Emily finally decided to go and ask Charlotte directly what the police were doing. There had been a lot more questions put, mostly to servants, but if anyone were either suspected or totally cleared, she had not heard of it.

Having sent a letter the day before to warn Charlotte she was coming, she put on a muslin from last year and sent for the carriage to take her. When she arrived, she told the coachman to drive around the corner and wait precisely two hours before returning to pick her up.

She found Charlotte expecting her, and busy preparing tea. The house was smaller than she had remembered, the carpets older, but it had an air of being lived in that made it pleasant, along with the smell of wax polish and roses. It did not occur to her to wonder whether the roses had been bought specially for her.

Jemima was sitting on the floor, crooning to herself, as she built a precarious tower out of colored blocks. Thank heaven it seemed as if she were going to look like Charlotte rather than Pitt!

After the usual greetings, which she meant most sincerely—in fact she was coming to value Charlotte's friendship more and more lately—she launched straight into news of the Walk.

"No one else even talks of it!" she said heatedly. "At least not to me! It's as if it had never happened! It's like a dinner table where someone has made a personal noise—a moment's embarrassed silence, then everyone begins to talk again a little bit more loudly, to show that they haven't noticed."

"Don't the servants talk?" Charlotte was busy with the kettle. "Servants usually do, among themselves. The butler wouldn't know. Maddock never did." She recalled Cater Street vividly for a moment. "But ask one of the maids, and they'll tell you everything."

"I never thought of asking the maids," Emily admitted. It was a stupid oversight. At Cater Street she would have done so without the need for Charlotte to tell her. "Perhaps I'm getting too old now. Mama never knew half as much as we did. They were all afraid of her. I think perhaps my maids are afraid of me. And they're terrified of Aunt Vespasia!"

That Charlotte could well believe. Quite apart from Aunt Vespasia's personality, no social climber was more impressed by a title than the average housemaid. There were the expections, of course, those who saw the trivialities and the flaws behind the polished front. But these servants were usually not only perceptive but also awake enough to their own advantage not to allow their perception to be known. And there was always loyalty. A good servant regarded his master or mistress almost as an extension of himself, his property, the mark of his own status in the hierarchy.

"Yes," she agreed aloud. "Try your lady's maid. She's seen you without your stays or your hair curled. She's the least likely to be in awe of you."

"Charlotte!" Emily banged the milk jug on the bench. "You say the most appalling things!" It was an undignified and uncomfortable reminder, especially of her increasing weight. "In your own way you are as bad as Fulbert!" She drew breath quickly. Then as Jemima began to whimper at the sharp noise, she swung around and picked her up, jiggling her gently till she began to gurgle again. "Charlotte, he's been going around in the most awful way, letting out little jibes at people, nothing you could exactly say was accusing, but you know from their faces that the people he's talking about know what he means. And inside himself he's laughing all the time. I know he is."

Charlotte poured the water onto the tea and put on the lid. The food was already on the table.

"You can put her down now." She pointed at Jemima.

"She'll be all right. You mustn't spoil her, or she'll want holding all the time. Who is he talking about?"

"Everyone!" Emily obeyed and put Jemima back with her bricks. Charlotte gave her daughter a finger of bread and butter, which she took happily.

"All of the same things?" Charlotte said in surprize. "That seems a little pointless."

They both sat down and waited for tea to brew before eating.

"No, all different things," Emily answered. "Even Phoebe! Can you imagine? He implied that Phoebe had something she was ashamed of and one day all the Walk would know. Who could be more innocent than Phoebe? She's positively silly at times. I've often wondered why she doesn't hit back at Afton. There must be something she could do! On occasions he is quite beastly. I don't mean he strikes her or anything." Her faced paled. "At least, good heavens, I hope not!"

Charlotte chilled as she remembered him, his cold, probing eyes, the impression he gave of a bitter humor, and a contempt.

"If it's anybody in the Walk," she said with feeling. "I sincerely hope it's him—and that he is caught!"

"So do I," Emily agreed. "But somehow I don't think it is. Fulbert is perfectly sure it isn't. He keeps saying so, and with great pleasure, as if he knew something horrid that amused him."

"Perhaps he does." Charlotte frowned, trying to hide the thought, and failing. It would come out in words. "Perhaps he knows who it is—and it is not Afton."

"It's too disgusting to think of," Emily shook her head. "It will be some servant or other, almost certainly someone hired for the Dilbridges' party. All those strange coachmen milling about, with nothing to do but wait. No doubt one of them refreshed himself too much, and, when he was in liquor, he lost control. Perhaps in the dark he thought Fanny was a maid, or something. And then, when he discovered she wasn't, he had to stab her to keep her from giving him away. Coachmen do carry knives quite often, you know, to cut harness if it gets caught, or get stones out of horses' hooves if they pick them up, and all sorts of things.'' She warmed to her own excellent reasoning. ''And after all, none of the men who live in the Walk, I mean none of us, would be carrying a knife anyway, would we?''

Charlotte stared at her, one of her carefully cut sandwiches in her hand.

''Not unless they meant to kill Fanny anyway.''

Emily felt a sickness that had nothing to do with her condition.

''Why on earth would anyone want to do that? If it had been Jessamyn, I could understand. Everyone is jealous of her because she is always so beautiful. You never see her put out, or flustered. Or even Selena, but no one could have hated Fanny—I mean—there wasn't enough of her to hate!''

Charlotte stared at her plate.

''I don't know.''

Emily leaned forward.

''What about Thomas? What does he know? He must have told you, since it concerns us.''

''I don't think he knows anything,'' Charlotte said unhappily. ''Except that it doesn't seem to have been any of the regular servants. They can all pretty well account for themselves. And none of them have a past trouble he can find. They wouldn't, would they? Or they wouldn't be employed in Paragon Walk!''

When Emily returned home, she wanted to talk to George, but she did not know how to begin. Aunt Vespasia was out, and George was sitting in the library with his feet up, the doors open to the garden, and a book upside down on his stomach.

He looked up as soon as she came in and put the book aside.

"How was Charlotte?" he asked immediately.

"Well." She was a little surprised. He had always liked Charlotte, but in a rather distant, absent way. After all, he very seldom saw her. Why the keenness today?

"Did she say anything about Pitt?" he went on, moving to sit upright, his eyes on her face.

So it was not Charlotte. It was the murder and the Walk he was thinking about. She felt that intense moment of reality when you know a blow is coming but it has not yet landed. The pain is not quite there, but you understand it as surely as if it were. The brain has already accepted it. He was afraid.

It was not that she thought he had killed Fanny; even in her worst moments she had never believed that. She did not know or sense in him the capability for such violence or, to be honest, for the fierceness of emotion to ignite such a train of events. If she were honest, he was not stirred by great tides. His worst sins would be indolence, the unintentional selfishness of a child. His temper was easy; he liked to please. Pain distressed him; he would go to much trouble to avoid his own and, as much as he had energy for, that of others. He had always possessed worldly goods without the need to strive for them, and his generosity frequently bordered on the profligate. He had given Emily everything she wanted and taken pleasure in doing so.

No, she would not believe he could have killed Fanny— unless it were in the heat of panic, and he would have given himself away immediately, terrified as a child.

The blow she felt was that he had done something else that Pitt would uncover in searching for the killer, some thoughtless gratification, not intended to hurt Emily, just a pleasure taken because it was there, and he liked it. Selena—or someone else? It hardly mattered who.

Funny, when she had married him, she had seen all that so clearly and accepted it. Why did it matter now? Was it her condition? She had been warned it might make her oversensitive, weepy. Or was it that she had come to love George more than she had expected to?

He was staring at her, waiting for her to answer the question.

"No." She avoided his eyes. "It seems as if most of the servants are accounted for, but that's all."

"Then what in hell is he doing?" George exploded, his voice sharp and high. "It's damn near a fortnight! Why hasn't he caught him? Even if he can't arrest the man and prove it, he ought at least to know who it is by now!"

She was sorry for him because he was frightened, and sorry for herself. She was also angry because it was his stupid thoughtlessness that had given him cause to fear Pitt, self-indulgence he had had no need to take.

"I only saw Charlotte," she said a little stiffly, "not Thomas. And, even if I had seen him, I could hardly have asked him what he was doing. I don't imagine it is easy to find a murderer when you have no idea where to begin, and no one can prove where they were."

"Dammit!" he said helplessly. "I was miles away from here! I didn't come home until it was all over, finished. I couldn't have done anything or seen anything."

"Then what are you upset about?" She still did not face him.

There was a moment's silence. When he spoke again his voice was calmer, tired.

"I don't like being investigated. I don't like half London being asked about me, and everyone knowing there is a rapist and murderer in my street. I don't like the thought that he's still loose, whoever he is. And, above all, I don't like the thought that it could be one of my neighbors, someone I've known for years, probably even liked."

That was fair. Of course, he was hurt. He would have been callous, even stupid, not to have been. She turned and smiled at him at last.

"We all hate it," she said softly. "And we're all frightened. But it might take a long time yet. If he's one of the coachmen or footmen, he won't be easy to find, and if it's one of us—he will have all sorts of ways of hiding himself. After all, if we've lived with him all these years and have no idea, how can Thomas find him in a few days?"

He did not reply. Indeed, there was no argument to make.

Still, regardless of tragedy, there were certain social obligations to be honored. One did not abandon all discipline simply because there had been loss, still less if the loss had been accompanied by scandalous circumstances. It would be unseemly to be observed at parties quite so soon, but afternoon calls, discreetly made, were an entirely different matter. Vespasia, prompted by interest and justified by duty, called upon Phoebe Nash.

She had intended to convey sympathy. She was genuinely sorry for Fanny's death, although the idea of dying did not appall her as it had in her youth. Now she was resigned to it, as one is to going home at the end of a long and splendid party. Eventually it must happen, and, perhaps by the time it did, one would be ready for it. Though doubtless that could hardly have been the case for Fanny, poor child.

Her real sympathy for Phoebe, however, was for her misfortune in having made an excessively trying marriage. Any woman obliged to live under one roof with Afton Nash was deserving at the least of commiseration.

She found the visit more trying to her patience. Phoebe was more than ordinarily incoherent. She seemed forever on the edge of some confidence which never actually formed itself into words. Vespasia tried concerned interest and

103

appreciative silence in turn, but on every occasion Phoebe dived off into some altogether unrelated subject at the final moment, twisting her handkerchief in her lap until the thing was not fit to stuff a pincushion.

Vespasia left as soon as duty was fulfilled, but outside in the blistering sun she walked very slowly and began to reflect on what might be causing Phoebe such distraction of mind. The poor woman seemed unable to keep her wits on anything for more than a moment.

Was she so overcome with grief for Fanny? They had never appeared especially close. Vespasia could not recall more than a dozen occasions when they had gone calling together, and Phoebe had never accompanied her to any balls or soirees, or held any parties for her, even though this was her first Season.

Then a new and very unpleasant thought occurred to her, so ugly she stopped in the middle of the path, quite unaware of being stared at by the gardener's boy.

Was Phoebe aware of something from which she guessed who it was that had raped and murdered Fanny? Had she seen something, heard something? Or more likely, was it some episode remembered from the past that had led her to understand now what had happened, and with whom?

Surely the idiot woman would speak to the police. Discretion was all very well. Society would disintegrate without it, and everyone naturally disliked having anything to do with something as distasteful as the police. Still, one must recognize the inevitable. To fight against it only made the final submission the more painful—and obvious.

And why should Phoebe be prepared to protect any man guilty of such a horrendous crime? Fear? It hardly showed sense. The only safety lay in sharing such a secret, so it could not die with you!

Love? Unlikely. Certainly not for Afton.

Duty? Duty to him, or to the Nash family, perhaps even

duty to her own social class, paralysis in the face of scandal. To be the victim was one thing—it could be overlooked in time—to be the offender, never!

Vespasia started to walk again, head down, frowning. All this was speculation; the reason could be anything, even as simple as the dread of investigation. Perhaps she had a lover?

But it was beyond doubt in her mind now that Phoebe was profoundly frightened.

To call upon Grace Dilbridge was unavoidable, but it was a dreary task and consisted of the usual almost ritual commiserations over Frederick's bizarre friends and their incessant parties and the indignities to which Grace felt herself subjected, as she was excluded from gambling and whatever else unmentionable went on in the garden room. Vespasia rather overdid the vehemence of her sympathy and excused herself, just as Selena Montague was arriving, brilliant-eyed and quivering with life. She heard Paul Alaric's name mentioned before she was quite out of the door and smiled to herself at the obviousness of youth.

It was necessary, of course, to call upon Jessamyn. Vespasia found her very composed and already out of total black. Her hair shimmered in the sun through the French windows, and her skin had the delicate bloom of apple blossom.

"How good of you, Lady Cumming-Gould," she said politely. "I'm sure you would like some refreshment—tea or lemonade?"

"Tea, if you please," Vespasia accepted, sitting down. "I still find it pleasant, even in the heat."

Jessamyn rang the bell and gave orders to the maid. After she had gone, Jessamyn walked gracefully over toward the windows.

"I wish it would cool down." She stared out at the dry

grass and dusty leaves. "This summer seems to be going on forever."

Vespasia was so practiced in the art of small conversation that she had an appropriate remark for any circumstance, but, faced with Jessamyn's composure and delicate, stiff body, she knew she was in the presence of powerful emotion, and yet she did not fathom precisely what it was. It seemed far more complex than simple grief. Or perhaps it was Jessamyn herself who was complex.

Jessamyn turned and smiled. "Prophecy?" she inquired.

Vespasia knew immediately what she meant. It was the police investigation she was thinking of, not the summer weather. Jessamyn was not a person with whom to be evasive; she was far too clever, and too strong.

"You may not have intended it as such when you spoke." Vespasia looked straight back at her. "But I dare say it will be the case. On the other hand, summer may slide quite imperceptibly into autumn, and we shall hardly notice the difference until one morning there is a frost, and the first leaves fall."

"And it is all forgotten," Jessamyn came back from the window and sat down. "Just a tragedy from the past that was never fully explained. For a while we shall be more careful about the manservants we hire, and then presently even that will pass."

"It will be replaced by other storms," Vespasia corrected. "There must always be something to talk about. Someone will make or lose a fortune; there will be a society marriage; someone will take a lover, or lose one."

Jessamyn's hand tightened on the embroidered arm of the sofa.

"Probably, but I prefer not to discuss other people's romantic affairs. I find them a quite private matter, and not my concern."

For a moment Vespasia was surprized, then she recalled

106

that she never had heard Jessamyn gossiping of loves or marriages. She could only remember conversation of fashion, parties, and even on rare occasions matters of weight like business or politics. Jessamyn's father had been a man of considerable property, but naturally it had all gone to her younger brother, since he was the male. It had been said at the time the old man died, years ago, that the boyhad inherited the money, and Jessamyn the brains. He was a young fool, so far as she heard. Jessamyn had the better part.

The tea came, and they swapped polite reminiscences of the previous Season and speculations as to what the next turn of fashion might be.

Presently she took her leave and met Fulbert at the gateway to the drive. He bowed with amused grace, and they exchanged greetings, hers decidedly cool. She had had enough visiting and was about to continue on her way home when he spoke.

"You've been calling upon Jessamyn."

"Obviously!" she replied tartly. Really, he was becoming fatuous.

"Most entertaining, isn't it?" His smile widened. "Everyone is rushing back to their own private sins, to make sure they are still covered. If your policeman, Pitt, were the least interested in voyeurism, he would find this better than a peepshow. It is rather like undoing one of those Chinese boxes; each comes apart in a different way, and nothing is what it seems."

"I have no idea what you mean," she said coldly.

It was plain from his face that he knew she was lying. She understood him with exactness, even if she had no better than educated guesses as to what the sins in question might be. He did not seem to be offended. He was still smiling, and there was laughter in his face, even in the angle of his body.

"There is a great deal goes on in this Walk you don't

dream of," he said softly. "The carcass is full of worms, if you break it open. Even poor Phoebe, although she's too frightened to speak. One of these days she'll die of pure fright, unless, of course, someone murders her first!"

"What on earth are you talking about?" Now Vespasia hovered between fury at his adolescent pleasure in shocking and a chill of quite real fear that indeed he knew something beyond even the worst imaginings of her own.

But he simply smiled and turned to walk up the driveway toward the door, and she was obliged to proceed on her way without an answer.

It was nineteen days after the murder that Vespasia came to the breakfast table with a frown on her face and an extraordinary wisp of hair trailing across her head completely out of place.

Emily stared at her.

"My maid tells me a most peculiar story." Vespasia seemed not quite sure where to begin. She never ate a heavy breakfast, and now her hand hovered over the toast rack, then the fruit, but could not settle for either.

Emily had never seen her so out of countenance before. It was disturbing.

"What sort of story?" she demanded. "Something to do with Fanny?"

"I've no idea." Vespasia's eyebrows went up. "Not apparently."

"Well, what is it?" Emily was growing impatient, not sure whether to be afraid or not. George had put down his fork and was staring at her, his face tight.

"It seems Fulbert Nash has disappeared," Vespasia spoke as if she herself could hardly believe what she was saying.

George breathed out in a sigh, and the fork clattered from his hand.

"What on earth do you mean, disappeared?" he said slowly. "Where has he gone?"

"If I knew where he had gone, George, I would hardly say he had disappeared!" Vespasia said with unusual acerbity. "No one knows where he is! That is the point. He did not come home yesterday, although he had no dinner engagement that anyone knows of, and he has not been home all night. His valet says he has no clothes with him other than the light suit he was wearing for luncheon."

"Are all the coachmen or footmen at home?" George demanded. "Did anyone take a message or call a cab for him?"

"Apparently not."

"Well, he can't simply have vanished! He must be somewhere!"

"Of course." Vespasia frowned still more and at last took herself a piece of toast and spread it with butter and apricot preserve. "But no one knows where. Or, if they do, they are not prepared to say."

"Oh God!" George gasped at her. "You're not suggesting he's been murdered!"

Emily choked on her tea.

"I'm not suggesting anything." Vespasia waved her arm at Emily, for George to do something about her. "Slap her, for goodness' sake!" She waited while George obliged and Emily pushed him away, finding her breath again. "I simply don't know," Vespasia finished. "But doubtless there will be suggestions, all of them unpleasant, and that will be one of them."

And it was, although Emily did not hear it until the following day. She had called upon Jessamyn and found Selena already there. So soon after Fanny's death, social visits were being kept very much within their own immediate circle, possibly as a matter of good taste, but more likely so that they might be freer to discuss it if they wished.

"I suppose you have heard nothing whatever?" Selena asked anxiously.

"Nothing," Jessamyn agreed. "It is as if the ground had opened up and swallowed him into it. Phoebe came this morning, and naturally Afton has inquired as much as is possible, discreetly, but he is not at any of his clubs in town, and no one else can be found who has spoken to him."

"Is there no one in the country he might have visited?" Emily asked.

Jessamyn's eyebrows shot up.

"At this time of the year?"

"It's the height of the Season!" Selena added, a little disparagingly. "Whoever would leave London now?"

"Perhaps Fulbert," Emily was stung to reply. "He seems to have left Paragon Walk without a word of explanation to anyone. If he were in London, why should he be anywhere but here?"

"That makes sense," Jessamyn admitted, "since he is not at any of the clubs, and he does not seem to be visiting any other friends up for the Season."

"The alternatives are too dreadful to contemplate." Selena shivered, then instantly contradicted herself. "But we must."

Jessamyn looked at her.

Selena was not going to draw back now.

"We must face it, my dear. It is possible he has been done away with!"

Jessamyn's face was very pale, very fine.

"You mean murdered?" she said quietly.

"Yes, I'm afraid I do."

There was a moment's silence. Emily's mind raced. Who would murder Fulbert, and why? The other possibility was, at once, worse and also an infinite relief—except that she dared not say it—suicide. If he had after all been the one who killed Fanny, maybe he had taken this desperate way to escape.

Jessamyn was still staring. In her lap her long slender hands were stiff, as if she could neither feel with them nor move them.

"Why?" she whispered. "Why would anyone murder Fulbert, Selena?"

"Perhaps whoever killed poor Fanny killed him also?" Selena replied.

Emily could not say what was in her mind. She must lead them to it, gently, until one of them had to say it for herself.

"But Fanny was—molested," she reasoned aloud. "She was only killed after that—perhaps because she recognized him, and he could not then let her go. Why should anyone kill Fulbert—if indeed he is dead? He is only missing, after all."

Jessamyn smiled very faintly, something like gratitude warming her pallor.

"You are quite right. There is hardly anything to suggest it was the same person. In fact, there is not really anything to prove they are connected at all."

"They must be!" Selena exploded. "We could not have two entirely unconnected crimes in the Walk in the space of a month. That is straining credulity too far! We must face it—either Fulbert is dead, or he has run away!"

Jessamyn's eyes were very bright, her voice came slowly, as if from far away.

"Are you saying that it was Fulbert who killed Fanny, and he has now run away in case the police find him?"

"Someone did." Selena would not be put off. "Perhaps he is mad?"

Another thought occurred to Emily.

"Or perhaps it was not him, but he knows who it was, and he is afraid?" she said it before she considered what effect it might have.

Jessamyn sat absolutely still. Her voice was soft, almost sibilant. "I don't think that's very likely," she said slowly.

"Fulbert was never very good at keeping a secret. Nor was he especially brave. I don't think that can be the answer."

"It's ridiculous!" Selena turned on Emily sharply. "If he knew who it was, he would have said so! And enjoyed it! And why on earth should he protect them? After all, Fanny was his sister!"

"Perhaps he didn't have the chance to tell anyone?" Emily was growing annoyed at being spoken to as if she were foolish. "Perhaps they killed him before he could get away?"

Jessamyn took a deep breath and let it out in a long, silent sigh.

"I think you must be right, Emily. I hate to say so—" Her voice faded for a minute, and she was obliged to clear her throat. "—but I think it is inescapable that either Fulbert killed Fanny and has run away, or else—" She shivered and seemed to shrink into herself. "—or else whoever so dreadfully murdered Fanny knew that poor Fulbert knew too much and killed him before he could speak!"

"If that is true, then we have a very dangerous murderer living in the Walk," Emily said quietly. "And I am very glad I have no idea who he is. I think we should all be extremely careful whom we speak to, what we say, and whom we find ourself alone with!"

Selena gave a little whimper, but her face was flushed and there were very fine beads of sweat on her face. Her eyes were bright.

The day seemed darker, the heat more suffocating. Emily rose to go home; the visit was no longer any pleasure.

The day after, it was not possible to keep the matter from the police. Pitt was informed of it and returned to the Walk, feeling tired and unhappy. It was a mark of his failure that something so unforeseen should have happened, and he had no explanation to offer for it. Of course, there were volumes of theories. He had no niceties to keep his mind from coming first to the most obvious and the most ugly. He had seen far too much crime for anything to surprize him, even incestuous rape. In the rookeries and teeming slums incest was all too common. Women bore too many children and died young, often leaving fathers with elder daughters to bring up a brood of little ones. Loneliness and reliance slipped easily into something else more intimate, more urgent.

But he had not expected to find it in Paragon Walk.

Then there was the possibility that it was not escape, or suicide, but another murder. Perhaps Fulbert had known too much and been foolish enough to say so? Perhaps he had even tried blackmail and paid the ultimate price for it.

Charlotte had told him something about Fulbert's remarks, the sly, cutting cruelty of them, the "whited sepulchers." Perhaps he had chanced on a secret more dangerous than he knew and been killed for that—nothing to do with Fanny at all? It would not be the first time one crime had planted the seed of an idea for another, where motives were completely unconnected. Nothing invites imitation like apparent success.

The only place he could start was with Afton Nash, the person who had reported Fulbert as missing and who had lived in the same house. Pitt had already sent men to check on the clubs and houses of other sorts, where a man might be who was indulging himself, had taken more to drink than was good for him, or wished to be anonymous for a while.

He was received with chilly civility at the Nash house and conducted to the morning room, where a few moments later Afton appeared. He looked tired, and there were harsh lines of irritation around his mouth. Afflicted by a summer cold that obliged him to keep dabbing at his nose, he looked at Pitt with disfavor.

"I presume you are now here with reference to my

brother's apparent disappearance?'' he said, and sniffed. "I have no idea where he is. He gave no indication of intending to leave." He pulled his mouth down. "Or of being afraid."

"Afraid?'' Pitt wanted to allow him room and time to say anything he would.

Afton looked at him with contempt.

"I am not going to avoid the obvious, Mr. Pitt. In view of what has happened here recently to Fanny, it is not impossible that Fulbert is also dead."

Pitt sat sideways on the arm of one of the chairs.

"Why, Mr. Nash? Whoever killed your sister cannot possibly have had the same motive."

"Whoever killed Fanny did so to keep her silent. Whoever killed Fulbert, if indeed he is dead, will have done so for the same reason."

"You think Fulbert knew who that was?"

"Don't treat me like a fool, Mr. Pitt!" Afton dabbed at his nose again. "If I knew who it was, I would have told you. But it is only rational to consider the possibility that Fulbert knew, and was killed for it."

"We will have to find a body or some trace of it before we can assume murder, Mr. Nash," Pitt pointed out. "So far there is nothing to indicate that he did not simply choose to go away."

"With no clothes, no money, and alone?" Afton's pale eyes widened. "Unlikely, Mr. Pitt." His voice was soft, weary with Pitt's stupidity.

"He may have done quite a few things we had thought unlikely," Pitt pointed out. But he knew that, even when people change the major direction of their lives, they do not often alter the small thing: a mall will still keep his personal habits, his tastes in food, the pleasures that entertain or bore him. And he doubted Fulbert was careful enough, or desperate enough, to have left without thought for his creature comfort. He had been used to clean clothes all his life and a valet to lay them out for him. And if he were leaving London he would assuredly need money.

"Still," Pitt agreed, "you're probably right. Who was the last person to see him, that you know of?"

"His valet, Price. You can speak to the man if you want, but I've already questioned him, and he can't tell you anything of use. All Fulbert's clothes and personal possessions are still here, and he had no engagement that evening that Price knew of."

"And I presume he would know, because he would be required to set out Mr. Fulbert's clothes, if he were going out?" Pitt added.

Afton looked slightly surprised that Pitt should know such a thing, and it irritated him. He dabbed at his nose and then winced; it was becoming raw with the constant friction.

Pitt smiled, not enough for levity, but enough to let Afton know he had understood.

"Quite," Afton agreed. "He left here at about six in the evening, saying he would be back for dinner."

"But he didn't say where he was going?"

"If he had, Inspector, I should have told you!"

"And he didn't come back, nor did anyone see him again?"

Afton glared at him.

"I imagine someone saw him!"

"He could have walked to the end of the road and taken a cab," Pitt pointed out. "There are quite often hansoms even around here."

"Where to, for heaven's sake?"

"Well, if he is still in the Walk, Mr. Nash, where is he?"

Afton looked at him with slow comprehension. Apparently he had not considered it before, but there were no rivers or wells, no woods, no gardens large enough for one to dig unnoticed, no untenanted cellars or sheds. There were always gardeners, footmen, butlers, kitchenmaids or boot-boys to find something left. There was nowhere to hide a body.

"Find out whose carriage left the Walk that evening, or the following morning," he ordered waspishly. "Fulbert was not a very big man. Anyone could have carried him if they had needed to—except perhaps Algernon—especially if he were already unconscious or dead."

"I intend to, Mr. Nash," Pitt answered him. "And to question cabbies, errand boys and send out a directive to every other police station in the force, also a description of him to all the railway stations and especially the cross-channel ferry. But I shall be surprized if we turn up anything of use. I have already begun a search of hospitals and morgues."

"Well, good God, man, he's got to be somewhere!" Afton exploded. "It's not as if he could have been eaten by wild animals in the middle of London! Do all those things, by all means—I suppose they are necessary—but you'd get furthest by asking a few damned awkward questions right here! Whatever's happened to him has to do with Fanny. And much as I would like to imagine it was some drunken coachman from the Dilbridges' party, it would be straining credulity a little too far. If it were, Fulbert would not know of it, and so it could be of no conceivable danger to the man."

"Unless he saw something," Pitt pointed out.

Afton looked at him with icy amusement.

"Hardly, Mr. Pitt. Fulbert was with me all that evening, playing billiards, as I believe I told you when you first asked."

Pitt met his eyes perfectly calmly.

"As I understand, sir, from both of you, Mr. Fulbert did leave the billiard room on at least one occasion. Is it not possible that while passing a window he observed something unusual, which afterwards he realized to be of significance?"

Dull anger crept up Afton's face. He hated to be in the wrong.

"Coachmen are not significant, Inspector. They are about the street all the time. If you had one, you would know. I suggest you press a little more closely on the Frenchman, for a start. He said he was at home all evening. Perhaps he was not, and it was he whom Fulbert saw? One lie springs from another! Find out what he was really doing. He's far too easy with women. He's managed to seduce the minds of nearly every woman in the Walk. I think he is a great deal older than he pretends. Spends all his time inside, or going out at night—but see his face in the daylight.

"One expects women to be frail, to look no further than a man's features or his manners. Perhaps Monsieur Alaric's tastes run to something young and innocent like Fanny. But she was not duped by his charm. Maybe the loose and sophisticated women like Selena Montague bored him. If Fulbert sensed that, and was rash enough to let Alaric know he had seen him out—" He sniffed savagely and choked. "If he did," he added.

Pitt listened. The flow was poisonous, but there might be some germ of truth in it, even so.

Afton continued.

"Selena always was a—a strumpet. Even when her husband was alive, she did not know how to conduct herself. Lately she has sought after George Ashworth, and he's been fool enough to dally with her! I find it disgusting. Perhaps it does not offend you?" He glared at Pitt with curled lip. "Nevertheless, it is true."

It was what Pitt had been fearing. He had already read it through Charlotte's words, although of course he had not told her. Perhaps he could still keep it from Emily. He said

117

nothing to Afton, just looked at him, his face attentive, as he struggled to keep expression out of it.

"And you should take a good deal closer look at Freddie Dilbridge's party," Afton went on. "Not only coachmen drink more than they can hold. He has some very strange guests. I don't know how Grace puts up with it, except of course it is her place to obey him, and, good woman that she is, she abides by it. But, good God, do you know his daughter is keeping company with some Jew, and Freddie allows it, just because the man has money! I ask you, some money-grubbing little Jew, with Albertine Dilbridge!" He turned around sharply, his eyes narrowed. "Or perhaps you don't understand that? Although even the lower classes don't usually mix their blood with foreigners. To do business with them is one thing, even to have them in one's house, when one must, but that is utterly different from permitting one of them to court one's daughter." He snorted and was obliged to blow his nose. He flinched in pain as the linen of his handkerchief rubbed the red flesh.

"You had better start doing your job a little more effectively, Mr. Pitt. Everyone here is suffering appallingly. As if the heat and the Season were not enough! I loathe the Season, with its endless simpering young women dressed by their mothers and taught to parade like cattle at a fat stock show, young men gambling away their money, whoring around, and drinking till they cannot even remember which idiocy they were at the night before. Do you know I went to see Hallam Cayley at half past ten on the morning Fulbert disappeared, to inquire if he had seen him, and he was still insensible from the previous night? The man is only thirty-five, and he's a dissipated wreck! It's obscene!"

He looked at Pitt without pleasure. "One thing to be said for your type, I suppose, at least you are too busy to become drunk, and you cannot afford it."

Pitt straightened up and put his hands into his pockets to hide the clenching of his fists. He had seen every kind of moral and spiritual wreck thrown up with the flotsam of London's underworld, but nothing that offended him, as did Afton Nash, without stirring up a modicum of pity. There must be some deep and dreadful scar on this man he did not even guess.

"Does Mr. Cayley drink a great deal, sir?" he asked with soft voice.

"How the devil should I know?" Afton snapped. "I do not frequent that sort of place. I know he was drunk the other morning when I called, and he behaves like a man who has indulged himself beyond the point his stomach can bear." He jerked his head up to look at Pitt again. "But look at the Frenchman. There is something sly and over intimate about him. God only knows what foreign aberrations he has! There is no one in his house but his own servants. He could be doing anything in there. Women are incredibly foolish. For God's sake, protect us from this—this obscenity!"

Six

Emily did not mention Fulbert's disappearance to Charlotte, and she heard of it from Pitt. There was nothing she could do about it so late in the evening, or indeed the following day. Since Jemima was grizzly with cutting teeth, Charlotte did not feel it fair to ask Mrs. Smith to look after her. However, by midafternoon she was so distracted by Jemima's crying that she slipped over the street to ask Mrs. Smith if she had any remedy for it, or at least something to ease the pain sufficiently for the child to rest.

Mrs. Smith clucked with disapproval at Charlotte and took herself off into the kitchen. A moment later she came back with a bottle of clear liquid.

"You put that on 'er gums with a piece of cotton, an' it'll soothe 'er in no time, you just see."

Charlotte thanked her for it profusely. She did not ask what was in the mixture, feeling she would probably prefer not to know, as long as it was not gin, which she had heard some women gave their babies when they could bear the crying no longer. Still, she imagined she would recognize the smell of that.

"And 'ow's your poor sister?" Mrs. Smith asked, glad of a few moments' company and wanting to keep it.

Charlotte seized the chance to prepare the ground to visit Emily again.

"Not very well," she said quickly. "I'm afraid the brother of a friend has disappeared quite without trace, and it is all very distressing."

"Oooh!" Mrs. Smith was entranced. " 'Ow dreadful! Ain't that extraordinary, wherever can 'e 'ave gorn?"

"Nobody knows." Charlotte sensed that she had won already. "But tomorrow, if you will be kind enough to look after Jemima, and I hardly like to ask you when—"

"Never you mind!" Mrs. Smith said instantly. "I'll look after 'er, don't you worry. She'll 'ave them teeth cut in a week or two, and poor little thing'll feel the world better. You just go and see to your sister, love. Find out what 'appened!"

"Are you sure?"

" 'Course, I'm sure!"

Charlotte gave her a dazzling smile, and accepted.

Actually she was going as much for curiosity as in any belief that she could help Emily. But she might help Pitt, and perhaps that was what was in her heart. After all, Fulbert's disappearance could hardly make anything worse for George. And she had a great desire to speak again with Aunt Vespasia. As Vespasia frequently pointed out, not always at happy moments, she had known most of the people in the Walk since childhood and had a prodigious memory. So often, small clues, threads from the past, could point to something in the present that would otherwise be overlooked.

She arrived at Emily's house at the traditional time for afternoon tea and was shown in by the maid, who recognized her now and ushered her in.

Emily already had Phoebe Nash and Grace Dilbridge with her, and Aunt Vespasia joined them from the garden almost at the same time as Charlotte came in at the other door. The usual polite greetings were exchanged. Emily told the maid she might bring in the tea, and a few minutes later it arrived: the silver service and bone china cups and saucers, minute cucumber sandwiches, little fruit tarts, and sponge cakes spread with fine sugar and whipped cream. Emily poured the tea, and the maid waited to hand it around.

"I don't know what the police are doing," Grace Dilbridge said critically. "They don't seem to have found the slightest trace of poor Fulbert."

Charlotte had to remind herself that, of course, Grace had no idea that the police in question included Charlotte's husband. The notion of having a social connection with the police was unthinkable. She saw a bright spot of color in Emily's cheek, and surprizingly it was Emily who came to their defense.

"If he does not wish to be found, it would be extremely difficult even to know where to begin," she pointed out. "I would have no idea where to start. Would you?"

"Of course not." Grace was put out by the question. "But then I am not a policeman."

Vespasia's magnificent face was perfectly calm except for a faint surprize, but her eye flickered over Charlotte for an instant before fixing on Grace.

"Are you suggesting, my dear, that the police are more intelligent than we are?" she inquired.

Grace was momentarily floored. It was certainly not what she had intended, and yet somehow she seemed to have said it. She took refuge in a sip of tea and then a nibble at a cucumber sandwich. A look of confusion passed over her face, followed by polite determination.

"But everyone is so appallingly upset," Phoebe murmured to fill the gap. "I know I miss poor Fanny still, and the whole household seems to be at sixes and sevens. I jump every time I hear a strange sound. I simply cannot help myself."

122

Charlotte had wanted to see Aunt Vespasia alone in order to put some questions to her frankly; there would be no point at all in trying to be devious. But she would have to wait until tea was properly accomplished and the visitors excused themselves. She took one of the cucumber sandwiches and bit into it. It was unpleasant, faintly sweet, as if the cucumber were bad, and yet is was crisp enough. She looked at Emily.

Emily had one also. She stared at Charlotte, consternation on her face.

"Oh dear!"

"I think you had better have a word with your cook," Vespasia suggested, putting down one of the cakes. She reached for the bell herself. They waited until the maid came and was duly sent to fetch the cook.

When the cook came, she was a buxom woman with a good color, who normally might well have been handsome enough, but today looked hot and untidy, although it was long before time for the preparation of dinner.

"Are you feeling unwell, Mrs. Lowndes?" Emily began carefully. "You have put sugar in the sandwiches."

"And, I fear, salt on the cakes," Vespasia touched one delicately with her finger.

"If you are," Emily continued, "perhaps you would prefer to take to your bed for a while. One of the girls can prepare some vegetables, and I am sure there is a cold ham or chicken we could eat. I cannot have dinner turning out like this."

Mrs. Lowndes stared at the cake stand in dismay, then let out a long wail of anguish, rising at the end. Phoebe looked alarmed.

"It's awful!" Mrs. Lowndes moaned. "You can't know, m'lady, 'ow awful it is down there, knowing as there's a maniac loose in the Walk. An' decent, God-fearin' people bein' a murdered one by one. Only the good Lord knows as who'll be next! The scullery maid's fainted twice today already, and me kitchen maid's threatening to leave if'e ain't found soon. Always been in decent employment, all of us! Never 'ad anything like this in all our lives! We won't never be the same again, none of us! Aoow—eee!" she wailed, even more shrilly, and tore a handkerchief out of her apron pocket. Her voice rose higher and louder, and the tears streamed down her face.

Everyone looked stupefied. Emily was aghast. She had no idea at all what to do with this enormous woman rapidly nearing the verge of complete hysteria. For once even Aunt Vespasia seemed at a loss.

"Aowoo!" Mrs. Lowndes howled. "Ooooh!" She began to shake violently and threatened to collapse on the carpet.

Charlotte stood up and seized the vase of flowers from the sideboard. She took the blooms out with her left hand and felt a satisfactory weight remaining. With all her strength she hurled the water into the cook's face.

"Be quiet!" she said firmly.

The howl ceased in mid-breath. There was total silence.

"Now control yourself!" Charlotte went on. "Of course, it is unpleasant. Do you not think we all feel distressed? But it is up to us to behave with dignity. You must set an example to the younger women. If you lose control of yourself, what on earth can we expect of the maids? A cook is not merely someone who knows how to mix a sauce, Mrs. Lowndes. She is head of the kitchen; she is there to keep order and to see that everyone conducts themselves as they ought. I'm surprised at you!"

The cook stared at her. The color brightened in her face, and slowly she drew herself up to her full height, throwing her shoulders back.

"Yes, ma'am."

"Good," Charlotte said stiffly. "Now Lady Ashworth will look to you to stop any silly chatter among the girls. If

124

you keep your head and behave with the dignity appropriate to the senior member of the female staff, then they will all take courage and follow your example."

Mrs. Lowndes lifted her chin a little and her bosom swelled, remembering her own importance.

"Yes, m'lady. I'll take it kindly, m'lady," she looked at Emily, "if you'd overlook my momentary weakness, and not mention it in front of the other servants, ma'am?"

"Of course not, Mrs. Lowndes," Emily said quickly, taking Charlotte's cue. "Quite understandable. It's a heavy burden of responsibility you carry for so many girls. The less said, the better, I think. Perhaps you would have the parlormaid bring us some fresh cakes and sandwiches?"

"Yes, m'lady, most certainly." With great relief she picked up the two plates and sailed out, dripping with water, and ignoring Charlotte, still standing with the flowers in one hand and the empty vase in the other.

After Phoebe and Grace had gone, Emily immediately took herself to the kitchen, against Vespasia's advice, to make sure that Charlotte's counsel had been taken, and dinner would not be another disaster. Charlotte turned to Vespasia. There was no time for subtlety, even were she capable of it.

"It seems even the servants are in a turmoil over Mr. Nash's disappearance," she said directly. "Do you think he has run away?"

Vespasia's eyebrows rose in slight surprize.

"No, my dear, I do not for a moment think so. I imagine that his tongue has at last earned him the fate he has so long sought by it."

"You mean someone has murdered him?" Of course it was what she had expected, but to hear it spoken so plainly by someone other than Pitt was still startling.

"I should think so." Vespasia hesitated. "Except that I have no idea what they have done with his body." Her nostrils flared. "A peculiarly unpleasant thing to think of, but ignoring it will not change it. I suppose they took him out in a hansom and left him somewhere, perhaps the river."

"In that case, we'll never find him." It was an admission of defeat. With no body, there was no proof of murder. "But that is not the most important thing, what matters is who!"

"Ah," Vespasia said softly, looking at Charlotte. "Indeed, who? Naturally I have given the subject a great deal of consideration. In fact I have been able to think of little else, although I have avoided speaking of it in front of Emily."

Charlotte leaned forward. She was not sure how to express herself without seeming forward, even callous, and yet she must. Delicacy was of no service now. "You have known these people most of their lives. You must know things about them the police could never discover, or understand if they did." It was not intended as flattery, simply fact. They needed Vespasia's help—Pitt needed it. "You must have opinions! Fulbert used to say fearful things about people. He said to me once that they were all whited sepulchers. I don't doubt most of it was for effect, but judging from their reactions, there was a germ of truth!"

Vespasia smiled, and there was dry, faraway humor and regret in her face, an infinity of memories.

"My dear girl, everyone has secrets, unless they have lived no life at all. And even they, poor souls, imagine they have. It is almost an admission of defeat not to have a secret of some kind."

"Phoebe?"

"Hardly one to kill over," Vespasia shook her head slowly. "The poor soul is losing her hair. She wears a wig."

Charlotte recalled Phoebe at the funeral, her hair sliding one way and her hat the other. How could she feel so sharply sorry for her and at the same time want to laugh? It was so unimportant, and yet it would be painful to Phoebe. Unconsciously she touched her own hair, thick and shining. It was her best feature. Perhaps if she were losing it, it would matter enormously. She too would feel insecure, belittled, somehow naked. The laughter vanished.

"Oh," there was pity in the word, and Vespasia was looking at her with appreciation. "But as you say," Charlotte collected herself and went on, "hardly a matter to murder over, even if she were capable of it."

"She wouldn't be," Vespasia agreed. "She is far too silly to do anything so big so successfully."

"I was thinking of the purely physical side," Charlotte replied. "She couldn't manage that, even if she'd a mind to."

"Oh, Phoebe is stronger than she looks," Vespasia sat back in her chair, staring up at the ceiling in recollection. "She could murder him all right, with perhaps a knife, if she had lured him somewhere she could simply leave him. But she has not the nerve to carry it off afterward. I remember when she was a girl, about fourteen or fifteen, she took her elder sister's lace petticoat and pantaloons and cut them down to fit herself. She was as cool as you like doing it, but then, when she came to wear them, she was so stricken with fear, she wore her own on top in case anything should catch her skirt and the better ones be seen. As a result she looked ten pounds heavier and not in the least attractive. No, Phoebe might do it, but she has not the endurance to carry it off."

Charlotte was fascinated. How little one guessed of people when one saw them only in the single dimension of a few days or weeks; how they lacked all the substance of the past. They seemed almost flat, like cardboard, with all the depth gone.

"What other secrets are there?" she asked. "What else did Fulbert know?"

127

Vespasia sat up and opened her eyes wide.

"My dear child, I wouldn't begin to guess. He was unbearably nosy. His main preoccupation in life was to acquire uncharitable information about others. If at last he found something too big for him, I cannot but say he richly deserved it."

"But what else?" Charlotte was not going to give up so easily. "Who else? Do you think he knew who killed Fanny, and that was it?"

"Ah!" Vespasia breathed out slowly. "That, of course, is the real question. And I'm afraid I have no idea. Naturally I have been over and over everything I know. To tell the truth, I expected you to ask me." She looked at Charlotte hard. Her old eyes were very clear, very clever. "And I would warn you, my girl, to keep your tongue a little stiller than you have done so far. If indeed Fulbert did know who killed Fanny, it served him ill. At least one of the secrets in Paragon Walk is a very dangerous matter indeed. I don't know which of them brought Fulbert Nash to his death, so leave them all alone!"

Charlotte felt the cold ripple through her, as if someone had opened an outside door on a winter day. She had not thought of personal danger before. All her anxieties had been for Emily, that she might learn of weakness, selfishness in George. She had not feared violence, not even to Emily, let alone to herself. But, if there were a secret so dreadful in Paragon Walk that Fulbert had lost his life merely because he knew it, then to betray curiosity at all would be dangerous, and knowledge itself would be fatal. Surely the only secret like that must be the identity of the rapist. He had killed Fanny to protect that. There couldn't be two murderers in the Walk—could there?

Or had Fulbert stumbled on some other secret, and his victim, already prompted by the one so-far-successful murder, simply copied the same resolution to his problem?

Thomas had said that crime begot crime; people imitated, especially the weak and sick in mind, the opportunists.

"Do you hear me, Charlotte?" Vespasia said somewhat abruptly.

"Yes! Oh, yes, I do." Charlotte recalled herself to the present, the sunlit withdrawing room and the old lady in ecru-colored lace sitting opposite her. "I don't speak to anyone except Thomas about it. But what else? I mean, what other secrets do you know?"

Vespasia snorted. "You won't be told, will you!"

"Don't you want to know?" Charlotte met her eyes squarely.

"Of course, I do!" Vespasia snapped. "And if I die for it, at my time of life it doesn't matter! I shall almost certainly die soon anyway. If I had anything useful to say, don't you think I would have said it? Not to you, but to your extraordinary policeman." She coughed. "George has been dallying with Selena. I have no proof of it, but I know George. As a child he played with other children's toys if he felt like it, and ate other children's sweets. He always gave the toys back, and he was always generous with his own. Used to everything being his anyway. Trouble with an only child. You have a child, don't you? Well, have another!"

Charlotte could think of no adequate reply to this. She had every intention of having another, when the good Lord should so choose. Anyway, her concern was for Emily now.

Vespasia guessed it.

"He knows that I know," she said gently. "He is far too frightened at the moment to do anything foolish. In fact he turns decidedly green every time Selena comes anywhere near him. Which isn't very often, except to try and show the Frenchman that she is sought after. Silly creature! As if he cared!"

"What other secrets?" Charlotte pressed.

"None of any value. I cannot think Miss Laetitia would

129

harm anyone because they knew she had a scandalous love affair thirty years ago."

Charlotte was stunned.

"Miss Laetitia? Laetitia Horbury?"

"Yes. Quite secret, of course, but very burning at the time. Haven't you noticed Miss Lucinda always making cutting little remarks to her about morals, and so forth? The poor creature is so jealous it is eating her alive. Now, if Laetitia had been killed, I could understand it. I have frequently thought that Lucinda would poison her in a shot, if she dared. Except she would be lost without her. Devising new ways of observing her own moral superiority is her chief enjoyment in life."

"But how can it hurt? Laetitia knows it is only envy?" Charlotte was fascinated.

"Good heavens, no! They never discuss it! They each imagine the other does not know! What would be the pleasure or the savor of it if it were all in the open?"

Again Charlotte was torn between pity and laughter. But then, as Vespasia had said, it was hardly a matter over which Fulbert could have lost his life. Even if all Society knew, it would do Miss Laetitia little harm; in fact it might rather enhance her interest. Miss Lucinda would be the one to suffer by comparison. Then her jealousy might well be unendurable.

Before she could pursue the matter any further, Emily returned from the kitchen hurt and in short temper. Apparently she had had some altercation with the scullery maid, who was frightened out of her wits that the bootboy was after her, and Emily had told her not to be so stupid. The girl was as plain as a coal scuttle, and the bootboy had his sights set a good deal higher.

Vespasia reminded her she had been advised not to go, which only added fuel to the fire of Emily's temper.

130

Charlotte excused herself as soon as she could, and in ill-grace Emily ordered her a carriage to take her home.

Of course Charlotte had regaled Pitt with everything she had heard, plus her own evaluation of it, almost as soon as he had come in the door, and although he knew that most of it would be irrelevant, no more than trivia to the case, yet momentous to those concerned, still he bore them at the back of his mind when he went out the following day to continue his investigations.

There had been no trace of Fulbert anywhere. Seven bodies had been found in the river, two of women, almost certainly prostitutes, one child, probably fallen in by accident and too feeble to cry out or splash for help; probably an unwanted mouth to feed anyway, put out to beg as soon as it was old enough to speak intelligently. The other four had been men but, like the child, beggars and outcasts. Certainly none of them could conceivably have been Fulbert, however abused or molested. It had taken more than a few days to bring them to such a degree of emaciation.

All the hospitals and morgues had been checked, even the workhouses. The sector of the police who were most familiar with the opium rooms and the brothels had been asked to keep an eye and an ear open—to ask questions would be pointless—but there had been no glimmer of him at all. To search the rookeries, of course, was impossible. As far as every human inquiry could ascertain, Fulbert Nash had disappeared from the face of London.

So there was nothing to do but go back to the Walk and pursue it again from there. Accordingly nine o'clock in the morning found him in Lord Dilbridge's morning room awaiting his lordship's pleasure. It was some quarter of an hour before he appeared. He was extremely neat—his valet would have seen to that—but there was a vague and rather disheveled look about his face. Obviously he was either unwell, or had had a wild night immediately previous. He stared at Pitt, as if he had trouble recalling precisely who the footman had said he was.

"Inspector Pitt, from the police," Pitt helped him.

Freddie blinked, then irritation focused in his eyes.

"Oh dear, is this still about Fanny? The poor child is gone, and the wretched creature who did it is miles away by now. I don't know what on earth you think any of us can do about it? The back streets of London are full of thieves and blackguards. If you fellows did your jobs properly and cleaned up some of them, instead of asking damn fool questions around here, this sort of thing wouldn't happen!" He blinked and rubbed something out of his eye. "Although I suppose, to be fair, we should be more careful who we hire as servants. But really, there isn't anything more I can do about it now, and certainly not at this time in the morning!"

"No sir," Pitt at last had the opportunity to speak without interrupting. "It isn't about Miss Nash. I called with regard to Mr. Fulbert Nash. We still have no trace of him—"

"Try the hospitals, or the morgue," Freddie suggested.

"We have done so, sir," Pitt said patiently. "And the doss houses, the opium rooms, the brothels, and the river. Also the railway stations, the port, the lighter men as far down the river as Greenwich and as far up as Richmond, and most of the cab drivers. No one has told us anything."

"That's ridiculous!" Freddie said angrily. His eyes were bloodshot, and he kept blinking. Freddie screwed up his face in an effort to think clearly. "He's got to be somewhere. He can't have vanished!"

"Quite," Pitt agreed. "So having searched everywhere I can to find him, I am obliged to come back here to see if I can deduce where he might have gone, or if not where, at least why."

"Why?" Freddie's face fell. "Well, I suppose he was—

well—no—I don't know what I suppose. Never really thought about it. Didn't owe money, did he? Nashes have always been well off, so far as I know, but he is the youngest brother, so maybe he hadn't so much."

"We thought of that, sir, and we checked. His bank gave us access to their records, and he is in good funds. And his brother, Mr. Afton Nash, assures us that he had no financial problems. We have found no mention of any debt in any of the usual gambling clubs."

Freddie looked worried.

"Didn't know you people could get into that kind of thing! What a man gambles is his own affair!"

"Certainly, sir, but where a disappearance is concerned, possibly a murder—"

"Murder! Do you think Fulbert was murdered? Well," he pulled a terrible face and sat down rather abruptly. He looked at Pitt through his fingers. "Well, I suppose we knew that, if we were honest. Knew too much, Fulbert, always was a bit too clever. Trouble is, he wasn't clever enough to pretend to be a little less clever."

"Very well put, sir." Pitt smiled. "What we need to know is which of all his clever remarks was the one that backfired on him? Did he know who raped Fanny? Or was it something else, possibly even something he didn't actually know, but implied he did?"

Freddie frowned, but the high color in his face fled, leaving the broken veins standing out. He did not look at Pitt.

"Don't know what you mean! If he didn't actually know it, why should anyone kill him? Bit risky, isn't it?"

Pitt explained patiently. "If he were to have said to someone, I know your secret, or words to that effect, he would not need to have spelled it out. If there really were something dangerous enough, the person would not wait to see if Fulbert would tell it or not."

"Oh. I see. You mean, just kill him anyway, be on the safe side?"

"Yes, sir."

"Rubbish! Few odd affairs, maybe, but no real harm in that. Good God! Lived in the Walk for years, every Season, of course, not in the winter, you understand?" The perspiration was standing out on his forehead and lip. He shook his head, as if he might at once clear it and drive out the loathsome idea. After a moment his face lit up. "Never thought of anyone like that. You'd better look at the Frenchman; he's the only one I don't know." He waved his hand as if he could wash Pitt away like a petty annoyance. "Seems to have plenty of means, and decent enough manners, if you like that sort of thing, bit too precise for me. But no idea where the man comes from, could be anywhere. A sight too easy with the women. And come to think of it, he never told us who his family was. Always be spacious of a fellow when you don't know who his family is. Look him up, that's my advice to you. Try the French police, maybe they'll help you?"

It was something Pitt had not thought of, and he mentally kicked himself for the oversight, the more so because it had taken a fool like Freddie Dilbridge to point it out to him.

"Yes sir, we shall do that."

"Might have been a rapist in France for all we know!" Freddie's own voice lifted as he warmed to the subject, pleased with his own sagacity. "Maybe Fulbert discovered it. Now that would surely be worth killing him for, wouldn't it? Yes, you find out about Monsieur Alaric before he came here. Guarantee you'll find the reason for your murder there! Guarantee it! Now, for heaven's sake, let me go and have some breakfast! I feel perfectly awful!"

Grace Dilbridge had an entirely different outlook on the subject.

"Oh no!" she said immediately. "Freddie is not himself

134

this morning, or I'm sure he would not have made such a suggestion. He is very loyal, you know. He would not wish to think of any of his friends as—as more than a little—indelicate. But I assure you, Monsieur Alaric is the most charming and civilized man. And Fanny, poor child, thought him quite devastating, as indeed did my own daughter, until quite lately when she has become fond of Mr. Isaacs. I really don't know what I'm going to do about that!" Then she blushed at having mentioned so personal a thing in front of what was after all no more than a tradesman. "But no doubt it will pass," she added hastily. "This is her first Season, after all, and it is natural she should be admired by a number of people."

Pitt felt he was losing the thread. He tried to pull her back.

"Monsieur Alaric—"

"Nonsense!" she repeated firmly. "My husband has known the Nashes for years, so naturally he is loath to admit it, even to himself, but it is quite obvious that Fulbert has run away because he himself was guilty of molesting poor Fanny. I dare say in the dark he mistook her for a maid, or something, and then when he discovered who she was, and she of course saw him, there was nothing he could do but kill her to keep her silent. It is perfectly awful! His own sister! But then men are perfectly awful, at times, it is their nature, and has been ever since Adam. We are conceived in sin, and some of us never rise above it."

Pitt searched his mind and found no answer to that, and anyway his thoughts were revolving on her earlier words and the thought that had never occurred to him before, that Fulbert could have mistaken Fanny for someone else, a maid, a kitchen girl, someone who would never dare to accuse a gentleman of forcing himself on her or, for that matter, might not even have minded, could possibly have encouraged him. And then, when he found it was his own

135

sister, the horror and the disgrace not only of rape but of incest would have panicked many a man into murder! And that applied equally to all three of the Nash brothers! His brain was in a whirl with the enormity of it, the vast new dimensions it opened up. Vista upon vista swam into his imagination and fell away endlessly. The whole problem would have to be started again almost from the beginning.

Grace was still talking, but he was not listening anymore. He needed time to think, to be outside in the sun where he could rearrange all that he knew in this new light. He stood up. He knew he was cutting across her speech, but there was no other way to escape.

"You have been extraordinarily helpful, Lady Dilbridge. I am most grateful." He smiled at her dazzlingly, leaving her a little startled, and swept out into the hallway and through the front door, coattails flapping, sending the maid on the step over backward, her broom at her shoulder like a guardsman presenting arms.

It was a long, hot and busy week later, when Charlotte announced to him that Emily was giving a soiree. He had very little idea what that was, except that it occurred in the afternoon, and that she had been invited to it. He was preoccupied with waiting for news from Paris about Paul Alaric and with the wealth of detail he had learned about the personal lives in the Walk, since he had begun, with Forbes's wide-eyed and willing assistance, to inquire all over again in the totally new light of Grace Dilbridge's suggestion. It seemed, if everyone was to be believed, that there were a great many more relationships of varying natures than he had suspected. Freddie Dilbridge was quite notorious. Something secret, and apparently thrilling to those who partook, was assumed to happen at some of his more riotous parties. And Diggory Nash had given way to temptation on more than a few occasions. There was much speculation about Hallam Cayley, especially since the death of his wife, but he had not yet sorted out the direct lies from the fantasies on that one, and had even less idea how much might actually be truth. Apparently George had at least had the good sense to keep his indulgences out of the servants' quarters, although it was beyond doubt he had certainly entertained feelings toward Selena, heartily reciprocated, which would deeply hurt Emily if she ever had to know. But if there were anything but wishful thinking about Paul Alaric, no one was prepared to speak of it.

He would dearly like to have discovered something to the discredit of Afton Nash, as he found the man incredibly unpleasant. However, although none of the maids seemed to feel kindly toward him, there was not even the barest suggestion he had been in the least familiar with any.

As for Fulbert himself, there were whispers, suggestions, but since his disappearance even the mention of his name produced such hysteria that Pitt had no idea what to believe. The whole Walk seethed in overheated imagination. The mind-dulling monotony of daily chores that stretched from childhood to the grave was made bearable only by the penny romances and the giggling stories swapped in tiny attic bedrooms when the long day was done. Now murderers and lust-crazed seducers lurked in every shadow, and fear, half-desire, and reality were hopelessly entangled.

He did not expect Charlotte to learn anything of value at Emily's party. He was convinced that the answer to the murders lay below stairs, far out of Charlotte's or Emily's reach, and all he said to her on the matter was in the nature of an exhortation to enjoy herself and a very firm command totally to mind her own business and make no inquiries or comments that might lead to anything but the most trivial of polite conversation.

She said, "Yes, Thomas," very demurely, which, had he been less consumed in his own thoughts, would have struck him immediately as suspicious.

The soiree was a very formal affair, and Charlotte was totally swept off her feet with delight at the gown Emily had had made for her as a present. It was of yellow silk, and it fitted her perfectly and was quite ravishingly beautiful. She felt like sunshine itself as she swept in through the doorway, head high, face glowing. She was surprized when no more than half a dozen people turned to look at her; she quite expected the whole room to fall silent and stare. However, she was conscious that Paul Alaric was one of those few who did look. She saw his elegant black head turn from Selena to where she stood on the step. She knew the color burned up her cheeks, and she lifted her chin a little higher.

Emily came over to welcome her straightaway, and she was pulled into the crowd, which must have numbered fifty or more, and drawn into conversation. There was no opportunity for any private exchange. Emily gave her a long, straight look, which said very plainly that she was to behave herself and think before she spoke, and the moment after she was called away to welcome another guest.

"Emily has asked a young poet to come and read us some of his work," Phoebe said with brittle cheerfulness. "I have heard it is most provoking. Let us hope we can understand it. It will give us food for much discussion."

"I hope it is not vulgar," Miss Lucinda said quickly. "Or erotic. Have you seen those quite dreadful drawings of Mr. Beardsley's?"

Charlotte would like to have commented on Mr. Beardsley, but since she had never seen any of his drawings, or indeed heard of him, she could not.

"I cannot imagine Emily choosing someone without doing all that one can to assure that he is neither," she replied, with an immediate edge to her voice. "Of course," she went on, "one is not able to control what one's guests say or do once they come, only to judge to the best of one's ability whom to invite."

138

"Of course." Lucinda colored faintly. "I did not mean to imply anything but mischance."

Charlotte remained cool.

"I believe he is political rather than romantic."

"That should be interesting," Miss Laetitia said hopefully. "I wonder if he has written anything about the poor or social reform?"

"I believe so." Charlotte was pleased to have caught. Miss Laetitia's interest. She rather liked her, especially since Vespasia had told her about the long past scandal. "They are the best things about which to try to stir people's consciences," she added.

"I'm sure we have nothing to be ashamed of!" It was a stout elderly lady who spoke, her body marvelously corsetted into a peacock-blue dress and her face above square-jawed and reminding Charlotte of a Pekinese dog, although vastly larger. She guessed her to be the Misses Horbury's permanent guest, Lady Tamworth, but nobody introduced her. "Poor Fanny was a victim of the times," she went on loudly. "Standards are falling everywhere, even here!"

"Do you not think it is up to the Church to speak to people's consciences?" Miss Lucinda asked with a slight flaring of the nostrils, although it was not clear whether her distaste was for Charlotte's political views or Lady Tamworth having brought up the subject of Fanny yet again.

Charlotte ignored the remark on Fanny, at least for the time being. Pitt had not said she must avoid political discussion, although of course Papa had outrightly forbidden it! But she was not Papa's problem now.

"Perhaps it is the Church that has stirred his will to speak in the way he is best equipped?" she suggested innocently.

"Do you not feel he is then usurping the Church's prerogative?" Miss Lucinda said with a sharp frown. "And

139

that those called of God for the purpose would do it far better?"

"Possibly," Charlotte was determined to be reasonable. "But that is not to say others should not do the best they can. Surely the more voices the better? There are many places where the Church is not heard. Perhaps he can reach some of those?"

"Then what is he doing here?" Miss Lucinda demanded. "Paragon Walk is hardly such a place! He would be better employed somewhere else, in a back street, or a workhouse."

Afton Nash joined them, his eyebrows raised in slight surprise at Miss Lucinda's rather heated comment.

"And who are you consigning to the workhouse, Miss Horbury?" he inquired, looking for a moment at Charlotte, then away again.

"I'm sure the back streets and the workhouses are already converted to the need for social reform," Charlotte said with a slight downward curve of her mouth. "And indeed for the ease of the poor. It is the rich who need to give; the poor will receive readily enough. It is the powerful who can change laws."

Lady Tamworth's eyebrows went up in surprise and some scorn.

"Are you suggesting it is the aristocracy, the leaders and the backbone of the country, who are at fault?"

Charlotte did not even think of retreating for courtesy's sake, or because it was unbecoming in a woman to be so contentious.

"I am saying there is no purpose in preaching to the poor that they should be helped," she replied. "Or to the workless and illiterate that laws should be reformed. The only people who can change things are the people with power and money. If the Church had already reached all of them, we would have achieved our reform long since, and there would be labor for the poor to earn their own necessities."

Lady Tamworth glared at her and turned away, affecting to find the conversation too unpleasant to continue, but Charlotte knew perfectly well it was because she could think of no answer. There was a delicate type of pleasure in Miss Laetitia's face, and she caught Charlotte's eye for a moment before also leaving.

"My dear Mrs. Pitt," Afton said very carefully, as if speaking to someone unfamiliar with the language, or a little deaf. "You do not understand either politics or economics. One cannot change things overnight."

Phoebe joined them, but he disregarded her entirely.

"The poor are poor," he continued, "precisely because they do not have the means or the will to be otherwise. One cannot denude the rich to feed them. It would be insane and like pouring water into the desert sand. There are millions of them! What you suggest is totally impractical." He managed a smile of condescension for her ignorance.

Charlotte seethed. It took all the self-will she possessed to master her face and affect an air of genuine inquiry.

"But if the rich and the powerful are unable to change things," she asked, "then to whom does the Church preach, and to what purpose?"

"I beg your pardon?" He could not believe what he had heard.

Charlotte repeated herself, not daring to look at Phoebe or Miss Lucinda.

Before Afton could form a reply to such a preposterous question, another voice answered instead, a soft voice with a delicate intonation of accent.

"To the purpose that it is good for our souls to give away a little, so that we may enjoy what we have, and still sleep easily at night, because we can then tell ourselves we have

141

tried, we have done our bit! Never, my dear, in the hope that anything will actually change!''

Charlotte felt the color sweep up her face. She had had no idea at all that Paul Alaric was so close and had heard her opinionated baiting of Afton and Miss Lucinda. She did not look at him.

"How very cynical, Monsieur Alaric." She swallowed. "Do you believe we are all such hypocrites?''

"We?" his voice rose very slightly. "Do you go to Church and feel better for it, Mrs. Pitt?"

She was caught in complete indecision. Certainly, she did not. Sermons in church, on the rare occasions she went, made her squirm with anger and a desire to argue. But she could not say so to Afton Nash and hope to be even remotely understood. And it would only hurt Phoebe. Damn Alaric for making a hypocrite of her.

"Of course I do," she lied, watching Phoebe's face. The anxiety ironed out of it, and she was immediately rewarded. She had nothing in common with Phoebe, and yet she felt an ache of pity for her every time her plain, pale face came to mind. Perhaps it was only because she imagined all the hurt Afton could do with his hard, thrusting tongue.

She turned to face Alaric and was shaken all over again by the humor in his eyes and the precise understanding of what she had said and why. Did he know she was not one of the rich, that she was married to a policeman and had barely enough to make ends meet, that her beautiful dress was a gift from Emily? And that the whole argument about giving to the poor was academic for her?

There was nothing but a charming smile on his face.

"If you will excuse me," Afton said stiffly. He almost pulled away Phoebe, who walked beside him as if her limbs were bruised and weak.

"A generous lie," Alaric said gently.

Charlotte was not listening to him. Her mind was on

Phoebe, and the painful, almost distant way in which she walked, holding herself in from Afton's touch. Was it just years of hurt; the instinctive withdrawal, as the burnt hand moves away from fire? Or did she know something new, perhaps only by instinct as yet? Was some memory stirring within her of a change in Afton, a lie remembered now, maybe something between him and Fanny—no, that was too obscene to think of! And yet it was not impossible! Perhaps in the dark he had not even known who it was, simply a woman to hurt. And he loved inflicting pain, that she knew herself as surely as any animal knows its predator by sight and smell. Did Phoebe know it, too? Was that why she walked afraid on the landing of her own house and called for the footman in the night?

Alaric was still waiting, composed, but a pucker of question between his brows. She had forgotten what he had said and was obliged to ask.

"I beg your pardon?"

"A most generous lie," he repeated.

"Lie?"

"To say that you feel better for going to church. I cannot believe it was the truth. You have not the enchantment of mystery, Mrs. Pitt. You are an open book. All your fascination lies in wondering what devastating truth you will deliver next. I doubt you could lie successfully, even to yourself!"

What did he mean by that? She preferred not to think. Honesty was her only skill, and her only safety against him.

"The success of the lie depends a great deal upon how much the hearer wishes to believe it," she replied.

He smiled very slowly, very sweetly.

"And therein lies the entire foundation of Society," he agreed. "How terrifyingly perceptive of you. You had better not tell anyone else. You will ruin the whole game, and then what will there be left for them to do?"

She swallowed hard and refused to meet his eyes. With

great care, she took the conversation back to the previous point.

"I lie very well, sometimes!"

"Which returns me to the sermons in church, does it not? The comfortable lies we repeat over and over again because we wish them to be true. I wonder what Lady Ashworth's poet will have to say? Whether we agree or not, I think the faces of the audience will be vastly entertaining, don't you?"

"Probably," she answered. "And I dare say his words will provide fuel for indignation for weeks to come."

"Oh indeed. We shall have to make a great deal of noise to convince ourselves all over again that we are right and that nothing really can or should be changed."

Charlotte stiffened. "You are trying to make me seem a cynic, Monsieur Alaric, and I find cynicism very unattractive. I think it is a rather facile excuse. One pretends nothing can be done; therefore, one can do nothing and feel perfectly justified. I think it is only another kind of dishonesty, and one I like even less."

He suddenly surprized her by smiling broadly and quite without disguise.

"I didn't think any woman could disconcert me, and you have just done it. You are quite appallingly honest; there is no way of entangling you in yourself."

"Did you wish to?" Why on earth should she feel so pleased? It was quite ridiculous!

Before he could reply, they were joined by Jessamyn Nash, her face as blemishless as a camellia and her cool eyes sweeping over Alaric before settling on Charlotte. They were wide, blazing blue, and intelligent.

"How charming to see you again, Mrs. Pitt. I had no idea you were going to visit us so often! Is not your own circle of society missing you dreadfully?"

Charlotte stared back at her without a flicker, smiling into the marvelous eyes.

144

"I hope so," she said lightly. "But I shall support Emily whenever I can, until this tragic business is resolved."

Jessamyn had more composure than Selena. Her face softened, the full mouth easing into a warm smile.

"How generous of you. Still, I dare say you may enjoy the change?"

Charlotte took her point perfectly, but kept up her innocence. She would match smile for smile if it choked her. She had no gift for guile, but she had always known that you catch more flies with honey than with vinegar.

"Oh quite," she agreed. "We have nothing so dramatic where I live. I don't think there has been a rape or a murder for years! In fact, maybe never!"

Paul Alaric tore out his handkerchief and sneezed into it. Charlotte could see his shoulders shaking with laughter, and the color burned up her face in exhilaration.

Jessamyn was white. Her voice, when it came, was as brittle as glass splinters.

"And perhaps not soirees like this, either? You must permit me to advise you, as a friend! One should circulate, speak to everyone. It is considered good manners, especially if one is in some degree or other a hostess, or connected with the hostess. You should not allow it to become obvious that you prefer one guest to another—however much you may do so!"

The shot was perfect. Charlotte had no choice but to leave, the heat flaming in her neck and bosom that Alaric might already imagine she had sought his company. And what was worse, her embarrassment now could only confirm it. She was furious and swore she would disabuse him of the idea that she was one of those stupid women who spent their time pursuing him! With a stiff smile she excused herself and sailed away, head so high she nearly fell over the step between the two reception rooms, and was still regaining her balance when she collided with Lady Tamworth and Miss Lucinda.

"I'm sorry," she stammered in apology. "I do beg your pardon."

Lady Tamworth stared at her, obviously noting her high color and the clumsiness of her deportment. Her thoughts regarding young women who drink too much in the afternoon were apparent in her face.

Miss Lucinda was on quite another tack. She grasped Charlotte fiercely with her plump little hand.

"May I ask you, quite confidentially, my dear, how well does Lady Ashworth know the *Jew*?"

Charlotte's eyes followed Miss Lucinda's to a slender young man with olive complexion and dark features.

"I don't know," she said immediately, glancing at Lady Tamworth. "If you like, I shall ask her?"

But they were not abashed.

"I should, my dear. After all, she may not be aware who he is!"

"No, she may not," Charlotte agreed. "Who is he?"

Lady Tamworth looked nonplussed for a moment.

"Why—he's a Jew!" she said.

"Yes, so you said."

Lady Tamworth snorted. Miss Lucinda's face dropped, her eyebrows puckered.

"Do you approve of Jews, Mrs. Pitt?"

"Wasn't Christ one?"

"Really, Mrs. Pitt!" Lady Tamworth shook with outrage. "I accept that the younger generation has different standards from our own." She stared once more at Charlotte's still glowing neck. "But I cannot tolerate blasphemy. Really, I can't!"

"That is not blasphemy, Lady Tamworth," Charlotte said clearly. "Christ was a Jew."

"Christ was God, Mrs. Pitt," Lady Tamworth said icily. "And God is most certainly not a Jew!"

Charlotte did not know whether to lose her temper

completely or laugh. She was glad Paul Alaric was out of earshot.

"Isn't He?" she said with a slight smile. "I never really thought about it. What is He then?"

"A mad scientist," Hallam Cayley said from over her shoulder, a glass in his hand. "A Frankenstein who didn't know when to stop! His experiment has got a little out of hand, don't you think?" he stared around the room, his face mirroring a disgust so deep it hurt him.

Lady Tamworth chewed her teeth in impotence, her rage too great for words.

Hallam regarded her with contempt.

"Do you really imagine this was what He intended?" he finished his glass and waved it round the room. "Is this bloody lot in the image of any God you want to worship? If we've descended from God, then we've descended a hell of a long way. I think I'd rather join Mr. Darwin. According to him, at least we're improving. In another million years we might be fit for something."

At last Miss Lucinda found speech.

"You must speak for yourself, Mr. Cayley," she said with difficulty, as if she, too, were a little drunk. "For myself, I am a Christian, and I have no doubts whatever!"

"Doubts?" Hallam stared into the bottom of his empty glass and turned it upside down. A single drop fell out onto the floor. "I wish I had doubts. A doubt would at least include room for a hope, wouldn't it?"

Seven

The soiree was a success; the poet spoke brilliantly. He knew exactly how much to titillate with excitement, to hint at daring and change, to provoke thoughts of the wildest criticism of others, and yet at the same time never to insist on the truly unpleasant disturbance of conscience in oneself. He provided the thrill of intellectual danger without any of its pain.

He was received rapturously, and it was obvious he would be talked about for weeks to come. Even next summer the affair would be recalled as one of the more interesting events of the Season.

But after it was all over and the last guests had taken their leave, Emily was too tired to savor her victory. It had been more of a strain than she expected. Her legs were tired from so much standing, and her back ached. When she finally sat down, she found she was shaking a little, and it no longer seemed to matter a great deal that she had given a party that was a resounding success. The realities had not changed. Fanny Nash was still violated and murdered, Fulbert was still missing, and none of the answers were any kinder or easier to bear. She was too weary to delude herself any longer that it was some stranger with no claim on their lives. It was someone in the Walk. They all had their trivial or sordid little secrets, the ugly sides of life that most people could continue to hide forever. Of course, they were guessed at; no one but a fool thought the surface smile was all there was to anyone. But for other people, where there was no crime, no investigation, they could be allowed to fester silently in the dark places where they had lain hidden, and no one willfully uncovered them. There was a mutual conspiracy, to overlook.

But with the police, especially someone like Thomas Pitt, whether the real crime was discovered or not, all the other grubby little sins would be turned over sooner or later. It was not that he would wish to, but she knew from the past, from Cater Street and Callander Square, that people have a habit of betraying themselves, often in their very anxiety to conceal. It is so easily done, only a word or a panicky, thoughtless action. Thomas was clever; he sowed seeds and allowed them to grow. His subtle, humorous eyes saw so very much—too much.

She lay in her chair, stretching her back, feeling the stiffness in it. Could the child within her make so much difference already? There was a dragging, an awkwardness. Perhaps Aunt Vespasia was right and she would have to loosen her stays. That would make her look thick. She was not tall enough to carry the extra weight gracefully. Funny, Charlotte had looked all right when she was carrying Jemima. But then Charlotte had not had fashionable clothes anyway.

Across the room George was sitting fiddling with the newspaper. He had congratulated her on the party, but now he was avoiding looking at her. He was not reading it; she knew that from the angle of his head, the curiously fixed stare he held. When he was really reading, he moved, his expression altered, and every so often he would rattle the sheets as if he were having a conversation with them. This time he was using the paper as a shield, to avoid the necessity of speaking. He could at once be both absent and present.

Why? There was nothing she wanted so much as to talk, even if it was about nothing, simply to feel that he wished to be with her. He could not possibly know that the solution would be all right, that it would not go on hurting, and yet she wanted him to say so, to tell her all the comforting words. Then she could repeat them all to herself over and over, till they drove out reason and doubt.

He was her husband. It was his child that made her feel so tired and lumpy and strangely excited. How could he sit there a few feet away and be totally unaware that she wanted him to speak, to say something foolish and optimistic to silence all the clamor inside her.

"George!"

He affected not to have heard.

"George!" Her voice was growing higher and there was a thread of hysteria in it.

He looked up. At first his brown eyes were innocent, as if his thoughts were still on the paper. Then slowly they clouded, and understanding could not be denied. He knew she was demanding something.

"Yes?"

Now she did not know what to say. Reassurance you have to ask for is no reassurance at all. It would have been better if she had said nothing. Her brain told her that, but her tongue would not keep still.

"They haven't found Fulbert yet." It was not what she was thinking, but it was something to say. She could not ask him why he was afraid, what it was that Pitt might find out. Would it destroy her marriage? Not anything like divorce, no one divorced, at least, no one decent. But she had seen any number of empty marriages, polite arrangements to share a house and a name. When she had first determined to marry George, she had thought that friendship and acceptance would be enough—but they were not. She had grown used to affection, to shared laughter, little understanding secrets, long, comfortable silences, even habits that became part of the security and rhythm of life.

Now all this was sliding away, like the tide going out, leaving stretches of empty shingle.

"I know," he replied, with a little frown of puzzlement. She knew he did not realize why she had made such an obvious and silly remark. She had to say something more to justify herself.

"Do you think he's run away completely?" she asked. "Like to France, or something?"

"Why ever should he?"

"If he killed Fanny!"

His face fell a little. Obviously he had not really considered that.

"He wouldn't kill Fanny," he said firmly. "I should think he's probably dead himself. Maybe he went into town to gamble or something, and had an accident. People do sometimes."

"Oh, don't be so stupid!" At last she lost her temper completely. It surprised and alarmed her that she should so suddenly snap. She had never dared speak to him like that before.

He looked startled and the paper slid to the floor.

Now she was a little frightened. What had she done? He was staring at her, his brown eyes very wide. She wanted to apologize, but her mouth was dry and her voice would not come. She took a very deep breath.

"Perhaps you had better go upstairs and lie down," he said after a moment. He spoke quite quietly. "You've had a very heavy day. Parties like that are exhausting. Maybe in this heat it was too much for you."

"I'm not sick!" she said furiously. Then to her horror the

151

tears started to run down her face, and she found herself crying like a silly child.

There was a second of pain in George's face, then suddenly the solution washed over him with a wave of relief. Of course, it was her condition. She saw it in him as clearly as if he had spoken it. It was not true! But she could not explain. She allowed him to help her to her feet and gently out into the hallway and up the stairs. She was still boiling, words falling over themselves inside her, and dying before she could make them into sentences. But she could not control the tears, and it was warm to feel his arm around her, and so much better not to have to make all the effort herself.

But when Charlotte called the next morning, largely to inquire how she was after the soiree, Emily was in an unusually sharp temper. She had not slept well and, lying awake in her bed, had thought she had heard George moving around in the next room. More than once she considered getting up and going to him, to ask him why he was pacing, what worried him so much.

But she did not yet feel she knew him well enough to take the rather forward action of going into his room at two o'clock in the morning. She knew he would consider it ingenuous, even immodest. And she was not even sure she wanted to know. Perhaps most of all she was afraid he would lie to her, and she would see through the lies and be haunted by truths she only guessed at.

So when Charlotte appeared looking slender and fresh, her hair shining, unbearably cool, although she was wearing only wash-cotton, Emily was in no mood to receive her graciously.

"I suppose Thomas still knows nothing?" she said acidly.

Charlotte looked surprized, and Emily knew what she was doing, but still could not hold her tongue.

"He hasn't found Fulbert," Charlotte answered, "if that's what you mean?"

"I don't really care whether he finds Fulbert or not," Emily snapped. "If he's dead, I can't see that it matters a lot where he is."

Charlotte kept her patience, which only irritated Emily the more. Charlotte holding her tongue really was the last straw.

"We don't know that he is dead," Charlotte pointed out. "Or, if he is, that he did not take his own life."

"And then hide his body afterwards?" Emily said with withering contempt.

"Thomas says that many bodies in the river are never found." Charlotte was still being reasonable. "Or, if they are, they are unrecognizable."

Emily's imagination conjured revolting pictures, bloated corpses with their faces eaten away, staring up through murky water. It made her feel sick.

"You are perfectly disgusting!" She glared at Charlotte. "You and Thomas may find such conversation acceptable over the tea table, but I do not!"

"You have not offered me any tea," Charlotte said with a ghost of a smile.

"If you imagine I shall, after that, you are mistaken!" Emily snapped.

"You had better have something yourself, and try something sweet with it—"

"If one more person makes another polite reference to my condition, I shall swear!" Emily said fiercely. "I do not want to sit down, or take a refreshing drink, or anything else!"

Charlotte was beginning at last to become a little acid herself.

"What you want and what you need are not always the same thing," she said smartly. "And losing your temper

153

will not help anything. In fact, you will say things you will wish afterwards you had not. And if anyone should know the folly of that, I should! You were always the one who could think before you spoke. For goodness' sake, don't lose that now when you need it the most.''

Emily stared at her, coldness in the pit of her stomach.

''What do you mean?'' she demanded. ''Explain what you mean!''

Charlotte stood perfectly still.

''I mean that, if you let your fears drive you into suspicion now, or allow George to think you do not trust him, you will never be able to replace what you have destroyed, no matter how much you may regret it afterward, or how trivial it may all seem when you know the truth. And you will have to prepare yourself that we may never know who killed her. Not all crimes are solved.''

Emily sat down sharply. It was appalling to think they might never know, that they might spend the rest of their lives looking at each other and wondering. Every affection, every quiet evening, every simple conversation, offer of company or help, would be marred by the dark stain of uncertainty, the sudden thought—could it have been he who killed Fanny, or she who knew about it?

''They'll have to find out!'' she insisted, refusing to accept it. ''Someone will know, if he is really one of us. Some wife, some brother, some friend will find a clue!''

''Not necessarily.'' Charlotte looked at her with a little shake of her head. ''If he has been secret so long, why not forever? Perhaps someone does know. But they do not have to say so, maybe not even to themselves. We do not always recognize things, when we do not wish to.''

''Rape?'' Emily breathed the word incredulously. ''Why in the name of heaven would any woman protect a man who had—''

Charlotte's face tightened.

154

"All kinds of reasons," she replied. "Who wants to believe their husband, or brother, is a rapist, or a murderer? You can prevent yourself from seeing that forever, if you want to badly enough. Or convince yourself that it will never happen again, and it was not really his fault. You've seen for yourself, half the people in the Walk have already made up their minds that Fanny was a loose woman, that she invited her own fate, somehow she deserved it—"

"Stop it!" Emily hauled herself up and faced Charlotte angrily. "You're not the only one who can tell the truth about anything, you know! You're so smug, sometimes you make me sick! We're not all hypocrites here in the Walk, just because we have time and money and dress well, any more than all of you are in your grubbly little street, just because you work all day! You have your lies and your conveniences as well!"

Charlotte was very pale, and instantly Emily regretted it. She wanted to put her hands out, put her arms around Charlotte, but she did not dare. She stared at her, frightened. Charlotte was the only person she could talk to, whose love was unquestioned, with whom she could share the secret fears and wants in every woman's heart.

"Charlotte?"

Charlotte stood still.

"Charlotte?" she tried again. "Charlotte, I'm sorry!"

"I know," Charlotte said very quietly. "You want to know the truth about George, and you're afraid of it."

Time stopped. For motionless seconds Emily hesitated. Then she asked the question she had to ask.

"Do you know? Did Thomas tell you?"

Charlotte had never been any good at lying. Even though she was the elder, she had never been able to dupe Emily, whose sharp, practiced eye had always seen the reluctance, the indecision before the lie.

"You do." Emily answered her own question. "Tell me."

Charlotte frowned.

"It's all over."

"Tell me," Emily repeated.

"Wouldn't it be better—"

Emily just waited. They both knew that truth, whatever it was, was better than the exhaustion of sweeping from hope to fear, the elaborate effort to deceive oneself, the indulging in awful imagination.

"Was it Selena?" she asked.

"Yes."

Now that she knew, it was not so bad. Perhaps she had known before, but simply refused to say so to herself. Was that really all George was afraid of? How silly. How very silly. She would put a stop to it, of course. She would take that smug look off Selena's face and replace it with something far less satisfied. She was not sure how yet, or even if she would allow George to know that she knew about it. She played with the idea of letting him go on worrying, allowing the fear to eat into him sufficiently so that he would not in a hurry forget how it hurt. Perhaps she would never tell him that she knew?

Charlotte was looking at her, her eyes anxious, watching for her reaction. She turned back to the moment, smiling.

"Thank you," she said composedly, almost cheerfully. "Now I know what to do."

"Emily—"

"Don't worry." She put her hand out and touched Charlotte, quite softly. "I shan't have a quarrel. In fact, I don't think I shall do anything at all, just yet."

Pitt continued his questioning in Paragon Walk. Forbes had dug up some surprizing information about Diggory Nash. Yet he should not have been surprized, and he was angry with himself, for having allowed his prejudice to form his opinions for him. He had looked at the outward grace, the comfort, and the money in the Walk and assumed that, because they all lived in the same manner, came to London for the Season, frequented the same clubs and parties, that they were all the same underneath their uniformly fashionable clothes, and behind their uniformly mannered behavior.

Diggory Nash was a gambler with wealth he had not earned, and a flirt, almost by habit, with any woman who was pleasant and available. But he was also generous. Pitt was startled and ashamed of his own facile judgment when Forbes told him that Diggory subsidized a house that gave shelter to homeless women. God knew how many pregnant service girls were thrown out of sober and upright employment every year, to wander the streets and end up in sweatshops, workhouses or brothels. How unforeseen that Diggory Nash, of all people, should have given a meager protection to a few of them. An old wound of conscience speaking, perhaps? Or a simple pity?

Either way, it was with a feeling embarrassment that Pitt waited in the morning room for Jessamyn. She could not know what his assumptions had been, but he knew himself, and that was enough to tie his usually easy tongue and to give him a rare self-consciousness. It was no salve to his mind that it was perfectly possible Jessamyn had no idea of Diggory's actions.

When she came in, he was amazed again at the emotional impact of her beauty. It was far more than a mere matter of color or the symmetry of brow and cheek. It was something in the curve of the mouth, the challenging blue blaze of her eyes, the fragile throat. No wonder she grasped for what she wanted, knowing it would be given her. And no wonder Selena could not come to terms with subordinacy to this supreme woman. It flickered through his mind, the moment before she spoke to him, to wonder what Charlotte would have made of her if there had ever been a true rivalry between them, if perhaps Charlotte had also wanted the Frenchman? Did any of them love the Frenchman, or was he merely the prize, the chosen symbol of victory?

"Good morning, Inspector," Jessamyn said coolly. She was dressed in pale summer green and looked as fresh and strong as a daffodil. "I cannot imagine what more I can do for you, but, if there is still something left to ask, of course I shall try to answer."

"Thank you, ma'am." He waited until she sat down, then he sat also, as usual, allowing his coattails to fall where they may. "I'm afraid we have still found no trace of Mr. Fulbert."

Her face tightened a little, a very little, and she looked down at her hands.

"I assumed you had not, or surely you would have told us. You cannot have come only to say that?"

"No." He did not wish to be caught staring, yet both duty and a natural fascination kept his eyes on her face. He was drawn to her as one is to a solitary light in a room. Whether one wills it or not, it becomes the focus.

She looked up, her face smooth, eyes clear and brilliantly frank.

"What else can I tell you? You have spoken to all of us. You must know everything we know about his last days here. If you have found no trace of him anywhere in the city, either he has eluded you and gone to the Continent, or he is dead. It is a painful thought, but I cannot escape it."

Before he set out, he had ordered in his mind the questions he meant to ask. Now they seem less ordered, even less useful. And he must not appear impertinent. She could so easily be offended and refuse all answers, and from silence he could learn nothing at all. Neither must he over-flatter; she was used to compliments, and he judged her far too intelligent, even too cynical, to be gulled by them. He began very carefully.

"If he is dead, ma'am, it is most probable he was killed because he knew something which his killer could not afford to have him tell."

"That is the obvious conclusion," she agreed.

"The only thing we know that is so monstrous as that is the identity of the rapist and murderer of Fanny." He must still not patronize her or let her once suspect he was leading her.

Her mouth twitched in bitter amusement.

"Everyone desires their privacy, Mr. Pitt, but few of us need it to the point where we will kill our neighbors to preserve it. I think it would be ridiculous, without evidence, to suppose there are two such appalling secrets in the Walk."

"Exactly," he agreed.

She gave a very small sigh.

"So that brings us back to who raped poor Fanny," she said slowly. "Naturally, we have all been thinking about it. We can hardly avoid it."

"Of course not, especially someone as close to her as you were."

Her eyes widened.

"Naturally, if you knew anything," he went on, perhaps a bit hastily, "you would have told us. But maybe you have had thoughts, nothing so substantial as a suspicion, but, as you say—" He was watching her closely, trying to judge exactly how much he could press, what could be put into words, what must remain suggestion. "—as you say, you cannot dismiss the matter from your mind."

"You think I may suspect one of my neighbors?" Her blue eyes were almost hypnotic. He found himself unable to look away.

"Do you?"

For a long time she said nothing. Her hands moved slowly in her lap, unwinding some invisible knot.

He waited.

At last she looked up.

"Yes. But you must understand it is only a feeling, a collection of impressions."

"Naturally." He did not want to interrupt. If it told him nothing of anyone else, at worst it would tell him something of her.

"I cannot believe anyone in their right mind, in their true senses, would do such a thing." She spoke as if weighing each word, reluctant to speak at all, and yet pressed by obligation. "I have known everyone here for a long time. I have gone over and over in my memory all that I know, and I cannot believe such a nature could have been hidden from all of us."

He was suddenly disappointed. She was going to come up with some impossible suggestion about strangers.

Her fingers were stiff in her lap, white against the green of her dress.

"Indeed," he said flatly.

Her head came up, and there was a flame of color in her cheeks. She took in a deep breath and let it out, collecting herself.

"I mean, Mr. Pitt, that it can only have been someone laboring under the influence of a quite abnormal emotion, or perhaps intoxicated. When they have had too much to drink, people sometimes do things that in sobriety they would never dream of. And I'm told that even afterwards they do not always recollect what has happened. Surely that would also account for an apparent innocence now? If whoever killed Fanny cannot clearly remember it—?"

He recalled George's blank about the night, Algernon Burnon's reluctance to name his companion, Diggory's anonymous gambling. But it was Hallam Cayley who had repeatedly been drunk so often lately that he overslept. In fact, Afton had said he had been in an alcoholic sleep at ten o'clock on the very morning Fulbert's disappearance had been discovered. It was not a foolish suggestion at all. It would explain the lack of lies, of any attempt to mislead or cover up. The murderer could not even remember his own guilt! There must be a black and dreadful void in his mind; he must wonder; in the night terrors must creep out to fill the space with fragments of violence, images, the smell and sound of horror. But more drink would bring more oblivion.

"Thank you," he said politely.

She took a deep breath again.

"Is a man to blame for what he does in drunkenness?" she asked slowly, a little frown between her brows.

"If God will blame him, I don't know," Pitt answered honestly. "But the law will. A man does not need to get drunk."

Her face did not change. She was continuing with some train of thought that had already begun.

"Sometimes, to cover pain, one drinks too much." Her words were very careful, weighted. "Perhaps pain or illness or pain of the mind, perhaps a loss."

He thought immediately of Hallam Cayley's wife. Was that what she meant him to think? He looked at her, but her face was as smooth now as white satin. He decided to be bold.

"Do you speak of someone in particular, Mrs. Nash?"

Her eyes moved away from his for a moment, and the brilliant blue clouded.

"I would prefer not to speak plainly, Mr. Pitt. I simply do not know. Please do not press me to accuse." She looked back at him, clear and blazingly frank again. "I promise you, if I should come to learn anything, I shall tell you."

He stood up. He knew there would be no more.

"Thank you, Mrs. Nash. You have been most helpful. Indeed, you have given me much to consider." He did not

161

make any trite remarks about having an answer soon. It would be an insult to her.

She smiled very slightly.

"Thank you, Mr. Pitt. Good day."

"Good day, ma'am," and he permitted the footman to show him out to the Walk.

He crossed over to the grass on the other side. He knew he was not supposed to stand on it—there was a very small notice to that effect—but he loved the live feel of it under the soles of his boots. Paving stones were insensate, unlovely things, necessary if a thousand people were to walk over them, but hiding the earth.

What had happened in this graceful, orderly Walk that night? What sudden chaos had erupted, and then subsided into so many totally misshapen pieces?

The emotions eluded his grasp. Everything he clutched at fragmented and disappeared.

He must go back to the practical things, the mechanics of murder. Gentlemen such as these in Paragon Walk did not normally carry knives with them. Why had the rapist so opportunely had one with him on this occasion? Was it conceivable that it had not been a blaze of passion at all, but something premeditated? Could it even be that murder had always been the intent, and the rape was incidental, an impulse, or a blind?

But why should anyone murder Fanny Nash? He had never found anybody more innocuous. She was heir to no fortune and was no one's mistress, nor, as far as he could discover, had anyone shown the slightest romantic interest in her, apart from Algernon Burnon—and even that seemed a very staid affair.

Could it be that Fanny had innocently stumbled on some other secret in the Walk, and died for that? Perhaps without even realizing what it was?

And what had happened to the knife? Did the murderer

still have it? Was it hidden somewhere, possibly by now miles away, at the bottom of the river?

And the other practical question—she had been stabbed to death; he could still see in his mind's eye the thick gore of blood down her body. Why had there been no blood on the road, no trail leading back from the withdrawing room to where she had been attacked? There had been no rain since then. The murderer would have disposed of his clothes, they were easily explained, although Forbes had not been able to find—even with the most diligent questioning—any valet whose master's wardrobe was depleted or any signs that charred remains had been found in any boiler or fireplace.

But why no blood on the road?

Could it have happened here on this grass or in a flower bed, where it could have been dug in? Or in the bushes where it would not be seen? But neither he nor Forbes had found any sign of struggle, no trampled beds, no broken branches beyond the usual that were explained by a dog, someone stumbling in the dark, a clumsy gardener's boy, or even a maid and a footman indulging in a little horse-play.

If there had ever been anything, they had not found it or recognized it, and by now it was long covered either by the murderer, or by others.

He was back to reasons and characters. Why? Why Fanny?

His thoughts were interrupted by a discreet cough a few yards away from him, the other side of the roses. He looked up. An elderly and forlorn butler was standing uncomfortably on the path, staring at him.

"Did you want me?" Pitt inquired, affecting not to realize he was standing on the manicured grass.

"Yes, sir. If you please, Mrs. Nash would be obliged if you would call upon her, sir."

"Mrs. Nash?" his mind flew back to Jessamyn.

"Yes, sir." The butler cleared his throat. "Mrs. Afton Nash, that is, sir."

Phoebe!

"Yes, of course," Pitt replied immediately. "Is Mrs. Nash at home?"

"Yes, sir. If you would care to accompany me?"

Pitt followed him back across the roadway and along the footpath to Afton Nash's house. The front door opened before they reached it, and they were ushered in. Phoebe was in a small morning room toward the back. A long window looked onto the grass.

"Mr. Pitt!" she seemed almost startled, a little breathless. "How good of you to come! Hobson, send Nellie in with the tray. You will take tea, won't you? Yes of course. Please, do sit down."

The butler disappeared, and Pitt sat obediently, thanking her.

"It's still so dreadfully hot!" She flapped her hands. "I don't care for the winter, but right now I almost feel I should welcome it!"

"I dare say it will rain soon and be pleasanter." He did not know how to set her at ease. She was not really listening to him, and she had not looked at him once.

"Oh, I do hope so." She sat down and stood up again. "This is very trying. Do you not find?"

"You wanted to see me about something, Mrs. Nash?" She was obviously not going to come to the point herself.

"I? Well." She coughed and took some few moments over it. "Have you found trace of poor Fulbert yet?"

"No, ma'am."

"Oh dear."

"Do you know something, ma'am?" It appeared she was not going to speak without being pressed.

"Oh, no! No, of course not! If I did, I should have told you!"

164

"But you did call me here to tell me something," he pointed out.

She looked flustered.

"Yes, yes, I admit—but not as to where poor Fulbert is, I swear."

"Then what, Mrs. Nash?" He wanted to be gentle, but it was urgent. If she knew something, then he needed to hear it. He was stumbling around in the dark as much now as when he had first seen Fanny's body in the morgue. "You must tell me!"

She froze. Her hands went to her neck and the rather large crucifix hanging there. Her fingers wound on round it, her nails digging into her palms.

"There is something terrible and evil here, Mr. Pitt, something truly appalling!"

Was she imagining it, whipping herself into a hysteria? Did she know anything at all, or was it just vague fears in a frightened and silly mind? He looked at her, her face, her hands.

"What sort of evil, Mrs. Nash?" he asked quietly. Whether the cause was real or imaginary, he would swear the fear was genuine enough. "Have you seen something?"

She crossed herself.

"Oh, dear God!"

"What have you seen?" he insisted. Was it Afton Nash, and she knew it, but, because he was her husband, she could not bring herself to betray him? Or had it been Fulbert, incestuous rapist and suicide, and she knew that?

He stood up and put his hand toward her, not to touch her, but in a half-gesture of support.

"What have you seen?" he repeated.

She started to shake, first her head, in little twitches from side to side, then her shoulders, finally her whole body. She made little whimpering sounds, like a child.

"So foolish!" she said furiously between her teeth. "So very foolish. And now it's all real, God help us!"

"What is real, Mrs. Nash?" he said urgently. "What is it you know?"

"Oh!" she lifted up her head and stared at him. "Nothing! I think I have lost my wits! We will never win against it. We are lost, and it is our own fault. Go away, and leave us alone. You are a decent man, in your own station. Just go away. Pray, if you want to, but go now, before it reaches out and touches you! Don't say I didn't warn you!"

"You haven't warned me. You haven't told me what to beware of!" he said helplessly. "What? What is it?"

"Evil!" Her face closed, and her eyes were hard and dark. "There is a dreadful wickedness in Paragon Walk. Go away from it, while you can."

He could not think of anything else to do. He was still searching for something more to say when the maid came in with the tray of tea.

Phoebe disregarded it.

"I can't leave, ma'am," he answered. "I have to stay until I've found him. But I shall take care. Thank you for your concern. Good afternoon."

She did not reply, but stood staring at the tray.

Poor woman, he thought outside in the heat. The whole incident, first her sister-in-law and now her brother-in-law, had been too much for her. She had become hysterical. And doubtless she got little sympathy from Afton. It was a pity she had no work to do and no children to absorb her mind and keep it from fancies. There were moments, surprizing and disorienting him, when he was as sorry for the rich as for any of the poor. Some of them were as pathetic, as imprisoned in the hierarchy—welded to their function, or lack of function, in it.

* * *

166

It was late in the afternoon when the Misses Horbury called on Emily; in fact, it was later than was at all suitable for visiting. Emily was more than a little irritated when the maid came to announce them. She even debated with herself whether to say she was unavailable, but since they were close neighbors, and she was obliged to meet with them regularly, it was better not to give offense, in spite of this extraordinary behavior.

They came in in a cloud of yellow, which was peculiarly unbecoming on both of them, although for entirely different reasons. On Miss Laetitia it was too sallow, giving her skin a jaundiced look; on Miss Lucinda it clashed with her sandy yellow hair, lending her the appearance of a rather fierce little bird far gone in the process of moulting. She trailed bright wisps behind her as she bounced into the room, her eyes fixed on Emily.

"Good afternoon, Emily, my dear." She was unusually informal, in fact verging on the familiar.

"Good afternoon, Miss Horbury," Emily said coolly. "What a pleasant surprize"—she emphasized the word "surprize"—"to see you." She smiled distantly at Miss Laetitia, who was standing somewhat reluctantly a little further back.

Miss Lucinda sat down without being invited.

Emily was not going to offer them refreshment at this time in the afternoon. Had neither of them any sense of propriety?

"It doesn't look as if the police are going to discover anything," Miss Lucinda remarked, settling herself deeper the chair. "I don't think they have any idea, myself."

"They wouldn't tell us if they had," Miss Laetitia said to no one in particular. "Why should they?"

Emily sat down, resigned to being civil, at least for a while.

"I've no idea," she said wearily.

Miss Lucinda leaned forward.

"I think there is something going on!"

"Do you?" Emily did not know whether to laugh or be cross.

"Yes, I do! And I mean to discover what it is! I have visited this Walk every Season since I was a girl!"

Emily did not know what answer was expected to this. "Indeed?" she said noncommittally.

"And what is more," Miss Lucinda continued, "I think it is something perfectly scandalous, and it is our duty to put a stop to it!"

"Yes." Emily was floundering now. "It would be."

"I think it is something to do with that Frenchman," Miss Lucinda said with conviction.

Miss Laetitia shook her head.

"Lady Tamworth says it is the Jew."

Emily blinked. "What Jew?"

"Why, Mr. Isaacs, of course!" Miss Lucinda was losing patience. "But that is nonsense. Nobody would entertain him, except for business necessities. I think it has to do with those parties at Lord Dilbridge's. I don't know how poor Grace bears all of it."

"All of what?" Emily asked. She was not sure whether there was anything remotely worth listening to in all this.

"All that goes on! Really, Emily, my dear, you must concern yourself with what occurs in your immediate neighborhood, you know. How else can we control it? It is up to us to see that standards are maintained!"

"She has always been very concerned about standards," Miss Laetitia put in.

"It's as well!" Miss Lucinda snapped. "Someone needs to be, and there are more than enough of us who are not!"

"I have no idea what is going on." Emily was a little embarrassed by the obvious meaning between them. "I do not go to the parties at the Dilbridges', and quite honestly, I didn't know that they hold any more than most people do in the summer.''

''My dear, neither do I actually 'go' to them. And I dare say they don't. But it's not the number, it is the nature that matters. I tell you, Emily, my dear, there is something very strange going on, and I mean to uncover it!''

''I would be careful, if I were you,'' Emily felt obliged to caution her. ''Remember that there have been very tragic occurrences. Do not place yourself in danger.'' She was thinking rather more of the sensitivities of those Miss Lucinda might press with her curiosity than of any peril to Lucinda herself.

Miss Lucinda stood up, thrusting out her bosom.

''I am of dauntless courage when I see my duty clearly before me. And I shall expect your help, if you discover anything of importance!''

''Oh, indeed,'' Emily agreed, knowing perfectly well she would consider nothing that entered Miss Lucinda's realm of ''duty'' important.

''Good! Now I must call on poor Grace.''

And before Emily could find suitable words to point out the lateness of the hour, she gathered Miss Laetitia in her wake and swept out.

Emily was standing outside in the garden at dusk, her face upward toward the evening breeze, the frail, sweet scent of roses and mignonette drifting across the dry grass. There was a single, brilliant star out already, although the sky was blue-gray and there was still color in the west.

She was thinking about Charlotte, knowing she had no garden, no room for flowers, and feeling a little guilty that chance had given her so much for no effort of her own. She determined to find a graceful way of sharing it a little more, without making Charlotte feel aware of it—or Pitt. Apart from the fact that he was Charlotte's husband, Emily liked Pitt for himself.

169

She was standing quite still, facing the breeze, when it happened, a shrill, tearing scream that went on and on, shattering the night. It reverberated in the stillness, then came again, sickeningly, thick-throated.

Emily froze, her skin crawling. The evening was heavy with silence.

Then somewhere there was a shout.

Emily moved, picking up her skirts and running back into the house, through the withdrawing room, the hall, and out of the front door, shouting for the butler and the footman.

Out in the front driveway she stopped. Lights were coming on along the Walk, and a man's voice was calling out two hundred yards away.

Then she saw Selena. She was running along the middle of the road, her hair ragged down her back and the bosom of her dress ripped open, showing white flesh.

Emily started toward her. Already she knew in her heart what it was. There was no need to wait for Selena's gasping, sobbing words.

She fell into Emily's arms.

"I've been—violated!"

"Hush!" Emily held on to her hard. "Hush!" She was talking meaninglessly, but it was the sound of a voice that mattered. "You're safe now. Come on, come inside." Gently she led her, weeping, across the carriageway and up the stairs.

Inside she closed the withdrawing room door and sat her down. The servants were all outside, searching for the man, any stranger, anyone who could not explain themselves— although it did occur fleetingly to Emily that all the man need do was join in the hunt to pass into virtual invisibility!

Maybe when she had time to think, to compose herself, Selena would say less, be embarrassed or unclear.

Emily knelt down in front of her, taking her hands.

"What happened?" she said firmly. "Who was it?"

Selena lifted her face, flushed, her eyes wide and glittering.

"It was awful!" she whispered. "Violent hunger, like nothing I've ever known! I shall feel it—and smell it—as long as I live!"

"Who was it?" Emily repeated.

"He was tall," Selena said slowly. "And slender. And God, how strong he was!"

"Who!"

"I—oh, Emily, you must swear before God you will say nothing—swear!"

"Why?"

"Because," she swallowed hard, her body shivering, her eyes enormous, "I—I think it was Monsieur Alaric, but— but I cannot be sure. You must swear, Emily! If you accuse him, and you are wrong, we shall both be in terrible danger. Remember Fanny! I shall swear I know nothing!"

Eight

Pitt was called, of course, and he left home immediately in the same cab that had brought the message, but by the time he reached Paragon Walk, Selena was dressed in a discreet gown of Emily's and sitting on the big sofa in the withdrawing room. She was now much more composed. Her face was flushed, her hands white and knotted in her lap, but she told him quite coolly what had happened.

She had been returning from a brief visit to Grace Dilbridge, hurrying a little to be home before dark, when she had been attacked from behind by a man of above average height and quite phenomenal strength. She had been thrown to the ground on the grass by the rose bed, as near as she could judge. The next part was too appalling, and surely Pitt, as a delicate man, would not expect her to describe it? Sufficient to say she had been violated! By whom she did not know. She had not seen his face, nor could she describe anything else about him, except his enormous strength and the fierceness of his animal behavior.

He questioned her as to anything at all she might have noticed without realizing it: his clothing, was it of good texture or harsh; did he have a shirt beneath his jacket, white or dark? Were his hands rough?

She considered for only a moment.

"Oh," she said, with a little flutter of surprize. "Yes, you are right! His clothes were good. He must have been a gentleman. I recall white shirt cuffs. And his hands were smooth, but"—she lowered her eyes—"very strong!"

He pressed her further, but she could tell him nothing more. He had not spoken, and presently she grew distressed and became unable to say anything more.

He was obliged to give up and fall back on the ordinary routine chasing of details. In a long and exhausting night, he and Forbes questioned every man on the Walk, obliging them to leave their beds angry and frightened. As previously, everyone could account in a perfectly reasonable way for his whereabouts, but none had complete proof that they could not have been outside for those few, vital moments.

Afton Nash had been in his study, but it opened onto the garden and, there was no reason why he could not have slipped out without being seen. Jessamyn Nash had been playing the piano and could not say whether Diggory was in the room all evening or not. Freddie Dilbridge had been alone in his garden room; he had said that he was considering some decorating changes. Grace was not with him. Hallam Cayley and Paul Alaric lived alone. The only bright aspect was that George had been in town, and it really did seem wildly improbable that he could have returned unseen to the Walk.

All the servants were questioned, and all the answers compared. A few had been occupied in activities they would have preferred to keep secret; there were three separate affairs and a card game where money of quite a high order had changed hands. Possibly there would be dismissals in the morning! But most either could account for themselves or were precisely where one would expect them to be.

At the end of it all, in a still, warm dawn, eyes gritting

with sleep, his throat dry, Pitt knew nothing more of any worth.

It was two days after that that Pitt at last received his answer from Paris regarding Paul Alaric. He stood in the middle of the police station with it in his hands, more confused than ever. The Paris police could find no trace of him and apologized for the delay in their reply, explaining that they had sent to every major center in France inquiring, but still they could find no definite news. There were, of course, one or two families of that name, but none of their members fitted the description as to age, appearance, or anything else. And their whereabouts were already accounted for. Most certainly they had no records of such a person accused, much less convicted, of any indecent assaults upon women.

Pitt wondered why Alaric should lie as to his origin?

Then he recalled that Alaric had never said anything about his origin. Everyone else had said he was French, but Alaric himself had said nothing at all, and Pitt had never seen reason to ask. Freddie Dilbridge's accusation was probably exactly what Grace had said it was—a desire to attract attention away from his own friends. Who easier to accuse than the only foreigner?

Pitt dismissed the Paris reply and went back to the practical investigation.

The investigation proceeded through the long, hot days, tedious question after question, and gradually Pitt was obliged to turn his attention to other crimes. The rest of London did not suddenly cease from robbery, deceit, and violence, and he could not spend all his hours on one mystery, however tragic or dangerous.

Life slowly resumed a more normal pattern in the Walk. Of course, Selena's ordeal was not forgotten. Reactions to it varied. Oddly enough, Jessamyn was the most sympathetic. It was as if the old enmity between them had been entirely swept away. It fascinated Emily, because not only did they show a new friendship towards each other, there seemed to be a glow of satisfaction about it in both of them, as if each felt in her own way she had won a signal victory.

Jessamyn was all solicitude for Selena's appalling experience and coddled her on every reasonable occasion, even prompting other people to the same concern. Of course, it did have the byproduct of allowing no one to forget the incident, a fact which Emily noted with some amusement and passed on to Charlotte when visiting her.

And curiously, Selena herself did not seem to mind. She colored deeply and her eyes were bright when it was referred to, always obliquely, of course—no one could wish to be vulgar enough to use unpleasant words—but she seemed to take no offense at its mention.

Naturally there were others who regarded it quite differently. George studiously avoided the subject altogether, and Emily permitted him to do so for some time. She had originally decided to dismiss her knowledge of his involvement with Selena, provided it never happened again. Then one morning an opportunity presented itself which was too good to miss, and almost without being conscious of it, she found herself taking advantage.

George looked up over the breakfast table. Aunt Vespasia was down early this morning and had helped herself delicately to apricot preserve with walnuts in, and a little very thin toast.

"What are you going to do today, Aunt Vespasia?" George inquired politely.

"I shall endeavor to avoid Grace Dilbridge," she replied, "which will not be easy, since I have certain calls to make, as a matter of duty, and no doubt she will have the same ones. It will require some forethought to see that we do not come across each other at every step and turn."

175

George said the automatic thing, partially because he was not really listening.

"Why do you wish to avoid her? She's harmless enough."

"She is excessively tedious," Aunt Vespasia said smartly, finishing her toast. "I used to think that her suffering and the continuous, eyes-upturned expression of it was the nadir of boredom. But that was easy to take compared with her views on the subject of women who are molested, the general bestiality of men, and certain woman who contribute to everyone's misfortune by encouraging them. That is more than I can bear."

Emily spoke, for once, a fraction before she thought, her natural feelings for Selena stronger than her usual caution.

"I would have thought you might agree with her, at least in some respects?" she said, turning to Vespasia, a little edge to her voice.

Vespasia's gray eyes widened.

"To disagree with Grace Dilbridge and yet have to listen to her with civility is part of the normal trials of Society, my dear," she replied. "To be obliged by honesty, to agree with her, and to say so, is more than should be asked of anyone! It is the first and only time we have agreed about anything of moment, and it is intolerable. Of course Selena is no better than she should be! Even a fool knows that!" She stood up and dusted an imaginary crumb off her skirt.

Emily lowered her eyes for a long moment; then looked up at George. He turned from Aunt Vespasia, going out of the door, and back at Emily.

"Poor Aunt Vespasia," Emily said carefully. "It is most trying. Grace is so very self-righteous, but one has to admit that on this occasion she is right. I dislike speaking ill of my own sex, especially of a friend, but Selena has behaved in the past in a way to—not quite invite." She hesitated. "Misunderstanding as to her—" She stopped, her eyes

176

holding George's, staring across at him. His face was pale, stiff with apprehension.

"What?" He asked in the silence.

"Well—" She smiled very brightly, a cool, wise little smile. "Well, she has been a little—free—with herself, hasn't she, my dear? And that sort of person attracts—" She let it go. She knew from his face that he had understood perfectly. There were no more secrets.

"Emily," he began, knocking his teacup with his sleeve.

She did not wish to discuss it. Excuses were painful. And she did not want to hear him make them. She affected to suppose he was going to criticize her.

"Oh, I don't doubt you are going to say I should not speak of her in that way when she has had such a dreadful experience." She reached for the teapot to have something to do, but her hand was not as steady as he would have wished. "But I promise you what Aunt Vespasia says is quite true, and I know it for myself. Still—I'm sure after this it will not happen again. Everything will be quite changed for her from now on, poor creature!" She composed her face sufficiently to smile across at him and hold the teapot with hardly a quiver. "Would you care for some more tea, George?"

He stared at her, a mixture of incredulity and awe in his eyes.

She viewed it with a warm, delicious tingle of satisfaction.

For a moment they stayed motionless, understanding working through, completing itself.

"Tea?" she repeated at last.

He held out his cup.

"I expect you are right," he agreed slowly. "In fact I'm sure you are. It will definitely be quite different from now on."

Her whole body relaxed, she smiled at him dazzlingly

177

and let the tea pour right up the cup, far too full for good taste.

He looked at it with a slight surprize, then smiled as well, a wide, intense smile, like one who has been delightfully amazed.

Miss Laetitia said nothing about the affair of Selena, but Miss Lucinda more than made up for it, spilling opinions out like shopping from a burst basket, every color and shape, but all adding weight to her conviction that there was something incredibly wicked going on in the Walk, and she would devote every ounce of courage she possessed to discovering what it was. Lady Tamworth reinforced her volubly, but took no action.

Afton Nash was also of the opinion that the only women who get molested are those who invite such things and therefore deserve little sympathy. Phoebe wrung her hands and grew even more terrified.

Hallam Cayley continued to drink.

Immediately after the next event, Emily called her carriage in the morning and rushed around unannounced to regale Charlotte with the news. She almost tumbled out of the door onto the pavement, ignoring the footman's help in her excitement, and forgot to give him any instructions. She thumped on Charlotte's door.

Charlotte, apron up to her chin, dustpan in hand, answered it, her face blank with surprise.

Emily burst in past her, leaving the door open.

"Are you all right?" Charlotte pushed it shut and followed after her as Emily swept into the kitchen and planted herself on one of the kitchen chairs.

"I'm marvelous!" Emily replied. "You'll never imagine what has happened! Miss Lucinda has seen an apparition!"

"A what?" Charlotte stared at her in disbelief.

"Sit down," Emily commanded. "Make me some tea.

I'm dying of thirst. Miss Lucinda saw an apparition! Last night. She has taken to the chaise lounge in the withdrawing room in a state of complete collapse, and everyone is rushing around to call on her, simply aching to know what happened. She will be holding court. I would love to be there, but I had to come and tell you. Isn't it ridiculous?"

Charlotte had put on the kettle; the tea things were already prepared, as she had intended to have a cup herself in an hour or two. She sat down opposite Emily and gazed at her flushed face.

"An apparition? What do you mean? A ghost of Fanny, or something? She's mad. Does she drink, do you think?"

"Miss Lucinda? Good gracious, no! You should hear what she says about people who drink!"

"That doesn't mean she doesn't do it herself."

"Well, she doesn't. And no, not a ghost of anybody, but something hideous and evil, staring at her through her window, its face pressed against the glass. She said it was pale green, with red eyes, and had horns out the top of its head!"

"Oh Emily!" Charlotte burst out laughing. "She can't have! There isn't any such thing!"

Emily leaned forward.

"But that's not all," she said urgently. "One of the maids saw something running away, sort of loping, and it jumped clear over the hedge. And Hallam Cayley's dog howled half the night!"

"Maybe it was Hallam Cayley's dog in the first place?" Charlotte suggested. "And it howled because it was shut up again, and maybe beaten for running away."

"Rubbish! It's quite a small dog, and it isn't green!"

"She could have thought its ears were horns," Charlotte was not going to give up. Then she collapsed in laughter. "But I would love to have seen Miss Lucinda's face. I'll wager that was as green as anything at the window!"

Emily burst into giggles, too. The kettle was spouting steam all over the kitchen, but neither of them took any notice.

"It really isn't funny," Emily said at last, wiping away her tears.

Charlotte saw the kettle and stood up to make the tea, sniffing and dabbing at her cheeks with the end of her apron.

"I know," she agreed. "And I am sorry, but it's so silly I can't listen to it and keep a straight face. I suppose poor Phoebe will be even more terrified now."

"I haven't heard, but I wouldn't be surprised if she took to her bed as well. She wears a crucifix the size of a teaspoon all the time. I can't imagine a man who would attack and molest you in the dark being warded off by that!"

"Poor creature." Charlotte brought the teapot to the table and sat down again. "I wonder if they'll send for Thomas?"

"For apparitions? More like the vicar."

"An exorcism?" Charlotte said with delight. "I should love to see that! Do you think they really will?"

Emily raised her eyebrows and began to giggle again. "How else do you get rid of green monsters with horns?"

"A little more water and a little less imagination," Charlotte said tartly. Then her face softened. "Poor thing. I suppose she has little else to do. The only events of any meaning in her life are those she dreams up. Nobody really needs her. At least after this she'll be famous for a few days."

Emily reached over and poured the tea, but she did not reply. It was a pathetic and sobering thought.

At the end of August there was a dinner party at the Dilbridges' to which Emily and George were invited, along with the rest of the Walk. Surprizingly, the invitation also included Charlotte, if she would care to come.

It was only ten days since Miss Lucinda's apparition, and

180

Charlotte's interest was still very much alive. She was not even concerned as to how she would present a suitable appearance. If Emily passed on the invitation she would no doubt also have in mind some gown Charlotte could wear. As usual curiosity won over pride, and without hesitation she accepted yet another of Aunt Vespasia's gowns, considerably made over by Emily's lady's maid. It was a rich oyster shaded satin with a little lace on it, though much had been taken off and replaced with chiffon to make it appear younger. Altogether, turning slowly in front of the cheval glass, Charlotte was very pleased with it. And it was marvelous to have someone else to do her hair. It was extremely difficult to wind hair elegantly at the back of one's own head. Her hands always seemed to be at the wrong angle.

"That's fine," Emily said tartly. "Stop admiring yourself. You're becoming vain, and it doesn't suit you!"

Charlotte smiled broadly.

"It might not, but it feels wonderful!" She picked up her skirts, swishing them a little, and followed Emily down to where George was waiting for them in the hallway. It was an event Aunt Vespasia had chosen not to attend, although as a matter of course the invitation had included her.

It was a long time since Charlotte had been to a party at all, and in the past she had not enjoyed them much. But she felt quite differently about this. It was not a case of accompanying Mama so that she might be paraded before suitable potential husbands. This time she was secure in Pitt's love, not anxious what Society should think of her, and not especially concerned to impress. She could go and be quite naturally herself, and there was no effort required since she was essentially a spectator. The dramas in Paragon Walk did not affect her, because the main tragedy did not touch Emily, and if Emily wished to become involved in the minor farces, that was her own affair.

It was quite a small dinner by the Dilbridges' usual standards, not more than two or three faces that Charlotte did not already know. Simeon Isaacs was there, with Albertine Dilbridge, much to Lady Tamworth's obvious disapproval. The Misses Horbury were dressed in pink, and it looked surprisingly well on Miss Laetitia.

Jessamyn Nash floated in in silver gray, looking quite marvelous. Only she could have contrived at once to warm the color with life, and at the same time leave untarnished its wraithlike essence. For a moment Charlotte envied her.

Then she saw Paul Alaric, standing next to Selena, his head bent a little to listen to her, elegant and faintly humorous.

Charlotte raised her chin a little higher and approached them with a dazzling smile.

"Mrs. Montague," she said brightly, "I'm so glad to see you looking so well." She did not want to be obvious, above all not in front of Alaric. Waspishness might amuse him, but he would not admire it.

Selena looked slightly surprised. Apparently it was not what she had expected.

"I am in excellent health, thank you," she said, with eyebrows raised.

They swapped polite nothings, but, as Charlotte looked more closely at Selena, she realized that her initial words had been perfectly true. Selena did appear in excellent health. She looked nothing like a woman who had recently suffered the violence and obscenity of rape. Her eyes were brilliant, and there was a flush on her cheeks that was so high and yet so delicate Charlotte was convinced it owed nothing to art. She moved a little quickly, small gestures of her hands, eyes glancing round the room. If this was a display of courage, a defiance of the tacit consensus that a women ravished was somehow justly despoiled and must remember it all her life, then, for all her dislike, Charlotte could only admire it.

She did not allude to the incident again, and the conversation passed to other things, small items in the news, trivia of fashion. Presently she drifted away, leaving Selena still with Alaric.

"She looks remarkably well, don't you think?" Grace Dilbridge observed with a small shake of her head. "I don't know how the poor creature bears it!"

"It must take a great deal of courage," Charlotte replied. It did not come easily to her to praise Selena, but honesty obliged it. "One cannot help admiring her."

"Admire!" Miss Lucinda spun round, her face flushed with anger. "You must admire whom you choose, Mrs. Pitt, but I call it brazen! She is disgracing the whole of womanhood! I really think next Season I must go somewhere else. It will be extremely hard for me, but the Walk has become defiled beyond endurance."

Charlotte was too surprised to answer immediately, and Grace Dilbridge did not seem to know what to say either.

"Brazen," Miss Lucinda repeated, staring at Selena, now walking on Alaric's arm across the floor toward the open French doors. Alaric was smiling, but there was something in the angle of his head that betrayed courtesy rather than interest. He seemed even faintly amused.

Miss Lucinda snorted.

Charlotte found her tongue at last.

"I think that is a most unkind thing to say, Miss Horbury, and quite unjust! Mrs. Montague was the victim, not the perpetrator, of the crime."

"What utter nonsense!" It was Afton Nash, pale-faced, eyes glittering. "I find it hard to imagine you can really be so naive, Mrs. Pitt. Feminine charms may be considerable—to some." He raked her up and down with a contempt that seemed to strip her of her gorgeous satins and leave her naked to the prying and derision of everyone. "But if you imagine they are such as to drive men to force themselves upon the unwilling, you overrate your own sex." He smiled icily. "There are enough willing, positively eager, for titillation, who even find a perverse pleasure in violence and submission to it. No man need risk his reputation by assaulting the unwilling, whatever any given woman may choose to say afterward."

"That's a disgusting thing to say!" Algernon Burnon had been close enough to overhear. Now he stepped forward, ashen faced, his slight body shaking. "I demand that you withdraw it, and apologize!"

"Or you will—what?" Afton's smile did not alter. "Request me to choose between pistols and swords? Don't be ridiculous, man! Nurse your offense, by all means, if you must. Believe whatever you want to about women; but don't try to make me believe it too!"

"A decent man," Algernon said stiffly, "would not speak ill of the dead, nor insult another man's grief. And whatever anyone's most private weaknesses or shame, he would not make public mock of it!"

To Charlotte's amazement Afton did not reply. His face drained of all blood, and he stared at Algernon as if no one else existed in the room. Seconds ticked by, and even Algernon seemed frightened by the intensity of Afton's frozen hatred. Then Afton turned on his heel and strode away.

Charlotte breathed out slowly; she did not even know why she was frightened. She did not understand what had happened. Neither, apparently, did Algernon himself. He blinked and turned to Charlotte.

"I'm sorry, Mrs. Pitt. I'm sure we must have embarrassed you. It is not a subject we should have discussed in front of ladies. But," he took in a deep breath and let it out. "I am grateful to you for defending Selena—for Fanny's sake—you—"

Charlotte smiled.

"I understand. And no person who is worth counting a friend would think otherwise."

His face relaxed a little.

"Thank you," he said quietly.

A moment later she found Emily at her elbow.

"What happened?" Emily demanded anxiously. "It looked dreadful!"

"It was unpleasant," Charlotte agreed. "But I don't really know exactly what it meant."

"Well, what did you do?" Emily snapped.

"I praised Selena for her courage," Charlotte replied, looking at Emily very directly. She had no intention of going back on it, and Emily might as well know.

Emily's brows wrinkled, her mood changed in the instant from anger to puzzlement.

"Yes, isn't it extraordinary. She seems almost—elated! It is as if she had won some secret victory that none of the rest of us know about. She is even nice to Jessamyn. And Jessamyn is nice to her, too. It's ridiculous!"

"Well, I don't like Selena either," Charlotte admitted. "But I am obliged to admire her courage. She is defying all the bigoted little people who say she is somehow to blame for what happened to her. Whoever had the fire to do that would have my regard."

Emily stood staring across the enormous room to where Selena was talking to Albertine Dilbridge and Mr. Isaacs. A few feet away from them, Jessamyn stood with a champagne glass in her hand, watching Hallam Cayley take what must have been his third or fourth rum punch since his arrival. Her expression was unreadable. It could have been pity or contempt, or it might have had nothing to do with Hallam at all. But when her eyes moved to Selena, there was nothing in them but pure, delicious laughter.

Emily shook her head.

"I wish I understood," she said slowly. "Perhaps I'm mean-spirited, but I really don't think it's just courage. I've never seen Selena in that way. Maybe it's my fault, but I don't know. That's not defiance; she's pleased with herself. I swear it. You know she's set her cap at Monsieur Alaric?"

Charlotte gave her a withering look.

"Of course I know it! Do you think I'm blind and deaf, too?"

Emily ignored the barb.

"Promise you won't tell Thomas, or I shan't tell you!"

Charlotte promised immediately. She could not possibly forego the secret, whatever conflicts followed afterward.

Emily pulled a face.

"On the night it happened I was the first person there, as you know—"

Charlotte nodded.

"Well, I asked her straightaway who it was. Do you know what she told me?"

"Of course, I don't!"

"She made me swear not to accuse him, but she said it was Paul Alaric!" She stood back and waited for Charlotte's amazement.

Charlotte's first feeling was one of disgust, not for Selena, but for Alaric. Then she rejected the whole idea, thrusting it away.

"That's ridiculous! Why on earth should he attack her? She is chasing him so hard, all he would need to do is stop running away, and he would have her for the asking!" She knew she was being cruel, and she intended it.

"Exactly," Emily agreed. "Which only makes the mystery greater! And why does Jessamyn not care? If Monsieur Alaric is really so passionate about Selena that he ravished her in the Walk, surely Jessamyn would be beside herself with rage—wouldn't she? But she isn't; she is laughing, I can see it in her eyes every time she looks at Selena."

"So she doesn't know," Charlotte reasoned. Then she thought more deeply. "But rape is not a matter of love, Emily. It is violence, possession. A strong man, a man who is capable of caring, does not force a woman. He takes love as it is offered, knowing that that which is demanded has no meaning. The essence of strength is not in overpowering others, but in mastering oneself. Love is giving, as well as receiving, and when one has once known love, one sees conquest as the act of a weak and selfish person, the momentary satisfaction of an appetite. And then it is no longer attractive, merely rather sad."

Emily frowned, and her eyes were clouded.

"You are talking about love, Charlotte. I was only thinking of physical things. They can be quite different, without any love at all. Perhaps there is even a little hate in them. Maybe Selena did secretly rather enjoy it. To have lain with Monsieur Alaric willingly would be a sin. And even if Society did not particularly care, her friends and family would. But to be the victim excuses her, at least in her own mind. But if it was not so dreadful, and she was excited by it when she knew she should have been revolted, then she has had it both ways! She is innocent of the guilt, and yet she has had the pleasure!"

Charlotte thought about it for a few moments, then discarded it, perhaps not with reason but because she did not wish it to be true.

"I don't think it can be a pleasure. And why is Jessamyn so amused then?"

"I don't know," Emily gave up. "But it is not as simple as it seems." She moved away, going over toward George, who was trying unsuccessfully to reassure Phoebe, muttering something soothing to her and obviously highly embarrassed. Phoebe had taken to speaking much about religion and was never without a crucifix. He had no idea what to say to her and was overwhelmed with relief when Emily took over, determined to turn the conversation away from salvation to something more trivial, such as how to train a good parlormaid. Charlotte watched in admiration at the skill with which it was done. Emily had learned a lot since Cater Street.

"The play amuses you?" It was a soft voice, very beautiful, just behind her.

Charlotte spun round a little too quickly for grace. Paul Alaric raised his eyebrows very slightly.

"It hovers between tragedy and farce, doesn't it?" he said with a slow smile. "I fear Mr. Cayley is destined for tragedy. There is a pervading darkness in him that will engulf him altogether before long. And poor Phoebe—she is so terrified, and she has no need."

Charlotte was confused. She was unprepared to discuss reality with him. In fact she was not sure even now whether he was speaking seriously, or merely playing verbal games. She searched for an answer that would not commit her.

He waited, his eyes soft, Latin dark, but without the overt sensuality she always associated in her mind with Italy. They seemed to look inside her without effort, to read her.

"How do you know she has no need?" she asked.

His smile broadened.

"My dear Charlotte, I know what she is afraid of—and it does not exist—at least not here in Paragon Walk."

"Then, why don't you tell her so?" She was angry, feeling for Phoebe's panic.

He looked at her with patience.

"Because she would not believe me. Like Miss Lucinda Horbury, she has convinced herself."

"Oh, you mean Miss Lucinda's apparition?" Suddenly, she was weak with relief.

He laughed outright.

"Oh, I don't doubt she saw something. After all, if she will go poking her virtuous nose into other people's affairs, it is too much temptation for someone to resist putting something there for her to sniff at. I imagine it was very real, her green monster—at least for the occasion."

She wanted to disapprove, but even more than that she wanted to believe him.

"That's quite irresponsible," she said, in what she imagined to be a stiff voice. "The poor woman might have had a seizure with fright."

He was not fooled for an instant.

"I doubt it. I think she is a remarkably durable old lady. Her indignation will keep her alive, even if only to find out what is going on."

"Do you know who it was?" she asked.

His eyes widened.

"I don't even know that it happened at all. I have only deduced it."

She did not know what else to say. She was very aware of him standing close to her. He did not need to touch her or to speak for her to be conscious of him above and beyond everyone else in the room. Had he attacked Fanny, and then Selena? Or had it been someone else, and Selena had merely wished herself into believing it was he? She could understand that. It removed the assault from the realm of the sordid and humiliating to something dangerous but not without thrill.

To pretend, even to herself, that his company was not without deep and rather disturbing undertones of excitement, a kind of dominance, would be dishonest. Was it unconscious perception of violence in him that fascinated her? Was it true that women in some primitive depth they must deny, actually longed for rape? Did they all, even herself, secretly hunger for him?

"Woman wailing for her demon lover"—a line of verse, ugly and appropriate, intruded into her mind. She shook it away, forcing herself to smile, although it felt artificial and grotesque.

"I can't imagine anyone dressing up in such a ludicrous fashion," she said, trying to be light. "I think it was more likely to have been a stray animal, or even the branches of some shrub or other in the gaslight."

"Perhaps," he said gently. "I won't argue with you."

Indeed, they were prevented from continuing with the subject any further by the arrival of the Misses Horbury themselves and Lady Tamworth.

"Good evening, Miss Horbury," Charlotte said politely. "Lady Tamworth."

"How resolute of you to come," Alaric added, and Charlotte could have kicked him.

Miss Lucinda's face flushed for a moment. She disapproved of him, and therefore disliked him, but she could not refuse praise.

"I knew it to be my duty," she replied soberly. "And I shall not return home alone." She looked at him pointedly, her pale blue eyes wide. "I would not be foolish enough to go unaccompanied in Paragon Walk!"

Charlotte saw Alaric's fine brows rise very slightly and knew precisely what he was thinking. She felt a desperate desire to giggle. The idea of any man, least of all Paul Alaric, willfully accosting Miss Lucinda was preposterous.

"Very wise," Alaric agreed, meeting her challenging look squarely. "I doubt anything at all would have the temerity to attack three of you."

The faintest suspicion crossed her face that he was somehow amused by her, but, since she saw nothing funny herself, she dismissed it as a foreign joke and not worthy of attention.

"Certainly not," Lady Tamworth agreed enthusiastically. "There is no limit to what can be accomplished if we band together. And there is so much to be done, if we are to preserve our Society." She glanced balefully across at Simeon Isaacs, head bent to Albertine Dilbridge, his face alight. "And we must act quickly, if we are to succeed! At least that abominable Mr. Darwin is dead and can do no more harm."

"Once an idea is published, Lady Tamworth, its originator does not need to survive," Alaric pointed out. "Anymore than the seed need the sower in order to flourish."

She looked at him with distaste.

"Of course you are not English, Monsieur Alaric. You could not be expected to understand the English people. We will not take seriously such blasphemies."

Alaric affected innocence.

"Was not Mr. Darwin an Englishman, then?"

Lady Tamworth shrugged her shoulder sharply.

"I know nothing about him, nor do I wish to. Such men are not a fit subject for the interest of decent people."

Alaric followed the line of her eye.

"I'm sure Mr. Isaacs would agree with you," he said with a faint smile, and Charlotte was forced to stifle a giggle by pretending to sneeze. "Being a Jew," Alaric continued, avoiding her eye, "he would not countenance Mr. Darwin's revolutionary theories."

Hallem Cayley drifted up, his face heavy, another glass in his hand.

"No," he looked at Alaric with dislike. "The poor sod believes man is made in the image of God. I think the ape far more likely, myself."

"You are surely not saying now that Mr. Isaacs is a Christian?" Lady Tamworth bridled.

"A Jew," Hallam answered carefully and distinctly, then took another drink. "The Creation belongs to the Old Testament. Or haven't you read it?"

"I am of the Church of England," she said stiffly. "I don't read foreign teachings. That is primarily what is wrong with society these days: a great deal of new foreign blood. These are names now that I never heard of when I was a girl! No breeding. Heaven only knows where they come from!"

"Hardly new, ma'am." Alaric was standing so close to Charlotte, she fancied she could feel the warmth of him through the thick satin of her gown. "Mr. Isaacs can trace his ancestry back to Abraham, and he back to Noah, and so back to Adam."

"And so back to God!" Hallam drained his glass and dropped it on the floor. "Impeccable!" He glared triumphantly at Lady Tamworth. "Makes the rest of us look like yesterday's bastards, doesn't it?" He grinned broadly and turned away.

Lady Tamworth shook with rage. Her teeth clicked quite audibly. Charlotte felt a pity for her, because her world was changing, and she did not understand it; it had no place for her. She was like one of Mr. Darwin's dinosaurs, dangerous and ridiculous, beyond its time.

"I think he has had too much to drink," she said to her. "You must excuse him. I don't suppose he meant to be so offensive."

But Lady Tamworth was not mollified. She could not forgive.

"He is appalling! It must have been associating with men like that that gave Mr. Darwin his ideas. If he does not leave, then I shall."

"Would you care for me to escort you home?" Alaric asked instantly. "I doubt Mr. Cayley will leave."

She looked at him with loathing, but forced herself to refuse civilly.

Charlotte burst into giggles, covering her face with her hands.

"You were quite dreadful!" she said to him, furious with

192

herself for laughing. She knew it was the pressure of fear and excitement as much as humor, and she was ashamed.

"You do not have the sole prerogative to be outrageous, Charlotte," he said quietly. "You must allow me a little fun as well.'

A few days later Charlotte received a note from Emily, written in haste and some excitement. From something that Phoebe had said, Emily was now perfectly convinced that, in spite of her self-righteous prying, Miss Lucinda was right, and there was something going on in the Walk. She herself had certain more practical ideas as to how its nature could be uncovered, especially if it had something to do with Fanny and with Fulbert's disappearance. And it was hard to believe it had not.

Of course, Charlotte made immediate arrangements for Jemima, and by eleven o'clock in the morning she was at Emily's door. Emily was there as soon as the maid. She almost scurried Charlotte into the morning room.

"Lucinda's right," she said urgently. "She is dreadful, of course, and all she wants is to discover some piece of scandal she can tell everyone else and feel thoroughly superior about. She'll dine out on it for the rest of the Season. But she won't find out anything, because she's going about it all the wrong way!"

"Emily!" Charlotte took hold of her, gripping her arm. She could only think of Fulbert. "For heaven's sake, don't! Look what happened to Fulbert!"

"We don't know what happened to Fulbert," Emily said reasonably. She shook Charlotte's arm off with impatience. "But I want to find out—don't you?"

Charlotte wavered.

"How?"

Emily scented victory. She did not push. She tried a little honest flattery.

"Your suggestion—I suddenly realized that was the way. Thomas can't do it. It would have to be casual—"

"Who?" Charlotte demanded. "Explain yourself, Emily, before I explode!"

"Maids!" Emily was leaning forward now, her face shining. "Maids notice everything, between them. Maybe they don't know what all the different pieces mean, but we might!"

"But Thomas—" Charlotte started, although she knew Emily was right.

"Nonsense!" Emily brushed it aside. "No maid is going to talk to the police."

"But we can't just go questioning other people's maids!" Emily was exasperated.

"For goodness' sake, I shan't be so obvious! I shall go for some quite different reason, a recipe I admire, or I could take some old dresses I have for Jessamyn's maid—"

"You can't do that!" Charlotte said in horror. "Jessamyn will give her her own old things. She must have dozens! You couldn't explain any reason—"

"Yes, I could. Jessamyn never gives her old dresses away. She never gives anything away. Once it has been hers, she keeps it or burns it. She doesn't allow anyone else to have her things. Besides, her lady's maid is about the same size as I am. I have looked out a muslin from last year that will be perfect. She can wear it on her afternoon off. We shall go when I know that Jessamyn is out."

Charlotte was very dubious about the idea and feared it might prove embarrassing, but since Emily patently intended going regardless, her curiosity obliged her to go as well.

She had misjudged Emily. They learned nothing that seemed of any value at Jessamyn's, but the maid was delighted with the dress and the whole interview appeared as natural as a chance conversation with no purpose at all but pleasantry.

They proceeded to Phoebe's, arriving at the only time of the day when she was to be absent, and learned of an excellent mixture for making furniture wax with a most pleasing smell. It seemed Phoebe had taken to visiting the local church at odd hours, lately as often as every other day.

"Poor creature," Emily said as they left. "I think all these tragedies have quite turned her mind. I don't know whether she is praying for Fanny's soul, or what."

Charlotte did not understand the idea of praying for the dead, but there was nothing difficult in sympathizing with the need for comfort, a quiet place where faith and simplicity had found refuge over the generations. She was glad that Phoebe had discovered it, and, if it gave her calm, helped hold at bay the terrors that crowded in on her, so much the better.

"I'm going to see Hallam Cayley's cook," Emily announced. "You know the weather is quite different today. I am thoroughly cold, even though I put on a warmer dress. I do hope we aren't going to have a wretched spell, the Season isn't nearly over!"

It was true, here was an east wind, and it was definitely chill, but Charlotte was not interested in the weather. She pulled her shawl tighter and kept up with Emily.

"You can't just walk in and ask to speak to his cook! What on earth excuse have you? You'll make him suspicious, or else he will just think you ill-mannered."

"He won't be in!" Emily said impatiently. "I told you, I have chosen my times with great care. She cannot cook pastry to save herself; you could shoe horses with it. That's why Hallam always eats pastry when he is out. But she is a genius with sauces. I shall beg her for a recipe to impress Aunt Vespasia. That will flatter her, and then I can pass on to general conversation. I am convinced Hallam knows

195

about what is going on. He has behaved like a man haunted for the last month or more. I think, in his own way, he is as frightened as Phoebe!''

They were almost to the door. She stopped to let her shawl fall a little more gracefully, adjusted her hat, and then pulled the bell.

The footman opened the door immediately; his face fell with surprize when he saw two unaccompanied women.

''Lady—Lady Ashworth! I'm sorry, ma'am, but Mr. Cayley is not at home.'' He ignored Charlotte. He was not sure who she was and had more than enough to deal with without her.

Emily smiled disarmingly.

''How unfortunate. I was wondering if he might be kind enough to permit me to speak with your cook. Mrs. Heath, isn't it?''

''Mrs. Heath? Yes, m'lady—''

Emily favored him with a dazzling look.

''Her sauces are quite famous, and, as I have my husband's aunt, Lady Cumming-Gould, staying for the Season, I wanted to impress her with something special now and then. My cook is excellent, but—I know it is an impertinence, but I wondered if Mrs. Heath would be generous enough to share a recipe? Of course, it would not be the same, not made by her, but it would still be remarkable!'' She smiled hopefully.

He thawed. This was his realm and understandable.

''If you care to wait in the withdrawing room, m'lady, I'll ask Mrs. Heath to come up and see you.''

''Thank you, I'm obliged.'' Emily swept in, and Charlotte followed behind her.

''You see!'' Emily said triumphantly when they were seated and the footman had disappeared. ''All it needs is a little forethought.''

When Mrs. Heath arrived, it was immediately apparent

that she had decided to revel in her moment of glory. Negotiations were going to be protracted, and she would require every possible compliment before parting with the secret of her creations. It was equally obvious that she would share them; the fame already glittered in her eyes.

They were about at the point of accomplishment, when a small, very smutty maid came clattering down the stairs and burst into the withdrawing room, mobcap askew and hands black.

Mrs. Heath was outraged. She drew breath to deliver a blast of rebuke, but the girl spoke before her.

"Mrs. Heath, please, mum! The chimney's on fire in the green room, mum. I lit the fire to get rid of that smell like you told me to, and now it's all smoke everywhere, and I can't put it out!"

Mrs. Heath and Emily looked at each other in consternation.

"It's probably a birdnest in the chimney," Charlotte said practically. Since her marriage, she had had to learn about such things. She had called the sweep more than once for her own house. "Don't open the windows, or you'll make the draught worse, and it'll really burn. Get a long handled broom, and we'll see if we can dislodge it."

The maid stood, unsure whether to obey a strange woman or not.

"Well, go on, girl!" Mrs. Heath decided she would have given the same advice, if good manners had not prevented her from speaking first. "I don't know why you had to ask me!"

Emily seized the chance to reinforce her advantage, rather than risk being cut short before her real purpose by an inopportune domestic emergency.

"It may be quite far up. Perhaps we had better see if we can help. If it is not done properly there may be a real fire." And without waiting for agreement, she marched out of the

197

door and followed the scuttering maid up the stairs. Charlotte went as well, curious to see more of the house, and to hear anything that might be said, not that she shared Emily's expectation of any useful information regarding Fulbert or Fanny.

The green bedroom was indeed full of smoke, and the fumes caught in their throats as soon as they opened the door.

"Oh!" Emily coughed and stepped back. "Oh, that's awful. It must be a very big nest."

"Perhaps you'd better get a bucket of water and put the fire out," Charlotte said sharply to the maid. "Can you fetch a pitcher from the bathroom, and be quick. Then when it is out we can open all the windows."

"Yes, mum." The girl scurried away, now thoroughly frightened, in case she should be blamed for the whole affair.

Emily and Mrs. Heath stood coughing, happy for Charlotte to take command.

The girl came back and offered the pitcher to Charlotte, eyes wide and alarmed. Mrs. Heath opened the door, then, when she saw no flames, decided to reassert herself. She took the pitcher and strode in, hurling the contents on the billowing fireplace. There was a belch of steam and soot flew out, covering her white apron. She leapt back, furious. The girl stifled a giggle and turned it into a choke.

But the fireplace was dead and black, running trickles of sooty water into the hearth.

"Now!" Mrs. Heath said with determination. She had a personal vendetta with the thing, and it was not going to beat her, especially not in front of visitors and her own upstairs maid. She seized the broom the girl had been using to sweep the floor and advanced on the chimney. She launched a brisk swipe up the cavernous hold and struck something unyielding. Her face fell in surprise.

"It's an awful big nest! I shouldn't wonder if the bird's still there, by the feel. You were right, miss." She poked fiercely at it again and was rewarded with a fall of soot. She momentarily forgot her language and abused it roundly.

"Try poking to one side, and see if you can unbalance it," Charlotte suggested.

Emily was watching closely, her nose wrinkled.

"It doesn't smell very pleasant," she said unhappily. "I'd no idea wet fires were so—so sickly!"

Mrs. Heath put the broom in slightly sideways and jabbed hard. There was another trickle of soot, a scraping noise, and then, quite slowly, the body of Fulbert Nash slithered down the chimney and fell spreadeagled across the wet fireplace. It was blackened with soot and smoke, and maggots had infested the flesh. The smell was unspeakable.

Nine

Pitt found no pleasure at all in the discovery of Fulbert's body, not even the satisfaction of solving a mystery. He had expected Fulbert to be dead, but the deep stab wound in his back made suicide impossible, even if someone else had disposed of the body by stuffing it up the chimney. Although he could think of no reason why any innocent person should do so, except perhaps Afton Nash, to hide his brother's guilt. To everyone else, a suicide was the perfect answer to the rape and murder of Fanny.

And Fulbert had been dead a long time, probably since the night he disappeared. The body was decomposed in the heat of summer and riddled with maggots. It was not possible he could have been alive to attack Selena.

It was another murder.

They brought a closed coffin and took him away. Then Pitt turned to the inevitable. Hallam Cayley was waiting. He looked appalling; his face was gray and running with sweat, and his hands shook so badly the glass rattled against his teeth.

Pitt had seen shock before; he was used to watching while people came face to face with horror or guilt or overwhelming grief. He had never learned to tell one kind of shock from another. Looking at Cayley now, he did not know what the man felt, except that it was total and appalling. Pitt's mind observed and thought of questions to ask, but a feeling of pity drenched him and put reason into a silent background.

Hallam set the glass down.

"I don't know," he said hopelessly. "So help me God, I did not kill him."

"Why did he come here?" Pitt asked.

"He didn't!" Hallam's voice was rising; his control was thin, slipping away. "I never saw him! I don't know what the hell happened!"

Pitt had not expected admission, at least not yet. Perhaps he was one of those who would deny everything, even when there was proof. Or it was conceivable he really did know nothing. Pitt would have to speak to all the servants as well. It would be long and wretched. Finding guilt was always finding tragedy. When he had first joined the police, he had thought it would be dispassionate, the solution of mysteries. Now he knew otherwise.

"When did you last see Mr. Nash?" he asked.

Hallam looked up, surprised, his eyes bloodshot.

"Good God, I don't know! It was weeks ago! I don't remember when I saw him, but not the day he was killed. I do know that."

Pitt raised his eyebrows slightly.

"You believe he was killed when he disappeared?" he asked.

Hallam stared at him. The color rushed up his face, then ebbed away again. The sweat stood out on his lip.

"Wasn't he?"

"I should imagine so," Pitt said wearily. "It's not possible to tell now. I suppose he could have stayed up there indefinitely, as long as that room wasn't used. The smell would have got worse, of course. Did you give the maids orders to clean in there?"

"For heaven's sake, man, I don't care about housekeeping! They clean when they want to. That's what I have servants for—not to have to think about things like that."

There was no point in asking him if his servants were acquainted with Fulbert in any personal way. That had all been gone into already, and everyone had denied it, which was to be expected.

It was Forbes who elicited a surprizing new fact or at least a statement. The footman admitted now that he had opened the door to Fulbert on the afternoon of his disappearance, while Hallam was out, and Fulbert had gone upstairs, saying he wished to speak to the valet. The footman had assumed that he had let himself out afterwards, but now it was obvious that he had not. He excused himself for the lie in his first account, by saying he did not believe it important and had not wished to implicate his master on so flimsy a coincidence, being naturally afraid for his employment.

It ended in an unsatisfactory impasse. The valet denied having seen Fulbert, and nothing could be proven. Forbes said there had long been all manner of rivalries and old feuds among the household staff, and he had no idea whom to believe. According to previous testimony, either of the manservants could conceivably have killed Fanny, if one or more were lying, and neither of them could have attacked Selena.

Finally Pitt went back to the station, posting a constable to see that none of the Cayley servants moved from the Walk. The whole thing left a sour and unfinished taste in his mouth, but he could accomplish no more with questions now.

Fulbert was buried immediately, and the funeral was a small and somber affair, almost as if the dreadful corpse were in full view, instead of discreetly nailed into a polished dark, wood box.

Pitt attended, this time not out of pity for the dead, but because he needed to observe the mourners. Charlotte had not come, and neither had Emily. They were both still suffering from the horror of discovering the body, and in truth Charlotte had known him so little, her presence might be interpreted not so much as respect but rather as mere curiosity. Emily's condition gave her ample excuse to remain at home. George, grim and white-faced, body stiff against the wind, was the only representative of the family.

Pitt borrowed a black coat to cover his own rather multicolored clothes and stood discreetly at the back, half under the yew trees, hoping no one would do more than glance at him, possibly even assume him to be part of the undertaking party.

He waited as the cortege arrived, black crepe fluttering in the wind. No one spoke except the minister, and his sing-song voice floated over the hard clay and the withered grass between the gravestones.

There were no women except the immediate family, Phoebe and Jessamyn Nash. Phoebe looked appalling; her skin was ashen, and there were dark blotches under her eyes. She stood with shoulders hunched; from the back she might have been an old woman. He had seen abused children with that same resigned look, terrified, and yet too sure of the blow to bother to run.

Jessamyn was totally different. Her back was as straight as a soldier's, her chin high, and even the drifting black veil over her face could not hide the luminosity of her skin and the glittering eyes, fixed on the yew branches shifting in the wind at the far side, where the walk went down to the lych-gate. The only betrayal of emotion was the hard-clenched hands, so hard that, but for the gloves, surely the nails would have bitten into the skin.

All the men were there. Pitt studied them one by one, his memory turning over everything he knew about them, searching for reasons, inconsistencies, anything from which to distill an answer.

Fulbert had been murdered because he knew who had raped Fanny, and then Selena. Surely there could be no other cause, no other secret in the Walk worth killing for?

Could it have been Algernon Burnon? It would have needed no great strength to strike the blow, a single plunge with a knife. He was close to the open grave, his face sober, no passion in it. It was unlikely he had cared much for Fulbert. Probably, he was thinking of Fanny. Had he loved her? Whatever grief he had felt had been masked behind generations of careful composure. Gentlemen did not make exhibitions of their feelings. It was unbecoming, effeminate to show obvious distress. A gentleman managed even to die with dignity.

Who had decided on the long engagement? Surely, if he had felt such violent hunger for her, he could have insisted the marriage take place sooner? Many women married at Fanny's age, or younger; there was nothing hasty or improper about it. Looking at Algernon's calm face now, Pitt found it too difficult to believe there lay behind it ungovernable passion of any sort.

Diggory Nash was next to him, close to Jessamyn but not touching her. Indeed she looked so unlike a woman who needed any supporting arm, it would almost have been an impertinence, an intrusion to have offered her one. She was isolated in whatever feeling gripped her, unaware of the rest of them, even of her husband.

Did she know something about Diggory that they did not? Pitt stared at him from the discreet shelter of the yews. It was a less proportionate face than Afton's and yet so much warmer. There was no laughter in it now, but the lines were there, and a gentleness in the mouth—perhaps not the power of Afton? Had some weakness of appetite, years of easy gratification, led him to a mistaken identity in the dark, rape of his own sister, and murder to hide it?

Surely such a character would have betrayed itself before now? Guilt and terror would have wracked him, haunted his solitude, kept him awake, ended in some desperate folly and downfall? All Forbes's questions had elicited no complaint from any maid as to Diggory's behavior. Admittedly, there had been advances, but no unwelcome ones had been pressed. Refusal had been accepted, on the rare occasions it was offered, with humor and resignation.

No, Pitt could not believe Diggory was more than exactly what he seemed.

And George? He knew now why George had been so evasive in the beginning. He had simply been too drunk to remember where he had been—and too embarrassed to say so. Perhaps the fright would have done him good, at least for Emily's sake?

Freddie Dilbridge. He had his back to Pitt now, but Pitt had watched him as he walked down the path behind the coffin. His face had been anxious, confused rather than grieved. If there was fear, it was of the unknown, the inexplicable, not the all-too-plain fear of one who knows precisely what is wrong, and what the vengeance for it will be.

And yet there was something about Freddie that troubled Pitt. He had not yet discovered what it was. Dissolute parties were not exceptional. There were always those who were bored, occupied by no necessity to earn their bread or even to administer their property, driven by no ambition, who found entertainment in satisfying their own appetites, or the more bizarre appetites of others. Voyeurism was not novel, even a little moral blackmail afterward, a feeling of superiority.

Although that picture fitted his mind's perception of

Afton Nash better. There was cruelty in him, a delight in the frailty of others, especially the sexual frailty. He was a man who might well pander to tastes he despised, for the pleasure of reveling in his own superiority at the same time. Pitt could not think of anyone he had disliked as much. To be the victim of one's own faults, however grotesque, he could find a pity for. But to delight in and prey upon the weakness of others was beyond the realm of any compassion he could muster.

Afton was standing at the head of the grave, his eyes on the minister, grim and hard. But then he had buried a brother and had a sister murdered in one short summer. Was it conceivable he was the arch-hypocrite and had violated and killed his own sister, then stabbed to death his brother to keep his secret? Was that why Phoebe was disintegrating in terror before their eyes, descending from eccentricity into madness? Dear God, if it were, Pitt must catch him, prove it, and have him taken away. Pitt had never enjoyed hanging. It was commonplace, a part of society's mechanics to purge itself of a disease, but still he found it repellent. He knew too much about murder, about the fear or the madness that impelled it. He had seen and smelled the grinding poverty, the unnumbered deaths from and diseases of starvation in the rookeries, and he knew there were forms of murder that never soiled the hands, long-distance extermination that blind society and profit never looked at. Death from hunger happened a hundred yards from death from obesity.

And yet he felt, if Afton were guilty, he could have sent him to the gallows without any personal pity.

The Frenchman, Paul Alaric, was there, if indeed he were French? Perhaps he came from one of the African colonies? He was far too smooth, too wry and subtle to be from the great wind-and-snow-driven plains of Canada. There was something incredibly old in him; Pitt could not

206

conceive of him belonging to the New World. Everything about him spoke of centuries of civilization, roots deep enough to cling to the very core and heart of old cultures and rich, dark history.

He stood now with black head bent and the rising wind, sleek and beautiful even in this graveyard. He mirrored respect for the dead, courteous observance of custom. Was that all he was here for? Pitt had discovered no relationship between him and Fulbert except that of neighbors.

Could Alaric be the supreme actor? Was there unfulfilled hunger under that intelligent face, hunger so violent it had driven him to attack first Fanny and then the all-too-willing Selena? Or was Selena not really willing, when it came to the point?

He dared not dismiss it, it was his duty to consider everything possible, however unlikely. And yet he could not force himself to believe that Alaric was so different from every appearance. Over years of studying people, Pitt had become a skilled judge, and he had found most people do not hide much of themselves from a careful watcher, one who listens to every phrase, watches the eyes, the hands, the small deceptions to build the vanity, the tiny exhibitions of greed or ambition, the betrayals of essential selfishness, the straying eyes, the grubby innuendos.

Alaric might be a seducer, but a rapist Pitt could not believe.

That left Hallam Cayley. He was standing over the grave from Jessamyn, staring at her, as they at last began to shovel in the earth. The hard clay rubble clattered on the lid, sounding hollowly, almost as if there were no body inside. One by one they turned and walked away—the observances were over. Now it was the gravediggers' duty to finish, fill in the earth and stamp it down. A fine misty rain hung on the wind, slicking the paths and making them dangerous.

Hallam walked behind Freddie Dilbridge. As Pitt moved

from the yews, hurrying to keep pace with them, he saw Hallam's face. He looked like a man in a nightmare; the pock marks in his skin seemed to have become deeper, and he was pallid and sweating. His eyes were puffed, and even at that distance Pitt could see the nervous twitch in one lid. Was it excess of drink that racked him, and if so what torture had driven him to it? Surely loss of a dead wife would not have ravaged him so? From all that he and Forbes had learned through questioning neighbors and servants, the marriage had been no more than ordinary, a fondness for each other, but not a passion so consuming as to leave this devastation in its wake.

In fact the more Pitt thought about it, the less likely did it seem. Hallam had only been seen to drink more than most men in the last year, certainly not since the time of his wife's death. What had happened a year ago? He had so far discovered nothing.

He was level with them now, and Hallam turned for a moment and saw him. His face twisted with fear and recognition, as if the gravestone he was passing were his own, and he had read his name on it. He hesitated, staring at Pitt, then Jessamyn caught up with him. Her face was tight, all expression ironed out of it.

"Come, Hallam," she said quietly. "Take no notice of him. He is here because it is his duty. It means nothing." Her voice was quite flat. She had composed herself till every vestige of feeling was suppressed, controlled into what she wished it to be. She did not touch him, keeping herself apart, at least a yard from him. "Come," she said again. "Don't stand here. You're holding everyone up."

Reluctantly Hallam moved, not that he wished to obey or to leave so much as that there was no purpose in remaining.

Pitt stood still, watching their black-creped backs, as they wound up the damp path towards the lych-gate and out onto the street.

Could Hallam Cayley have raped Fanny? It was possible. Emily had said Fanny was boring, nondescript, not the sort of girl to excite anyone. But Pitt remembered the small white body lying on the morgue table. It had been very delicate, virginal, almost childlike, the bones small, the skin clear. Perhaps that very innocence had attracted. She would demand nothing; her own hungers would not have awoken yet; there would be no expectations to satisfy, no comparisons to be made with other lovers, not even with dreams, except the most limpid and unformed.

Jessamyn had said she was too guileless to interest, too young to be a woman. But perhaps Fanny had grown tired of being viewed as a child and had secretly started to think as a woman inside, while preserving outside the image everyone expected of her? Perhaps she had seen Jessamyn's glamour and decided to grasp for a little of it herself. Had she practiced her budding arts on Hallam Cayley, imagining him safe, and found one dark evening that he was not, that she had gone too far, succeeded in her temptation?

It was believable. More believable than that she had tempted some servant.

The other possibility, of course, was that she had been mistaken for someone else, a maid. There were several kitchen girls and between maids who were not unlike her in build, even in face. Only the clothes were radically different. Would the fingers of an obsessed man in the dark feel the difference between Fanny's silk and a servant girl's wash-cotton?

He had no idea.

But Fulbert's body had been found in Hallam's house. The servants had let him in; no one denied that—but why had he gone there, if not to see Hallam? Had he waited till Hallam came home, as he had said he would do, and then been killed for his knowledge? Or could it have been a manservant, the footman or the valet, again because of what he knew. They could have killed Fanny; it was not impossible.

He had not forgotten that someone else could have come in. It was not likely they had been let in by a servant. Any servant would tell of it, only too glad to widen the circle of suspicion, away from themselves. But the garden walls were not high. A man of average agility could climb over without difficulty. His clothes would be marked, brick dust, moss stains. They would be got rid of, but Pitt should ask valets. He must get Forbes to check again.

There were gates, of course, but he had already ascertained that Hallam's was kept locked.

He followed the last of the funeral out of the gate and turned up the street, away from the graveyard and back toward the police station. He believed it was Hallam. It was possible, and the horror of it was in his face. But he had not enough to prove it. If Hallam were simply to deny it, to say someone had followed Fulbert and seized the chance to murder him and leave the body in Hallam's house, there was nothing to prove him a liar. He could not arrest a man of Hallam Cayley's social position without a better case than that.

If he could not prove Hallam guilty, the next best thing he could do was to disprove any other possibility. It was a thin case—and unsatisfactory.

At the police station one small question was answered— why Algernon Burnon had been so reluctant to name the person in whose company he claimed to have been on the evening Fanny was killed. Forbes had at last run her down, a handsome and cheerful girl who in a higher class of society might have called herself a courtesan, but from her usual clientele was no more than a tart. No wonder Algernon had preferred the odd glance of halfhearted

210

suspicion to the surety that he had been paying for such indulgence while his fiancee was struggling for her life.

The day after, Pitt and Forbes went back to the Walk, quietly, going in by back doors and asking to see valets. No one's clothes showed stains of damp or moss, and there was no discernible brick dust, just the general dust of a dry summer. There had been one or two small tears, but nothing unaccountable. But then one could so easily say one had caught it getting in or out of a carriage, or in one's own garden. Rose thorns tore; one knelt on the grass to pick up a fallen coin or handkerchief.

He even went to Hallam Cayley's garden and asked permission to look at the walls on both sides, and a highly nervous footman escorted him around step by step, watching him with increasing tension and unhappiness, as no mark or disturbance was found. If anyone had climbed over these walls lately, they had done it with a padded ladder placed so carefully it had not crushed the moss nor scratched a brick, and they had smoothed out the holes left by the feet of the ladder in the ground. Such care seemed impossible. How could he have hauled the ladder after him back to his own side without leaving great runnels in the moss on top of the wall? And once back, what then of the ladder marks in the ground? The summer had been dry, but the garden earth was still deep and friable enough to mark easily. He tried it with the weight of his own foot and left an unmistakable print.

There was a door in the farthest wall onto the path beyond the aspen trees at the end, but it was locked, and the gardener's boy had the key and said it had never left him.

Hallam was out. Tomorrow Pitt would call and ask him about keys, if he had ever had another and given or lent it, but it was only a formality. He did not believe for a moment that anyone else had come along the pathway at the end and let themselves in to keep an appointment with Fulbert in

211

Hallam's house—and still less that it could have been a chance meeting.

He went home and told Charlotte nothing about it. He wanted to forget the whole affair and enjoy his own family, the peace and sureness of it. Even though Jemima was asleep, he demanded that Charlotte get her up, and then he sat in the parlor with her in his arms, while she blinked at him sleepily, unsure why she had been roused. He talked to her, telling her about his own childhood on the big estate in the country, exactly as if she understood him, and Charlotte sat opposite, smiling. She had some white sewing in her hands; he thought it looked like one of his shirts. He had no idea if she knew why he was talking like this—that it was to blot out Paragon Walk and what must be faced tomorrow. If she had, she was wise enough not to let him know.

There was nothing new at the police station. He asked to see his superior officers and told them what he intended to do. If there were no other explanation, no other key to the garden door, and no one had seen any other person, he would have to assume it was someone in Cayley's household and interrogate them in that light, not only the footman and the valet, but Hallam Cayley himself.

They were unhappy with the idea, especially of accusing Hallam, but they conceded that it seemed unavoidable that it was someone in the house—most likely the valet or the footman.

Pitt did not argue with them or give them all the reasons why he thought it was Hallam. After all, most of it was deduction and the misery in the man's face, the horror within him that was greater than anything outside. They could so easily have said it was simply the terrors of a man who drinks too much and cannot stop himself. And he could not have reasoned otherwise.

He arrived at the Walk in the late morning and went

straight to the house. He rang at the front door and waited. Incredibly, there was no answer. He tried again, and again there was nothing. Had some domestic crisis occupied the footman to the neglect of his usual duties?

He decided to go around to the kitchen door. There surely would be servants there; there were always maids in a kitchen, at any time of the day.

He was still yards short of the door when he saw the scullery maid. She looked up and gave a yelp, grabbing at her apron front and staring at him.

"Good morning," he said, trying to force a smile.

She stood frozen to the spot, speechless.

"Good morning," he repeated. "I can't make anyone hear at the front. May I come in through the kitchen?"

"The servants has got the day off," she said breathlessly. "There's just me and cook, and Polly. And Mr. Cayley in't up yet!"

Pitt swore under his breath. Had that fool of a constable allowed them all to leave the Walk—including the murderer?

"Where have they gone?" he demanded.

"Well, 'oskins, that's the valet, 'e's in 'is own room, I reckon. I ain't seen 'im today, but Polly took 'im a tray o' toast and a pot o' tea. And Albert, that's the footman, I reckon as 'e's probably gorn round to Lord Dilbridge's, 'cos 'e's got a fancy for their upstairs maid. Is anything wrong, sir?"

Pitt felt a wave of relief. This time the smile was real.

"No, I shouldn't think so. But I'd like to come in all the same. I dare say someone could wake Mr. Cayley for me. I need to see him to ask him about one or two things."

"Oh, I shouldn't, sir. Mr. Cayley, well, 'e's—'e won't like it. 'E in't very well in the mornings!" She looked anxious, as if she feared she would be blamed for Pitt's arrival.

"I dare say not," he agreed. "But this is police business,

and it can't wait. Just let me in, and I'll wake him myself, if you prefer?"

She looked very dubious, but she knew authority when she heard it and led him obediently through the kitchens and stopped at the baize door to the rest of the house. Pitt understood.

"Very well," he said quietly. "I'll tell him you had no choice." He pushed the door open and went into the hall. He had only got as far as the bottom stair when the barest movement caught his eye, just an inch or two, as of something unfixed among the straight wooden pillars of the stairway.

He looked up.

It was Hallam Cayley, swinging by his neck very, very slightly from his dressing gown cord, attached to the bannister where it ran along the landing.

Only for the first second was Pitt surprised. Then it all seemed dreadfully, tragically inevitable.

He started to climb up slowly until he reached the landing. Closer to, it was obvious Hallam was dead. His face was mottled but had not the purplish look of suffocation. He must have broken his neck as soon as he jumped. He was lucky. A man of his weight might easily have snapped the cord and ended up two stories below, broken-backed but still alive.

Pitt could not haul him up alone. He would have to send one of the servants for Forbes, and a police surgeon, the whole team. He turned around and went down slowly. What a sad, predictable end to a wretched story. There was no satisfaction in it, no sense of solution. He went through the baize door and told the cook and the girl simply that Mr. Cayley was dead and they were to go next door and ask one of the manservants to send for the police, a surgeon, and a mortuary coach.

There were fewer hysterics than he had expected.

214

Perhaps, after the discovery of Fulbert's body, they were not entirely surprized. Perhaps they had no more emotion left.

Then he went back upstairs to look at Hallam again and see if there were any letter, any explanation or confession. It did not take him long; it was in the bedroom on a small writing table. The pen and ink were still beside it. It was open and not addressed to anyone.

> *I did assault Fanny. I left Freddie's party and went out into the garden, then into the street. I found Fanny there quite by chance.*
>
> *It all began as a flirtation, weeks before that. She pursued it. I realize now she did not understand what she was doing, but at the time I was beyond thinking.*
>
> *But I swear I did not kill her.*
>
> *At least the day afterward I would have sworn it. The day after I was stunned as anyone.*
>
> *Nor did I touch Selena Montague. I would have sworn that. I don't even remember what I was doing that night. I was drinking. But I never cared for Selena; even drunk I would not have forced myself on her.*
>
> *I've thought about it till my mind reeled. I've woken in the night cold with terror. Am I losing my mind? Did I stab Fanny without even knowing what I was doing?*
>
> *I didn't see Fulbert alive the day he was killed. I was out when he called, and when I came back my footman told me he had shown him upstairs. I found him in the green bedroom, but he was already dead, lying on his face with the wound in his back. But, so help me God, I don't remember doing it.*
>
> *I did hide him. I was terrified. I did not kill him, but I knew they would accuse me. I put him up the chimney. It was large, and I am a great deal bigger*

than Fulbert. He was surprizingly light when I picked him up, even though he was dead weight. It was awkward getting him into the cavern of it, but there are niches up there for the sweeps' boys, and I managed it at last. I wedged him in. I thought he might stay there forever, if I locked the room off. I never thought of spring cleaning, and of Mrs. Heath having a master key.

Perhaps, I am mad. Maybe I killed both of them, and my brain is so clouded with darkness or disease I don't know it. I am two people, one tormented, lonely, full of regrets, not knowing the other half, and haunted by terrors of it—the other God, or the devil knows what? A savage, a madman, killing again and again.

Death is the best thing for me. Life has nothing but forgetfulness in drink between terrors of my other self.

I am sorry about Fanny, truly sorry. That I know I did.

But, if I killed her, or Fulbert, it was my other self, a creature I don't know, but he will at least die with me.

Pitt put it down. He was used to feeling pity, the wrench inside of a pain one could not reach, for which there was no balm.

He walked back onto the landing. There were police coming in at the front door. Now there would be the long ritual of surgeon's examination, search of his belongings, recording of the confession, such as it was. It gave him no sense of accomplishment.

He told Charlotte about it in the evening when he got home, not because he felt any ease over it, but because it concerned Emily.

216

For several moments she said nothing, then she sat down very slowly.

"Poor creature." She let out her breath quietly. "Poor haunted creature."

He sat down opposite her, looking at her face, trying to close Hallam and everything else to do with Paragon Walk out of his mind. For a long time there was silence, and it became easier. He began to think of things they might do, now that the case was over and he would have some time off. Jemima was big enough not to take cold; they might go for a trip up the river on one of the excursion boats, even pack a picnic and sit on the back and eat, if the weather stayed so fine. Charlotte would enjoy that. He could picture her now, her skirts spread around her on the grass, her hair bright as polished chestnuts in the sun.

Perhaps next year, if they were careful of every penny, they might even go to the country for a few days. Jemima would be old enough then to walk. She could discover all the beautiful things, pools of water in the stones, flowers under the hedges, perhaps a bird's nest, all the things he had known as a child.

"Do you think it was the loss of his wife that started his madness?" Charlotte's voice scattered his dream and brought him back rudely to the present.

"What?"

"The death of his wife," she repeated. "Do you think grief and loneliness preyed on his mind till he drank too much and became mad?"

"I don't know." He did not want to think about it. "Maybe. There were some old love letters among his things. They looked as if they had been read several times, edges a bit bent, one or two tears. They were very intimate, very possessive."

"I wonder what she was like. She died before Emily went there, so she never knew her. What was her name?"

217

"I don't know. She didn't bother to sign the letters. I suppose she just left them around the house for him."

Charlotte smiled, a tight, sad little gesture.

"How dreadful, to love someone so intensely, and then for them to die. His whole life seems to have disintegrated since then. I hope, if I died, you would always remember me, but not like that—"

The thought was horrible, bringing the darkness of the night inside the room, void and immense, never ending, cold as the distance to the stars. Pity for Hallam overwhelmed him. There were no words for it, just the pain.

She moved to kneel on the floor in front of him, taking his hands gently. Her face was smooth, and he could feel the warmth of her body. She did not try to say anything, find words to comfort, but there was a sureness in her quiet beyond his understanding.

It was several days before Emily called, and when she came in with a swirl of dotted muslin she was glowing as Charlotte had never seen her before. She was quite noticeably heavier now, but her skin was flawless, and there was a new shine in her eyes.

"You look wonderful!" Charlotte said spontaneously. "You should have children all the time!"

Emily pulled a dreadful face, but it was in mock, and they both knew it. Emily sat down on the kitchen chair and demanded a cup of tea.

"It's all over," she said determinedly. "At least that part of it is!"

Charlotte turned slowly, her own thoughts hardening and finding shape even as she swung from the sink to the table.

"You mean you're not happy about it either?" she asked carefully.

"Happy?" Emily's face fell. "How could I be—Charlotte! Don't you believe it was Hallam?" her voice was incredulous, her eyes wide.

"I suppose it must have been," Charlotte said slowly, pouring water into the kettle and over the top, spilling into the sink without noticing. "He admitted assaulting Fanny, and there was no other reason for killing Fulbert—"

"But?" Emily challenged.

"I don't know," Charlotte turned off the tap and emptied the excess out of the kettle. "I don't know what else."

Emily leaned forward.

"I'll tell you! We never discovered what it was that Miss Lucinda saw, and what it is that is going on in the Walk— and there is something! Don't try to tell me it was all something to do with Hallam, because it wasn't. Phoebe is still terrified. If anything, she is even worse, as if Hallam's death were just one more thread in the ghastly picture she can see. She said the oddest thing to me yesterday, which is partly why I came today, to tell you."

"What?" Charlotte blinked. Somehow all this seemed at once unreal, and yet as if it had been inevitable. All her vague unease was focused now. "What did she say?"

"That all the things that had happened had concentrated the evil in the Walk, and there was no way we could exorcise it now. She hardly dared to imagine what abominable thing would happen next."

"Do you think perhaps she is mad, too?"

"No, I don't!" Emily said firmly. "At least not mad the way you mean. She is silly, of course, but she knows what she's talking about, even if she won't tell anyone."

"Well, how are we going to find out?" Charlotte said immediately. The thought of not trying to discover never occurred to her.

Emily had also taken it for granted.

"I've worked it out, from all the things everyone has said." She got down to business now, decisions made in her

219

mind. "And I'm almost certain it is something to do with the Dilbridges, at least, with Freddie Dilbridge. I don't know who is involved and who isn't, except that Phoebe knows, and it terrifies her. But the Dilbridges are having a garden party in ten-days' time. George doesn't approve, but I mean to go, and you are coming, too. We shall break away from the party without being noticed and explore the house. If we are clever enough, we shall find something. If there is real wickedness in that place, it will have left something behind. Maybe we'll discover whatever it was that Miss Lucinda saw? It has to be there."

Memories of Fulbert's charred body slithering down the chimney flashed into Charlotte's mind. It would be a long time before she wished to poke into other people's rooms in search of answers, but then, on the other hand, neither could she possibly leave the question unanswered.

"Good," she said firmly. "What shall I wear?"

Ten

Charlotte went to the garden party feeling marvelous. Emily, high on the wave of her own well-being, had given her a new dress, all white muslin and lace, with tiny pin tucks at the yoke. She felt like daisies in the wind of a summer field, or the white foam of a mountain stream, inexpressible, shimmeringly clean.

Everyone in the Walk was there, even the Misses Horbury, as though they were making a determined effort to put everything sordid or tragic behind them, firmly in the past, and for a hot, still afternoon totally to forget it.

Emily was gowned in spring green, her best color, and she positively radiated delight.

"We are going to find out what it is," she said softly to Charlotte, gripping her by the arm as they walked across the grass toward Grace Dilbridge. "I haven't made up my mind yet whether she knows or not. I've been listening very carefully to everyone the last few days, and I rather think Grace doesn't wish to know, so she has made sure not to find out by accident."

Charlotte remembered what Aunt Vespasia had said about Grace and her enjoyment in being put upon. Perhaps if she discovered the secret, it would be too appalling for her to find any pleasure in it anymore. After all, if one's husband

221

sinned in an average way, only slightly more openly than most, one could be expected to endure it gracefully and be sympathized with. One's social position would not be jeopardized. But if the sin were extraordinary, something unacceptable, then one would be required to take action, even perhaps to leave—and that was altogether another matter. A woman who leaves her husband, for whatever reason, is not only financially a disaster, but socially quite beyond condoning. Invitations simply cease.

They were now in front of Grace Dilbridge, who was looking rather a poor color, in a purple that did not suit her. It was far too hot a shade for such a heavy day. There were tiny thunder flies in the air, and it was difficult not to forget one's manners and brush them away quite violently, as they itched the skin and caught in one's hair in a most unpleasant sensation.

"How charming to see you, Mrs. Pitt," Grace said automatically. "I'm so delighted you were able to come. How well you look, Emily, my dear."

"Thank you," they both replied together, then Emily went on, "I had no idea your garden was so large. How lovely it is. Does it extend beyond that hedge also?"

"Oh, yes, there is a herbaceous walk, and a small rose garden." Grace waved an arm. "I have sometimes wondered if we should try growing peaches on that south facing wall, but Freddie won't hear of it."

Emily's elbow poked Charlotte, and Charlotte knew she was thinking of the garden room. It must be somewhere behind that hedge.

"Indeed," Emily said with polite interest. "I do love peaches. I should insist, if I had such a place. There is nothing like a fresh peach, in the season."

"Oh, I couldn't," Grace looked uncomfortable, "Freddie would be most angry. He gives me so many things, he would think me most ungrateful if I were to make an issue of such a small matter.''

This time it was Charlotte who poked Emily discreetly, with her foot, under the clouds of her skirt. She did not want Emily to press too hard and make their interest obvious. They had already learned enough. The garden room was behind that hedge, and Freddie did not want peaches anywhere near it.

They excused themselves, after again saying how delighted they were to be there.

"The garden room!" Emily said as soon as they were out of earshot. "Freddie does not want her going there to pick peaches at awkward moments. He has his private parties out there, I'll wager you anything.''

Charlotte did not take her up.

"But parties are not much," she said slowly, "unless something quite awful goes on. What we need to know is who goes to them. Do you think Miss Lucinda recalls with any clarity at all what she saw? Or will it be so embroidered over with imagination by now that it isn't any use? She must have told it umpteen times.''

Emily bit her lip in irritation.

"I really should have asked her when it happened, but I was so annoyed by her, and so delighted that someone had given her a good fright, that I deliberately avoided her. And I didn't want to pander to her vanity. She was sitting up on the chaise lounge, you know, with smelling salts, an embroidered cushion with Chinese dragons behind her, so Aunt Vespasia said, and a whole jugful of lemonade, receiving callers like some duchess and insisting on telling the whole story right from the beginning to every one of them. I simply could not have been civil to her. I should have burst into laughter. Now I wish I'd had more self control.''

Charlotte was not in a position to criticize, and she knew

223

it. Without replying, she looked around the rose-hung garden to see if she could find Miss Lucinda. She was bound to be with Miss Laetitia, and they were always in the same color.

"There!" Emily touched her arm, and she turned. This time they were in forget-me-not blue, and it was far too young for either of them. The touches of pink only made it worse, like some confection that had become over-heated.

"Oh dear!" Charlotte said under her breath, stifling a gasp of laughter.

"It's got to be done," Emily replied severely. "Come on!"

Side by side, they attempted to look casual as they drifted over toward the Misses Horbury, hesitating on the way to compliment Albertine Dilbridge on her gown and exchange a greeting with Selena.

"How did she take it?" Charlotte asked the moment they were away from her.

"Take what?" Emily was for once confused.

"Hallam!" Charlotte said impatiently. "After all, it's a bit of a letdown, isn't it? I mean to be ravished in overwhelming passion by Paul Alaric is rather romantic, in a disgusting sort of way, but to be molested by Hallam Cayley when he was too drunk and wretched to know what he was doing and didn't even remember it afterward is just terrible"—she stopped, and all the mockery drained out of her—"and very tragic."

"Oh!" Emily obviously had not thought of it. "I don't know." Then the idea began to interest her. Charlotte saw it in her face. "But now that I consider it, she has rather gone out of her way to avoid me ever since then. Once or twice I have thought she was going to speak to me, then at the last moment she had suddenly found something else more pressing."

"Do you suppose she knew it was Hallam all the time?" Charlotte asked.

Emily screwed up her face.

"I'm trying to be fair." She was finding it an effort, and it showed. "I don't know what I think. I don't suppose it matters now."

Charlotte was not satisfied. Some small doubt, a question unresolved, gnawed at the back of her mind. But she suffered it to remain for the moment. They were approaching the Misses Horbury, and she must compose herself to pry discreetly and with grace. She fixed an interested smile on her face and plunged in before Emily had the opportunity.

"How nice to see you again, Miss Horbury," she gazed at Miss Lucinda with something like awe. "I do admire your courage after such an appalling experience. I am only beginning now fully to appreciate what you must have been through! So many of us lead sheltered lives, we have no imagination of the dreadful things there are so close to us— if only we knew!" She mentally kicked herself for being a hypocrite, the more so because she was rather enjoying it.

Miss Lucinda was too steeped in her own convictions to recognize a complete turn of character. She puffed herself out with satisfaction, reminding Charlotte of a pastel-colored pouter pigeon.

"How perceptive of you, Mrs. Pitt," she said solemnly. "So many people don't understand what dark forces there are at work, and how near to us they are!"

"Quite." For a moment Charlotte's nerve failed her. She caught sight of Miss Laetitia, her pale eyes wide, and was not sure whether there was laughter in them, or if it was only a reflection of the light. She took a deep breath. "Of course," she continued, "you must know better than the rest of us. I have been fortunate. I have never been brought face to face with pure evil."

225

"Few of us have, my dear," Miss Lucinda was warming to this new show of interest. "And I most sincerely hope you never have the misfortune to be one of us!"

"Oh, so do I!" Charlotte put a great deal of feeling into it. She deliberately creased her brow in anxiety. "But then there is the question of duty," she said slowly. "Evil will not go away because we choose not to look at it." She took a deep breath and faced Miss Lucinda squarely, meeting her rather round eyes. "You will never know how much I admire you for your conduct, your determination to get to the bottom of the circumstances here, whatever they may be."

Miss Lucinda flushed with satisfaction.

"How kind of you, and how very wise. I know few women of such sense, especially among the young."

"Indeed," Charlotte continued, ignoring a nudge from Emily. "I admire you for coming here today at all," she lowered her voice conspiratorially, "knowing what we have heard about parties here!"

Miss Lucinda blushed, remembering her previous remarks about Freddie Dilbridge and his dissolute gatherings. She struggled for an excuse for her presence.

With increasing delight, Charlotte gave it to her.

"It must require a lot of self-sacrifice," she said soberly. "But I do appreciate that you are determined, at any cost to yourself in embarrassment or even positive danger, that you must discover whatever dreadful thing it was you saw that night."

"Yes, yes, quite." Miss Lucinda fastened onto it eagerly. "It is a matter of Christian duty."

"Has anyone else seen it?" Emily managed to say something at last.

"If they have," Miss Lucinda said darkly, "they have not said so."

"Maybe they were too frightened?" Charlotte tried to get to her actual purpose at last. "What did it look like?"

226

Miss Lucinda was surprized. She had forgotten the actuality. Now she tried to picture it again.

"Evil," she began, wrinkling her face. "Most evil. It had a green face, like a creature half man and half beast. And there were horns on its head."

"How appalling," Charlotte breathed out, suitably impressed. "What manner of horns? Like a cow, or a goat, or—"

"Oh, like a goat," Miss Lucinda said immediately. "Curling back."

"And what manner of body?" Charlotte went on. "Did it have two legs like a man, or four like a beast?"

"Two, like a man, and it ran away and leapt over the hedge."

"Leapt over the hedge?" Charlotte tried not to sound disbelieving.

"Oh, it's quite a low hedge, just ornamental." Miss Lucinda was not as impractical as she appeared. "I could have jumped it myself, when I was a girl. Not that I would have, of course!" she added hastily.

"Of course not," Charlotte agreed, struggling desperately to keep a straight face. The picture of Miss Lucinda taking a flying leap at the garden hedge was too delicious to be denied. "Which way did it go?"

Miss Lucinda did not miss the point.

"This way," she said firmly. "Down the Walk, toward this end."

Emily saw Charlotte's face and rushed to rescue with noises of sympathy and horror.

It took them some time to break away without obvious discourtesy, and when at last they did, with an excuse that they must speak to Selena, Emily turned to Charlotte, pulling her back by the sleeve, in case they were upon Selena before having an opportunity to speak to each other in private.

227

"What on earth was it?" she hissed. "I thought at first she was inventing most of it, but now I really do believe she saw something. She isn't lying. I would swear to that."

Charlotte had already made up her mind.

"Someone dressed up to frighten her," she answered under her breath, not wanting any passerby to overhear them. Phoebe was only a few yards away, standing with a wan smile, listening to Grace's misfortunes.

"Away from what?" Emily smiled dazzlingly at Jessamyn as she floated past. "Something here?"

"That's what we have to find out." Charlotte added a gesture of greeting. "I wonder if Selena knows," she went on to Emily.

"We'll find out." Emily sailed forward, and Charlotte was obliged to follow. She still disliked Selena, in spite of the admiration for her courage. She faced the unpleasant possibility that her feeling was mainly provoked because Selena had said it was Paul Alaric who had assaulted her. Charlotte most intensely did not wish that to be true. Alaric was here this afternoon. She had not spoken to him yet, but she knew precisely where he was, and that at the moment Jessamyn was drifting casually over towards him in a froth of water-blue lace.

"How pleasant to see you again, Mrs. Pitt," Selena said coolly. If she was indeed pleased, there was nothing of it in her voice, and her eyes were as remote and chilly as a winter river.

"And in so much more fortunate circumstances." Charlotte smiled back. Really, she was getting to be a total hypocrite! Whatever was happening to her?

Selena's face became even colder.

"I am so happy for you that the entire matter is over," Charlotte continued, goaded on by the profound dislike inside her. "Of course, it was a tragedy, but at least the fear is past, no more mystery." She allowed her voice to be as cheerful as was decent. "No one need fear anyone else from now on. All is explained and in the open—such a relief."

"I had not realized you were afraid, Miss Pitt!" Selena looked at her with a distaste that suggested her fear was quite ungrounded, since she could have been in no possible danger.

Charlotte rose to the occasion.

"Of course, I was, and for Emily too. After all, if a woman of decorum and position such as yourself could be molested, who on earth could count themselves safe?"

Selena struggled to think of an answer that was not blatantly rude, and failed.

"And such a relief for the gentlemen," Charlotte went on relentlessly. "None of them are under suspicion anymore. We know now that not any of them were in the least way guilty. It must be a sad and distressing situation, to be obliged to suspect one's friends."

Emily's fingers were digging into Charlotte's arm, and she was shaking so hard with suppressed laughter she had to pretend to have a sneezing fit.

"The heat," Charlotte said sympathetically. "It really is most oppressive. I shouldn't be surprized if the weather breaks soon and we have a thunderstorm. I love thunderstorms, don't you?"

"No," Selena said flatly. "I find them vulgar. Exceedingly so."

Emily sneezed again violently, and Selena backed away. Algernon Burnon was passing with a sherbet in his hand, and she seized the chance to escape.

Emily came up from her handkerchief.

"You are absolutely appalling!" she said happily. "I've never seen her better confounded."

Charlotte's mind knew at last what it was that troubled her about Selena.

"You were the first to see her after she was attacked, weren't you?" she asked soberly.

"Yes. Why?"

"What happend—exactly?"

Emily was slightly surprized.

"I heard her scream. I ran out through the front of the house and saw her. I went to her, naturally, and took her inside. What do you mean? What is it, Charlotte?"

"What did she look like?"

"Look like? Like a woman who has been assaulted of course! Her dress was torn open, and her hair was all over the place—"

"How was her dress torn?" Charlotte insisted.

Emily tried to picture it in her mind. Her hand went up to the left side of her own dress and made as if to rip it.

"Like that?" Charlotte said quickly. "And was it muddy?"

"No, not muddy. There was probably dust, but I didn't notice. It was hardly the time."

"But you told me she said it had happened on the grass," Charlotte pointed out, "by the rose beds."

"It's a hot dry summer!" Emily waved her hands. "Anyway, what does it matter?"

"But those flower beds are watered," Charlotte persisted. "I've seen the gardeners doing it. If she had been thrown to the ground—"

"Well, maybe it wasn't there! Maybe it was on the path. What are you trying to say?" Emily was beginning to understand.

"Emily, if I tore my dress open and pulled my hair out, then came screaming along the road, how would I look different from the way Selena looked that night?"

Emily's eyes were very clear blue.

"Not at all different," she said, as perception dawned.

"I don't think anyone attacked Selena," Charlotte framed her words with deliberation. "She made it up, to draw attention to herself and to get even with Jessamyn. Only

Jessamyn guessed the truth. That was why she pretended to be so sorry for her, and yet it didn't trouble her at all. She knew Paul Alaric had never touched Selena!''

"And neither did Hallam?'' Emily answered her own question with the tone of her voice.

"Poor man.'' Tragedy overtook farce again, and Charlotte felt the chill of real terror and real death. "No wonder he was confused. He swore he didn't attack Selena, and it was the truth.'' Anger hardened inside her, for the mischief Selena had caused, albeit some of it unknowingly. Still, it was a selfish and callous thing to do. She was a spoiled woman, and part of Charlotte wanted to punish her, at least to let her know that someone else knew what had really happened.

Emily understood immediately. A look passed between them, and there was no need for explanations. In time, Emily would allow Selena to perceive very precisely both her anger and her contempt.

"We've still got to find out what is going on here,'' Emily began again after a few moments. "That is only one small mystery solved. It doesn't tell us what Miss Lucinda saw.''

"We'll just have to ask Phoebe,'' Charlotte answered.

"Don't you think I've tried that?'' Emily was exasperated. "If it were so easy, I would have known the answer weeks ago!''

"Oh, I know she won't tell us intentionally,'' Charlotte was not upset. "But she might let something slip.''

Obediently, but without any expectations, Emily led her to where Phoebe was sipping a lemonade and talking to someone neither of them knew. It took ten minutes of innocuous pleasantries before they could get Phoebe on her own.

"Oh, dear,'' Emily said with a sigh. "What a tedious

creature. If I hear one more word about her health, I shall be positively rude."

Charlotte seized her chance.

"She doesn't realize how fortunate she is," she said, looking at Phoebe. "If she had been obliged to endure the strain that you have, she would not make such an issue of a few sleepless nights." She hesitated, not quite sure how to phrase the question she intended so as not to be obvious. "When you know something dreadful has happened, and suspicion is directed at those in your own family, it must be a nightmare!"

Phoebe's face was vacant for a moment with unfeigned innocence.

"Oh, I was not worried over much. I did not think Diggory would do anything so cruel. He is not in the least unkind, you know? And I knew it could not have been Afton."

Charlotte was stunned. If ever there was an innately cruel man, it was Afton Nash. She would have suspected him still, if there were any crime unsolved, but, of all crimes, rape seemed to satisfy his character best.

"How can you know?" she said without thought. "He was alone some of that evening."

"I—" To Charlotte's amazement, Phoebe blushed scarlet, the color burning painfully up her face to the very roots of her hair. "I—" She blinked, and her eyes filled with tears and looked away. "I had confidence it could not be him—that—that is what I meant to say."

"But you do know there is something wrong in the Walk!" Emily took advantage of the moment, and Charlotte's sudden silence.

Phoebe stared at her, her eyes widening as her mind flooded with a great question.

"You know what it is?" she breathed.

Emily hesitated, unsure which was best, to lie, or to admit ignorance. She compromised.

"I know something. And I mean to fight it! Will you help us?"

It was masterly. Charlotte looked at her with admiration.

Phoebe took her arm, squeezing it till the pressure made her wince.

"Oh, don't, Emily! You can't realize what you are doing! The danger isn't over, you know. There will be more, and worse! Believe me!"

"Then we must fight it!"

"We can't! It is too big, and too dreadful. Just wear a cross, say your prayers every night and morning; and don't go out at night. Don't even look out of your windows. Just stay at home and don't inquire into anything! Do as I say, Emily, and maybe it won't come after you."

Charlotte wanted to say more, but she was hurt inside by such fear. She grasped Emily.

"Perhaps that is good advice." She swallowed her feelings. "If you will excuse us, we must speak to Lady Tamworth. We have not even acknowledged her yet."

"Of course," Phoebe murmured. "But, do be careful, Emily! Remember what I said."

Emily gave her a weak smile and walked reluctantly toward Lady Tamworth.

It was another half hour before they had the opportunity to fade behind the rosebeds and disappear, unobserved, into the private part of the garden. They were in a herbaceous walk, backed by an even taller hedge of beach, quite impenetrable.

"Where now?" Charlotte asked.

"Behind that," Emily answered. "There has to be a way around it or else a gate."

"I hope it isn't locked." Charlotte was annoyed at the thought. It would stop them completely. Oddly enough, it

233

had not occurred to her before, because she never locked doors herself.

They walked along side by side, searching the thick leaves till they found the door, almost overgrown.

"It looks as if it isn't used!" Emily said in disbelief. "This can't be it."

"Wait a minute." Charlotte looked at it more closely, studying the hinges. "It opens the other way. It must be all cleared on the other side, for it to swing. Try it."

Emily pushed. It did not move.

Charlotte felt her heart sink. It was locked.

Emily pulled a pin out of her hair and pushed it into the lock.

"You can't do it with that." Charlotte let all her disappointment into her voice.

Emily ignored her and went on poking. She took the pin out and straightened it, making a loop on one end, then tried again.

"There," she said with satisfaction, and pushed the flat surface of the door gently. It swung open without a sound.

Charlotte was staggered.

"Where did you learn to do that?" she demanded.

Emily grinned. "My housekeeper's always taking the keys with her, even to bed, and I hate being obliged to ask her to get into my own linen cupboard. I thought it was rather a nice trick. Come on, let's see what is through there."

They tiptoed through the door and swung it shut behind them. At first it was disappointing, just a large garden room set out in paved walkways with little plots of green herbs between. They went all the way round it, but there was nothing else.

Emily stopped, disgusted.

"Why on earth bother to lock the gate to this?" she said angrily. "There's nothing here!"

234

Charlotte bent to touch one of the herb leaves and crush it between her fingers. It smelled bitter and aromatic.

"I wonder if it is some sort of drug," she said thoughtfully.

"Nonsense!" Emily brushed it aside. "Opium comes from poppies, and they grow in Turkey, or China, or somewhere."

"There are other things." Charlotte refused to give up. "What a peculiar shape this garden is, I mean the way the stones are laid out. It must have taken someone an awful lot of work."

"It's only star-shaped," Emily replied. "I don't think it's very attractive. It's uneven."

"A star!"

"Yes, the other points are over there, and behind the room. Why?"

"How many points altogether?" Something was beginning to form in Charlotte's mind, a memory of a case Pitt had been working on more than a year ago, and a scar he had spoken of.

Emily counted.

"Five. Why?"

"Five! That means it is a pentacle!"

"If that's what you call it." Emily was not impressed. "What does it matter?"

"Emily," Charlotte turned to her, the idea hard, frightening inside her. "Pentacles are the shapes people use when they practice black magic! Maybe that's what they do here, at their parties?" Now she remembered when Pitt had mentioned the scar—on the body of Fanny—on the buttock. The place of most mockery.

"That's why Phoebe is so terrified," she went on. "She thinks they have begun by playing but have conjured up real devils!"

Emily screwed up her face.

235

"Black magic?" she said incredulously. "Isn't that a little far-fetched? I don't even believe in it!"

But it made sense, and the more Charlotte thought of it, the more sense it made.

"You haven't got any proof," Emily went on. "Just because the garden is set out in a star shape! Lots of people might like stars."

"Do you know any?" Charlotte demanded.

"No—but—"

"We've got to get inside that room." Charlotte stared at it. "That's what Miss Lucinda saw, someone dressed up in black magic robes, with green horns."

"That's ridiculous!"

"Bored people sometimes do ridiculous things. Look at some of your Society friends sometime!"

Emily squinted at her.

"You don't believe in black magic, do you, Charlotte?"

"I don't know—and I don't want to. But that doesn't mean that they don't."

Emily gave in.

"Then I suppose we had better see if we can get inside that room, if you think Miss Lucinda's monster could be in there." She led the way across the bitter herbs and took out her hairpin again, but this time there was no need. The door was not locked. It swung open easily, and they stood staring into a large rectangular room with a black carpet and black curtained walls with green designs on them. The sun streamed in through a totally glassed roof.

"There's nothing here," Emily sounded annoyed, now that she had come this far and was half convinced.

Charlotte squeezed past her and went in. She put her hand to the velvet curtains and brushed them slowly. She was more than halfway around before she came to the space behind and saw the black robes and hoods. There were crosses embroidered on them in scarlet, upside down,

236

symbols of mockery, like the one on Fanny. She understood immediately what they were, and it was as if they were still alive. The evil in them remained after the wearers had gone out of this place, stripped to their ordinary faces and their daily lives among other people. How many of them carried that scar on their buttock?

"What is it?" Emily asked from just behind her. "What have you found?"

"Robes," Charlotte said quietly. "Disguises."

"What about Miss Lucinda's monster?"

"No, it isn't here. Maybe they didn't keep it."

Emily's face was pale, her eyes shadowed.

"Do you think it really is black magic, devil worship, and that sort of thing?" She was struggling to disbelieve it herself, now that she actually saw it in its ugliness and absurdity.

"Yes," Charlotte said quietly. She reached out and touched one of the hoods. "Can you think of any other reason for all this? And the pentacle, and the bitter herbs? That must be why Phoebe wears a cross and keeps going to church all the time, and why she thinks we can't ever get rid of the evil now that it's here."

Emily started to say something, and it died on her tongue. They stood staring at each other.

"What can we do?" Emily said at last.

Before Charlotte could think of any answer, there was a sound at the door, and they both froze in horror. They had forgotten the possibility of someone else coming. There was no conceivable explanation they could make. They had unlocked the door in the hedge deliberately. There was no way they could have lost their way. And no one would believe they did not know or understand what they had found!

Very slowly they turned to face the door.

Paul Alaric stood there, black outlined against the sun.

"Well!" he said softly, stepping in and smiling.

Charlotte and Emily stood so close together their bodies touched. Emily was gripping hard, fingers digging in like claws.

"So you've found it," Alaric observed. "A little foolhardy, wasn't it—to come looking for such a thing, and alone?" He seemed amused.

At the back of her mind Charlotte had always known it was foolish, but curiosity had driven out awareness of danger and silenced warning in her brain. Now she stared at Alaric and felt for Emily's hand beside her. Was he the head of them, the warlock? Was that why Selena found it credible that he should have attacked her—or was it why Jessamyn knew he had not? Or could it be that the head was a woman—Jessamyn herself? Her mind whirled around all kinds of ugly thoughts.

Alaric was coming toward them, still smiling, but with a slight furrow between his brows.

"I think we had better get out of this room," he said gently. "It's an extraordinarily unpleasant place, and I, for one, do not wish to be found here if one of its regular users should chance to come."

"R—regular?" she stammered.

His smile broadened into a harsh laugh.

"Good heavens, you think I'm one of them! I'm disappointed in you, Charlotte."

For one idiotic moment she blushed.

"Then who is?" she demanded defensively. "Afton Nash?"

He took her by the arm and led her into the sun, Emily only inches behind her. He pushed the door closed and continued along the path between the bitter herbs.

"No, Afton is far too bloodless for anything of that sort. His form of hypocrisy is much subtler than that."

"Then who?" Charlotte was sure enough it was not George to be unafraid of his answer.

"Oh, Freddie Dilbridge," he said confidently. "And poor Grace studiously turns a blind eye, pretending it is just a normal excess of the flesh."

"Who else?" Charlotte kept up with him, leaving Emily behind on the narrow path.

"Selena, certainly," he replied. "And I should think, Algernon. Poor little Fanny, before she died—at least, I would guess so. Phoebe knows about it, of course—she is not as innocent of nature or people as she seems—and Hallam without doubt. And naturally Fulbert knew, from what he said, even though he was never invited."

It all fitted into place.

"What do they do?" she asked.

His mouth turned down at the corners, rueful, a little contemptuous.

"Nothing very much, play at a little wickedness, imagine they conjure demons."

"You don't think it could be—real?" She hesitated to ask such a question outside in the summer garden with the beach hedge fluttering green above them. It was getting hotter and stiller, and there was a faint overcast across the sky. The thunderflies were worse.

"No, my dear," he said, looking straight at her. "I don't."

"Pheobe thinks so."

"Yes, I know. She imagines a foolish and rather sordid game that has suddenly summoned up real spirits, and set them loose in the Walk, to bring murder and insanity up from the dark regions of the damned." His face was wry, utterly reasonable, dismissing such things to the realms of hysteria.

She frowned.

"Is there no such thing as black magic?"

239

"Oh, yes." He pushed the door open in the hedge and stood back for them to go through. "Most certainly there is. But this is not it."

They emerged into the color and normality of the garden party again. No one had seen them leave the beach hedge and pass along the herbaceous walk. Miss Laetitia was listening dutifully to Lady Tamworth expounding on the evils of marrying beneath one's station, and Selena was having what appeared to be heated words with Grace Dilbridge. Everything was as usual; they might only have been gone for moments. Charlotte had to shake herself to remember what she had seen. Freddie Dilbridge, standing so casually with a glass in his hand, next to the pink roses, dressed up in robes with a hood over his head and holding night parties inside a pentacle, pretending to summon devils, perhaps holding a black mass, stripping the virgin Fanny and branding her body with the crooked scar. How little one knew of the thoughts writhing behind the facile mask. She must make a surpreme effort to be civil to him now.

"Don't say anything," Emily warned.

"I'm not going to!" Charlotte snapped back. "There isn't anything to say."

"I was afraid you might try to point out how wicked it is."

"I presume that that is why they like it!" Charlotte picked up her skirts and swirled over toward Phoebe and Diggory Nash. Afton was standing just beyond them. Before she got there, she realized that, although he had his back to them, they were in the middle of a rather unpleasant conversation.

"—damn silly woman with an overheated mind," Afton said waspishly. "Ought to stay at home and find something useful to do."

"That's easy to say when it isn't you." Diggory's mouth turned down in contempt.

"It's hardly likely to be me!" Afton's eyebrows went up in a sarcastic arch. "It would be a clever rapist who tackled me!"

Diggory raked him with a look of infinite distaste.

"It would be a damn desperate one! Personally, I would sooner try the dog!"

"Then if the dog is raped, we shall know where to look," Afton said coldly, but without apparent surprize. "You keep some peculiar company, Diggory. Your tastes are becoming depraved."

"At least, I have tastes," Diggory snapped back. "I sometimes think you are so withered up you have no passions left for anything. I wouldn't find it hard to believe that all signs of life are repulsive to you, and anything that reminds you you have a body is unclean to your mind."

Afton moved fractionally away from him.

"There is nothing unclean in my mind, nothing I need to look away from."

"Then you've a stronger stomach than I have. What goes on in your brain terrifies me! Looking at you, I could believe in those fantasies of the 'undead' that are so popular these days, corpses that won't stay buried."

Afton held out his hands, palms up, as though weighing the sunlight.

"As usual you are not very thorough, Diggory. If I were one of your 'undead,' the sun would shrivel me." He smiled with slow derision. "Or didn't you read that far?"

"Don't be so obvious," Diggory's voice was weary and irritated. "I was talking about your soul, not your flesh. I don't know whether it was the sunlight that shriveled you, or just life. But, sure as hell waits, something did!" He moved away, heading toward a tray of peaches and sherbet. Phoebe dithered for a moment and then followed, leaving

241

Afton to notice Charlotte at last. His cold eyes looked through her.

"Has your over-frank tongue placed you all by yourself again, Mrs. Pitt?" he inquired.

"Possibly," she replied with equal chill. "But if so, no one else has been blunt enough to tell me so. But then to be alone is not always displeasing."

"You seem to be visiting us in the Walk rather frequently. You did not bother with us before the rapist. Does it still hold some fascination for you, perhaps? A titillation, an extravagance, a wallowing in emotions, hot dreams of violence and surrender without guilt?" His eyes traveled from her bosom down to her thighs.

Charlotte shivered, as if his hands had touched her. She looked at him with total loathing.

"You seem to imagine that women like to be raped, Mr. Nash. It is a monstrous piece of arrogance, a delusion to feed your vanity and excuse your behavior, and it is quite untrue. Rapists are not magnificent. They are pathetic men who are reduced to taking by force that which others can win for themselves. If they did not hurt others so much, one could pity such a creature. It's—it's a kind of impotence!"

His face froze, but there was raw, scalding hatred in his eyes, as primal as birth and death. If they had not been in this civilized garden, with its ritual conversations, the chink of glasses, and polite laughter, she felt he would have torn her open, hacked at her with the sharp blade of a knife, plunged it in hilt deep, and torn her open—

She turned away, sick with the taste of fear, but not before she knew he had seen the understanding in her eyes. No wonder poor Phoebe had never even considered him the rapist. And now Charlotte knew, too, and that was something for which he would have no forgiveness this side of the grave.

She moved away, unseeing, consumed with her knowledge. Silks hung limp in the still air. Flawless skins were blackspotted with minuscule thunder flies, and it was getting hotter all the time. Conversation flittered past her, and she heard its sound but not its words.

"You let it upset you too much. It's foolish, and I dare say ugly, but it need not touch you, or your sister."

It was Paul Alaric, holding out a glass of lemonade for her, his eyes concerned, but with the same inward gleam of humor as always.

She remembered the garden room.

"It has nothing to do with that," she shook her head. "I was thinking of something else, something real."

He offered her the lemonade and, with his other hand, brushed a thunder fly away from her cheek.

She took the glass, glad of it, and as she turned slightly, her eye caught Jessamyn Nash with a look of malevolence on her face. This time she knew almost before hand what it was—nothing complex, just ordinary jealousy, because Paul Alaric had touched her, because his concern was for her, and she knew it was real.

Overwhelmingly, Charlotte wanted to escape from it all, the politeness masking the envies, the airless garden, the silly conversations and the hatreds underneath.

"Where is Hallam Cayley buried?" she asked suddenly.

Alaric's eyes widened in surprise.

"In the same graveyard as Fulbert and Fanny, about a mile away. Or to be accurate, just outside it—unhallowed ground for a suicide."

"I think I'll go and visit it. Do you suppose anyone will notice if I pick a few flowers from the front as I go?"

"I doubt it. But do you care?"

"Not at all." She smiled at him, grateful for his not saying the expected, and not criticizing her.

She broke off some daisies, some sweet William, and a few long heads of lupins, already seeding a little at the

243

bottom but still bright, and set out along the Walk toward the road at the end and the church. It was not as far as she had expected, but the heat was getting more oppressive all the time. The clouds overhead were heavier, and the flies were everywhere.

There was no one else in the graveyard, and she passed unnoticed through the lych-gate and down the path, past the graves with their carved angels and their memories, and beyond the yews to the small plot kept for those without the blessing of the church. Hallam's grave was very new, the ground still bearing the scars of disturbance.

She stood looking at it for several minutes before she laid the flowers down. She had not thought to bring any kind of container, and there was nothing already here. Maybe they thought no one would want to bring flowers for such a person.

She stared down at the clay, still dry and hard, and thought about the Walk, all the stupidity and the unnecessary pain, and the loneliness.

She was still thinking when she heard another step and looked up. Jessamyn Nash was coming out of the shade of the yew trees, carrying lilies. When she recognized Charlotte, she hesitated, her face pinched and hard, her eyes almost black.

"What did you come here for?" she said very quietly, coming toward Charlotte now. She held the lilies and their leaves upright, and there was a silver gleam of scissors in her hand.

Without knowing why, Charlotte was afraid, as if the thunder and the electricity in the air had ripped through her. Jessamyn was standing opposite her, the grave between them.

Charlotte looked down at the flowers.

"Just—just to put these here."

Jessamyn stared at them, then slowly raised her foot and

trod on them, grinding them with the weight of her body, till they were crushed and smeared on the stone-hard clay. She lifted her head and faced Charlotte, then calmly dropped her own lilies on the same spot.

Above them there was a slow crackle of thunder, and the first drops of rain fell huge and wet through their dresses to the skin.

Charlotte wanted to ask her why she had done that. The words were quite clear inside her head, but her voice remained silent.

"You didn't even know him!" Jessamyn said between her teeth. "How dare you come here with flowers? You are an intruder. Get out!"

Thoughts whirled in Charlotte's mind, wild and amazing like flashes of light. She looked at the lilies on the ground and remembered that Emily had said Jessamyn never gave anything away, even when she did not want it anymore herself. If she was finished with it, she destroyed it, but she never let anyone else have it. Emily had been speaking of dresses.

"What difference does it make to you if I put flowers on his grave?" she asked as levelly as she could. "He's dead."

"That doesn't give you any rights," Jessamyn's face was getting whiter, and she did not even seem aware of the heavy drops now falling. "You don't belong in the Walk. Go back to your own Society, whatever that is. Don't try to force yourself in here."

But the thoughts were hardening, clearing in Charlotte's brain. All kinds of questions were at last falling into order, finding answers. The knife, why Pitt had found no blood on the road, Hallam's confusion, Fulbert, everything at last made a pattern, even the love letters Hallam had kept.

"They weren't from his wife, were they?" she said aloud. "She didn't sign them because she didn't write them. You did!"

Jessamyn's eyebrows rose in perfect arches.

"What on earth are you talking about?"

"The love letters, the love letters to Hallam that the police found. They were yours! You and Hallam used to be lovers. You must have had a key to the garden gate. That's how you went to him, and that's how you got in the day Fulbert was killed. Of course, no one saw you!"

Jessamyn's lip curled.

"That's idiotic! Why should I want to kill Fulbert? He was a miserable little wretch, but that's not worth killing for."

"Hallam admitted raping Fanny—"

Jessamyn winced, almost as if she had been struck a physical blow.

Charlotte saw it.

"You can't bear that, can you, that Hallam wanted another woman so much he took her by force, least of all innocent, ordinary little Fanny?" She was guessing now, but she believed it. "You sucked him dry with your possessiveness, and when he wanted to let go, you clung onto him, driving him to escape in drink!" She took a deep breath. "Of course, he didn't remember killing Fanny, and there was no knife and no blood on the road! He didn't kill her. You did. When she stumbled into your withdrawing room and told you what had happened, your rage and jealousy all spilled over. You had been put aside, rejected for your own insipid little sister-in-law. You took the knife—maybe as easy as the knife from the fruit plate on the sideboard—and you killed her, right there in your own room. The blood was all over your clothes, but you could explain that! And you just washed the knife and put it back in the fruit. No one even looked at that. So simple.

"And when Fulbert knew you too well, with his prying eyes, you had to get rid of him too. Perhaps he threatened you, and you told him to go to Hallam, if he dared, knowing

246

you could go there along the back path and surprise him. Did you even know Hallam was out that day? You must have.

"What a surprize you must have had when no one found the body. You knew Hallam must have hidden it, and you watched him come apart, tormented by fear of his own insanity."

Jessamyn's face was as white as the lilies on the grave, and they were both wet with the rain, their floating muslins clinging to them like shrouds.

"You're very clever," Jessamyn said slowly. "But you can't prove any of it. If you tell the police that, I'll just say you are jealous over Paul Alaric. You don't belong in the Walk." Her face narrowed. "And I know you don't. For all your airs, your dresses are made over ones of Emily's! You are trying to crash your way in here. You are saying these things out of revenge, because I know it!"

"Oh, the police will believe me," Charlotte felt a surge of power inside her and intolerable anger for Jessamyn's indifference to all the pain. "You see, Inspector Pitt is my husband. You didn't realize that? And there are the love letters. They are in your hand. And it is very hard to wash all the blood off a knife. It gets in the crevices where the handle fits the blade. They'll find all these things, you know, once they know what to look for."

Jessamyn's face changed at last. The alabaster calm broke and the hatred came flooding through. She lifted the scissors and plunged them toward Charlotte, missing her only by inches as her foot slipped on the wet clay.

Charlotte galvanized to life, turning and running back over the rough grass and the great roots of the yews, under them and into the graveyard, her wet clothes slapping and clinging to her legs. She knew Jessamyn was behind her. The rain was pouring down now, guttering in yellow rivers over the baked ground. She jumped over graves, caught her

247

feet in flowers, and banged herself on the wet marble of the gravestones. A plaster angel loomed up in front of her, and she shrieked involuntarily, plunging on.

Only once did she turn back to see Jessamyn yards behind her, light gleaming on the scissors, her corn silk hair in streamers.

Charlotte was bruised now, legs spattered, arms hurt on the protruding corners of the stones. Once she fell over, and Jessamyn was almost on top of her before she scrambled to her feet, fighting for breath, sobbing. If only she could reach the street, there might be someone there, someone sane and ordinary who would help her.

She was almost there, turning back one more time to make sure Jessamyn was not on her, when she banged into something hard and arms closed round her.

She screamed, imagination sending the scissor blades lunging through her flesh as they had through Fanny's, and Fulbert's. She struck out, kicking and punching.

"Stop it!"

It was Alaric. For a long, breathless second she did not know whether she was more afraid of him or less.

"Charlotte," he said quietly. "It's over. You were a fool to have come here alone, but it's over now—finished."

Very slowly she turned round and faced Jessamyn, mudstained and wet.

Jessamyn let the scissors fall. She could not fight both of them, and she could not hide anymore.

"Come on," Alaric put his arm round Charlotte. "You look appalling! I think we'd better call for the police."

Charlotte found herself smiling—yes, send for the police—get Pitt! More than anything else—get Pitt!

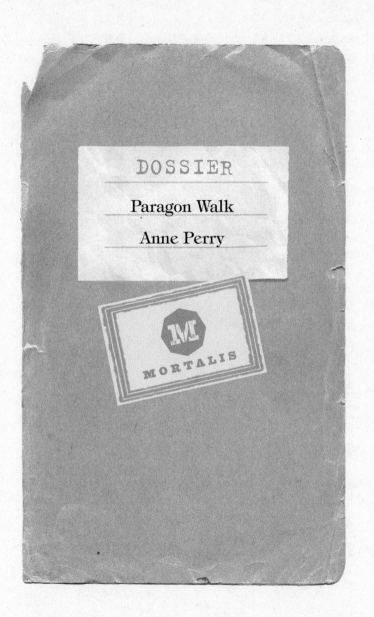

DOSSIER

Paragon Walk

Anne Perry

MORTALIS

Acclaimed writer Anne Perry spoke from her study in Scotland about her long-running series featuring Thomas and Charlotte Pitt, recreating Victorian London, and the craft of writing a killer mystery.

Mortalis: I'd love to have a mental picture of you at your writing desk; how and where do you write?

Anne Perry: I don't work at a desk, and my study is not on the ground floor but one up, on what Americans would call the second floor. There are windows on three sides, the walls are green, the floor is sand colored. There is a leather La-Z-Boy with a sheepskin on the back and a big pillow. I write my books by hand. I'm very particular about pens. I write on a legal-size pad with fine lines—white paper only, not yellow, as legal pads usually are, and the lines are much closer together. One of my handwritten pages types up to two book pages, about five hundred words. I sit here in the study with my feet up, occasionally playing classical music and looking at the view. I'm on a peninsula, with a lighthouse two miles away, looking westward to the valleys and mountains of Scotland, with a garden down below. I tell you, I suffer. It's a very nice environment. To write, you must be physically comfortable; you must not concentrate on where you are, but on where your mind is.

M: When did you know you wanted to be a writer?

AP: I can't remember that far back! Very possibly the idea started when I was three or younger. My mother was very good at telling stories. Of course she read to me but she was also good at telling stories, making them up. I remember one time during one story, she'd gone to sleep. I was rather small and could barely see over the edge of the bed but I hauled myself up and pulled her eyelid open, tapping her and saying, "Are you still in there?" and "What happened next?" So I grew up loving stories and was always more interested in telling them than in being told them. I remember saying in my twenties, "One day I'll write," and that I would write every day.

M: Your first novel, *The Cater Street Hangman,* came out in 1979. How old were you then?

AP: Thirty-eight or thirty-nine. It took a long time.

M: How did you stay motivated?

AP: There was no plan B. If you've got an alternative, it's easy to give up; but if you haven't, there's no plan to fall back on. When I want something, I want it very much.

M: What drew you to writing mysteries?

AP: Tension, conflict, characters, and what you discover about people you love under pressure. And perhaps what you discover about those you don't like; maybe you find out something else about them, something you didn't know that explains the way they are, some new understanding. Also, mysteries do so very well! I started writing Victorian mysteries because my stepfather had asked the question, Who was Jack the Ripper? I didn't take that up directly; I make fictional crimes. But I wondered how you might feel if such a crime was happening near you. It's a heck of a human story to tell.

M: So *The Cater Street Hangman* introduced readers to Inspector Thomas Pitt and his soon-to-be wife, Charlotte Ellison, now nearly thirty years ago. Twenty-five Pitt novels later, do Thomas and Charlotte have a special place in your heart?

AP: Oh yes, I'm very fond of them, and of all the peripheral characters, too. Great Aunt Vespasia is fun. She was a walk-on, walk-off character initially, but twenty books later I'm still in love with her. She was a renowned beauty of her generation, outrageous, very frank, very brave.

She is the old lady we'd all like to become. She'll never be old inside; and she's quick with the one-liners. The great thing about doing a long series is that you can have a minor character in one book, and then you can bring him back again many books later.

M: You have a beautiful sense for the atmosphere of Victorian London.

AP: It's a fun place to work with: the cobblestones, the gas lights, the gorgeous clothes. You've got such drama: the conflict of squalor and wealth, the poorest and the most glamorous. The fact that there is a grand queen in residence most of the time who was related to all the crowned heads of Europe, and yet there are also the poorest of the poor, living in the worst conditions. There is no limit to what you can do, to how magnificent or squalid a place can be. You can dine with a queen or starve to death, living twenty to a room.

The other thing is that London was just about the biggest city in the world at the time, in an empire that stretched around the world and back again. If you look at an old map, all the red bits were the British Empire; it was enormous. Consequently you can have almost any type of person turn up—any nationality, race, occupation. If you stood on the corner of Piccadilly, everyone who was anyone in the world would pass by. So you never run out of ideas of who you might deal with. I might not be able to have my characters travel (it might not be realistic), but almost anyone can come to London from, for example, the Congo, the heart of Africa. There were incredible Victorian wars all over Africa and India. You could travel from Cape Town to Cairo and get off British soil only once. The Empire encompassed the North African coast, Gibraltar, many small islands, Hong Kong. It was really quite enormous, and you can imagine people from any of these places turning up in London sooner or later. The Port of London was the biggest in the world, with trains going all over the place; anything on the face of the earth could turn up in London. It was a great time for social reform, for terrific theater, even for bringing new plants and horticulture into the country.

M: I feel like I've just traveled to London in a time machine.

AP: Yes, reading a book is the cheapest way to go, and you don't have to deal with the poor dentistry, poor plumbing, the disease, and all the rest.

M: Charlotte Ellison Pitt has fallen in love below her station and makes a love marriage. Are you a romantic?

AP: Oh yes, to marry for convenience or for a domestic situation is dreadful. Charlotte's lost quite a few things but gained far more. It's also much better to be able to like your husband as well as love him.

M: What do you think Charlotte loves, or likes, about her husband?

AP: That he can still surprise her, that he is an honest man, not just with others but also with himself. He has a sense of humor, a strong sense of compassion, and she can't boss him around. No woman wants that, not really.

M: Why is Thomas Pitt so extraordinarily untidy?

AP: Just to make him different, I suppose. He is not like anyone I know in particular. He is a creation, not built upon anyone—very few of my characters actually are. Monk, on the other hand, is a dandy; he cares very much how he looks. Pitt wouldn't know how to put it all together, except he does have good shoes—just a quirk. He knows his feet are important. Good shoes look after your feet.

M: Especially on those rainy London days. Your characters often complain about those "filthy" days, when they'd rather sit by a good fire. I like that.

AP: Good word, "filthy," I think. Yes, London was muddy, grimy, not with the air pollution and diesel fumes of today, but there was plenty of soot and the mess of horses in the streets. The chimney smoke from the factories was also pretty horrible. Fearful fogs then. We still have them today but I've never seen one on the trips I've taken to London; they're pretty rare. And the Thames is clean now and it wasn't then. The Thames is called the longest street in London, you know—

it stretches from the sea to the middle of England, with lots of bridges and tremendous traffic.

M: Charlotte certainly adds her own brand of wisdom and feminine knowledge to the Pitt novels. What would you say she brings to the table?

AP: Don't you think women and men observe people differently? This makes it possible to have a binocular view of people, not just a monocular one. In addition, when women are alone together, they behave quite differently than they do when men are present, much as men do when there are no women around. Surely you must have had the experience of seeing a man falling over a woman, and you've thought, *Can't you see she's playing you?* Or perhaps a man will see women admiring some other man and say, "Oh, you can't fancy him," but we women can see it. It's a much more layered way of looking at an event, to have this binocular view.

M: Does Pitt always appreciate this binocular view offered by Charlotte's assistance?

AP: Not when she gets in danger or makes a mess, but on the whole it's a good companionship and she does find useful information. Charlotte takes a backseat over the course of twenty-five novels and years down the line because Pitt is in Special Branch and she becomes a mother. In the next novel I'm working on, though, she takes a very front seat. Charlotte goes off to Ireland with Pitt's boss and Pitt gets stuck in France. It's all very complicated and a bit thriller-ish. Over the course of a series, you've got to change things up; it becomes tedious if too much remains the same, and it doesn't make much sense to have a very good detective who is never promoted and never challenged. So Pitt is eventually pulled off the force and put into Special Branch to learn new skills. It's the same with Monk; he starts as a policeman and then becomes a private detective. But he finds it difficult work with too erratic an income, so he takes a position with the Thames River Police. He has to learn a lot of new skills and it's all wonderfully atmospheric, with the major institutions on the river: the Archbishop of Canterbury's Palace, Westminster, Kew

Gardens, and the low society places like Limehouse, the Isle of Dogs, the terrible slums, the Royal Observatory, and the Royal Naval College in Greenwich. There are endless places to go.

M: Do your characters ever surprise you—do something you hadn't anticipated?

AP: I don't think characters do that as much as a situation might, and then their reaction is either in character and will work, or out-of-character and won't. My characters don't dictate; they're not real people. But the situation should be real and should affect your characters, and the characters should also then affect the situation. That's not an original comment by any means. Put people in a dramatic situation and they have an effect on it and they are changed. A character doesn't surprise you, but a situation draws something out of him or her that makes them act differently. If it works out in any other way, then it's my fault for not having foreseen it; characters can only behave within the character you've created for them.

M: How do you compose the anatomy of a crime? I'm wondering about the actual nitty-gritty of fashioning a mystery: Do you sketch out the crime, motive, and suspects at the outset, or does the whole thing evolve?

AP: You start with a crime in the middle of your composition because you may enter the story just before or just after the crime. Then you are unraveling what led up to it but doing so in real time, from the crime forward. The narrative thread goes in both directions, uncovering the past and creating the future. One mark of a mystery writer who's new at it is having a villain who's static. A character is going to react to what's going on, to the investigation, and not wait for you to unravel it. He may commit more crimes or interfere with the investigation. All the other characters are doing something as well, reacting to the situation. And you've got to have at least two reasonable suspects—better still, three—and then narrow it down to one. It's very difficult to mislead the reader without ever lying, but you mustn't lie.

Carefully, bit by bit, you have more ideas as you go along and you

256

rewrite as many times as necessary. Often I have great ideas at the end of a book and have to go back and weave them in from the beginning.

Also, no character is unimportant. No matter how peripheral, everyone is a real person who came from somewhere before he walked onto your page. Give him a face, a name, interests. Don't make him cardboard. Even if he's a postman delivering a letter, give him a blister, a limp, a new shirt—something that makes him real. All people are real.

Do you travel?

M: Me? Sure, I've been abroad a few times, and around the country. Why do you ask?

AP: Well, I travel a lot, and while sitting in a plane or a train or a bus I see a lot of people and discover that loads of them are interesting. You've got to be a people-studier and a people-liker to write well. I don't think "Life's a bitch and then you die." Yes, there is suffering, but I've found that even the most miserable people really have little to complain about.

M: Are you an optimist then? You sound refreshingly optimistic.

AP: Yes. I've been to America three times this year, from coast to coast, and to Canada, Spain, France, and Italy, and I haven't been to a place where people are rotten. I was just in Little Rock, Arkansas; the people were delightful and the weather was gorgeous! I also love L.A. I'm always treated so nicely there. In my experience, most people are pretty decent everywhere.

PHOTO: © DIANE HINDS

ANNE PERRY is the bestselling author of two acclaimed series set in Victorian England: the Charlotte and Thomas Pitt novels, most recently *Death on Blackheath* and *Midnight at Marble Arch,* and the William Monk novels, including *Blind Justice* and *A Sunless Sea.* She is also the author of the World War I novels *No Graves As Yet, Shoulder the Sky, Angels in the Gloom, At Some Disputed Barricade,* and *We Shall Not Sleep,* as well as eleven Christmas novels, most recently *A Christmas Hope.* Her stand-alone novel *The Sheen on the Silk,* set in the Byzantine Empire, was a *New York Times* bestseller. Anne Perry lives in Scotland.

www.AnnePerry.co.uk

35